BISON
BOOKS

The Home Ranch

By RALPH MOODY

Illustrated by Tran Mawicke

University of Nebraska Press
Lincoln and London

First Bison Book printing: 1994

Library of Congress Cataloging-in-Publication Data
Moody, Ralph, 1898–
The home ranch / by Ralph Moody; illustrated by Tran Mawicke.
p.   cm.
ISBN 0-8032-8210-9 (pa)
1. Ranch life—West (U.S.)—Fiction.   I. Title.
PS3563.05535H66   1994
813'.54—dc20
93-39762   CIP

Reprinted by arrangement with Edna Moody Morales and Jean S. Moody

∞

TO HAZEL

Contents

THE HOME RANCH

1

A Boy Needs a Man's Hand

I'D JUST come home from school, the last Monday in May, 1911, when Mother called to me, "Son, will you come up to my chamber for a few minutes? I'd like to talk to you."

Since Father had died, Mother sometimes called one of us up to her chamber for a talk. When she did, it was usually because we'd done something bad enough that she couldn't talk about it before the other children. She never scolded us up there, but she'd give us talking-to's that counted a good deal more than a scolding.

I put Lady, our horse, in the barn, and went to the house right away, but I didn't hurry too much. I couldn't be sure what Mother was going to talk about, and I needed a couple of minutes to sort of go over things in my mind.

In the summer of 1909, when I was ten, I'd worked as water boy on the Y-B spread, a big cattle ranch at the foot of the mountains west of Denver. I'd learned a lot about handling cattle up there, and riding bucking horses; and Hi Beckman, the foreman, had taught me to do trick riding. That Labor Day, riding together, we'd won the trick-riding contest at the Littleton roundup.

Then, in the summer of 1910, after we'd moved to Littleton and Father had died, I'd found whatever odd jobs I could around town. Sometimes I'd hire other boys, and make a few dollars by helping herders through town with their cattle. And sometimes I'd work a few days for Mr. Batchlett, the biggest cattle trader in town. But I'd made the most money at the race track, where I'd been pretty lucky in winning matched races. Grace, my older sister, had sort of worked that money into the grocery bill and other places, because we couldn't let Mother find out about my riding at the track.

Just the day before Mother called me up to her chamber, I'd ridden out to the Y-B ranch to see Mr. Cooper about getting my old water-boy job back. He had offered me twenty-five dollars a month, but while I was there Mr. Batchlett had ridden in, heard us talking, and offered me a dollar a day, man's wages, for a hundred straight days. He said he'd be making trading trips as far south as the New Mexico border, and could use me as a trail cowhand.

Anything better than five-cents-an-hour jobs were pretty hard for boys to get. To have both men wanting to hire me at high wages made me so proud I could have yipp-eed, but I didn't. I kept my face and voice as steady as I could, and said, "I'd like to work for both of you, but of course I can't, so I'll have to think it over. And maybe I can't work for either of you. Mother might need me at home. I'll have to ask her."

That was why I had to think a little before I went up to Mother's chamber. I hadn't talked to her about the jobs yet, but I was pretty sure she must have heard about the offers— or that somebody had told her about my riding in the matched races the summer before.

Mother was sitting on the edge of her bed when I went upstairs. She motioned for me to close the door, and said, "Sit down here beside me, Son. I think we should talk things over a little."

I said, "Yes, ma'am," and sat down with my hands folded in my lap.

When Mother really wanted something to soak in, she'd always let me sit and wait a couple of minutes. Then she'd clear her throat and begin. That time it seemed as though she waited an hour before she said, "Ralph, Mr. Batchlett called on me this afternoon. I understand you have been talking with him about going away from home to work this summer."

"No," I said, "I haven't. But he was talking to me about it yesterday. I just told him you might need me at home, and I'd have to talk to you about it."

"That's what we are up here for," she said.

I forgot all the things I'd planned to say, and the words just tumbled out in a heap: "Well, it's a dollar a day and he said it would be a hundred days and I'd be learning a trade and . . ."

"Yes, I know," Mother said, "but don't you think you're a little young for learning to be a livestock trader?"

"Well, I'm the top rabbit-dealer in Littleton now," I told her, "and I could make more money if I knew how to be a cattle-dealer too."

Mother put her arm around my shoulders and pulled me close against her. "I'm afraid my little boy is growing up too fast in some ways and not fast enough in others," she said. "How much do you weigh now, Son?"

"Well, I still weigh seventy-two pounds," I said, "but I've grown nearly an inch taller in the last year."

Mother let me sit up straight again, and squeezed one of my legs. "My! You're nothing but bone and sinew," she said. "I do wish you could put on a little flesh."

"I'm stouter than most any of the other fellows in my class at school," I said. "I can lift more and squeeze tighter with my knees and ride . . ."

"I know, I know, Son, but let's talk about this summer. A twelve-year-old boy is entirely too young to be away from home all summer with a crew of cattlemen. Particularly when they will be moving from place to place, and when there will be no woman who could take care of him in case he were sick."

It didn't look as though there was very much use in trying to argue, but I wanted to go with Mr. Batchlett so much that I said, "There wasn't any woman at the Y-B mountain ranch when I worked up there two years ago."

"Yes, I know, but you came home every week end then. And you were never so far away that they couldn't have brought you home in a few hours."

"But I never get sick," I told her. "When have I ever been sick—except when I had the measles?"

"Suppose you let me finish," Mother said. "As I was saying, a twelve-year-old boy is too young for such an undertaking. But I do realize that circumstances have given you a great deal more experience than most boys of your age. And I am sure that you are enough like your father that you will not be influenced by the roughness of the men you will be with, so I have told Mr. Batchlett you may go. However, I have told him that you can't go until after your school is out for the summer, and that you must be home when school opens in the fall."

If she hadn't dropped it so quickly, I could have acted more like a grown-up man. I didn't, though; I hugged my arms around her like a little kid. Mother didn't cry, but she had tears in her eyes, and before she told me to run along, she said, "I shall worry about you, and I realize that I may be criticized for letting you go, but a boy of your age needs a man's steadying hand on his shoulder."

Mr. Batchlett had a big ranch just north of Colorado Springs, and corrals and cow barns at Littleton. Lots of the people who lived on the outskirts of Denver kept a cow, but when her milk began to dry up they'd trade her to Mr. Batchlett—along with five or ten dollars—for a fresh one. In that way he got both the boot money and the calf, and everybody said he was getting rich.

The trading with the Denver people was done from Littleton, usually during the fall and early spring. At the end of the seasons Mr. Batchlett took the dry cows to his ranch, kept them there until they'd had calves, or were about ready to, then brought them back to Littleton for the Denver trade. In the summers he made his headquarters at the ranch, sending trading teams far to the south and up into the mountains to trade steers, bulls and young stock for more milk cows.

Mr. Batchlett had the reputation around town of being hard and tough, and some pretty rough men hung out around his corrals, so I was surprised that Mother had said I could go away to work for him. I think there were two or three reasons why she let me do it. One was that Mr. Batchlett had grown up in Texas with Hi Beckman, the foreman at the Y-B ranch. Hi came to our house often, and I'd heard him tell Mother, "Batch, he's hard on the outside because he's in a hard business, but he's just as soft as a woman on the inside."

Another reason was that she had known Mr. Batchlett only around his own home. The Batchletts lived within a block of us, the children were small, and Mrs. Batchlett was a frail little woman. Mother used to nurse her when she'd be sick, and once when she came home from there I heard her tell Grace, "In spite of what people say, I'm sure Hi must be right about Mr. Batchlett. It's wonderful to see how tender that big, rough man is with his wife and children."

As soon as I'd had my talk with Mother, I went right down to the corrals to see Mr. Batchlett, and found him getting ready to make his spring trip to the ranch. "I aim to get away from here bright and early on the first of June," he told me, "but your maw says you can't take off till your school's out. When'll that be?"

"Well, Friday's the last day," I said, "and that's June second. But on the last day we only have to go long enough to get our report cards. I'll be able to start out by half past nine."

"Fair enough!" he said. "I'll be taking fifty dry cows out to the home ranch, along with three men and a chuckwagon. Don't aim to push 'em too hard, and if you travel light you could catch up with us between Castle Rock and The Monument. I won't need you bad till we head off into the brush country."

Thursday at dawn I took my saddle, war bag, boots and chaps down to the corrals and put them in the chuckwagon, so Lady would only have my weight to carry the next morning. But we didn't get away next morning. The eighth grade had a graduation exercise, and school didn't let out until it was over. It was nearly noon before I got home, and Mother wouldn't let me start out that late in the day. "You may go just as early as you wish in the morning," she told me, "but you wouldn't be able to catch up with Mr. Batchlett this afternoon, and I won't have you sleeping out alone."

I figured it would be morning any time after midnight, so I said goodbye to the younger children when they went up to bed, and to Grace and Mother when I went a few minutes later. Before I crawled into bed beside Philip, I laid out my shirt, jumper, and overalls, and put a silver dollar in my overalls pocket.

I put the alarm clock where the moon would shine on it, but didn't set it. The third time I woke up it was five minutes after twelve, so I pulled my clothes on quietly, crawled out the window to the woodshed roof, and slipped to the ground. King, our dog, came out whining to go with me, but I stopped only long enough to tell him he was a good dog, and that I'd see him Labor Day. Then I shut him in the woodshed and went to the barn for Lady. I walked her on the grass till we were well away from the house, then let her into a swinging canter.

I don't know any more beautiful music than the beat of a cantering horse's hoofs on a crisp moonlit night, and Lady had one of the smoothest gaits of any horse that ever ran. The moon seemed only a few yards above the jagged outline of the mountains when we turned onto the Colorado Springs highroad. And there wasn't a sound in the world except the music of Lady's hoofs. I didn't push her, but let her take an easy swinging gait until she'd caught her second wind, then jogged her a mile, and let her lope again.

I suppose it's funny, but I could always visit with Lady better than I could with most people. I didn't have to be afraid I'd say something that would sound silly, and I didn't have to be ashamed of bragging a little bit if I wanted to. I guess I talked to Lady most of the night. I told her that I'd bet Mr. Batchlett would never be sorry he'd hired me at a full cowhand's wages, because I could ride as well as most of them, and because I'd make myself do anything they could do. And I told her a lot of other things I wouldn't have told any person. I don't remember them all, but I do remember telling her that when I grew up I was going to have a big ranch like Mr. Batchlett's, with a big brick house on it, and good cattle, and a pretty wife, and lots of children.

The moon set as we left the Platte Valley and climbed the long divide. There were no ranch houses up there, and the coyotes came out to sing their goodnight song to the moon. It was a lonely, sorrowful song, and I tried to tell myself I was sorry to be going away from home for a whole summer, that something might happen to Mother or one of the children while I was gone. But I could only keep it on my mind for a few seconds at a time. Then, before I knew it, I'd be thinking again that I was almost a man, and that for the first time I was going to be doing a man's job and getting a man's pay for it.

The top of the sun was just peeping over the hills when the houses at Castle Rock came into sight, and the general store opened as we came into town. Lady was going to need grain unless I stopped to let her graze for an hour or two, and I was getting pretty hungry myself. So I went into the store and bought two quarts of oats, a five-cent loaf of bread, and a can of deviled ham.

While I was eating my breakfast, the storekeeper told me that Mr. Batchlett's outfit had gone through town about noontime of the day before, and he asked me nearly a hundred questions. He seemed to hate all cattle, but milk cows most of all.

"Ain't no wonder Batch has to go to hirin' little kids for cow-hands," he told me. "Ain't no wonder he has to take on them as nobody else would hire. Wouldn't no self-respectin' cow-hand hire out to wrangle a mess of ornery milk cows. Might as leave try riding herd on the Ladies' Mish'nary Sassiety as on a parcel of breechy milk cows. Oh, Batch, he's doin' all right; he ain't no fool, but you got to be a fool to work for him."

2

Ornery Milk Cows

I FINISHED my breakfast in a hurry, and just as soon as Lady had finished hers I put her on the road again. I didn't feel nearly as good about my new job as I had during the night, and was anxious to find out what kind of a crew I'd be working with. I didn't talk to Lady any more, but kept her in a long swinging lope that ate into the miles. From the length of her shadow I guessed it to be about noon when we passed The Monument butte, and way ahead to the south I could see a haze of dust that I knew would be Mr. Batchlett's outfit.

The outfit had left the Colorado Springs highroad and turned off toward the mountains before I caught up with it. There was a good deal of scrub oak along there, so I was within half a mile before I could see anything more than the white top of the chuckwagon. But Mr. Batchlett saw us the minute Lady and I topped the rise. He waved his arm, then ya-hooed and swung his hat in a big circle above his head—the sign for making camp. With a couple of other riders, he began hazing the cows into a little green meadow, and the chuckwagon pulled to a stop.

By the time I'd ridden up, an old man with a gray walrus

19

mustache was unhitching the team, and Mr. Batchlett came loping in on his big chestnut horse. "Didn't get lost, did you?" he called. "Reckoned you'd come in about sundown last night."

"Mother wouldn't let me start till this morning," I called. Mr. Batchlett pulled his horse up so short he nearly sat it down. "Morning!" he said roughly. "You wasn't fool enough to . . ." Then he looked Lady over from head to croup, and asked, "What time this mornin'?"

"About ten minutes past twelve," I told him, "but it's morning any time after midnight, isn't it?"

Mr. Batchlett didn't answer, but swung out of his saddle, came over, and ran his hand along Lady's back and belly. I knew what he was looking for; if I had ridden her hard enough to do her any harm she'd be trembling, and the nerves under her skin would be twitching. "Guess she's all right," he said, "but a man could ruin an old mare like this with fifty miles in a straight stretch."

"Lady isn't very old," I told him, "only eight. And we did most of our traveling in the cool of the night and morning. And besides, I only w . . ."

"Yeah, I know. You only weigh as much as a hoptoad."

I was going to tell Mr. Batchlett that my weight wouldn't make any difference about handling cows, but the old man with the gray mustache cut in. "Fifty miles, huhh!" he snorted. "By dogies, a man would think . . . why, I recollect when I was the size of this here young'un I rid a flea-bit cayuse from . . ."

"I know, I know, Hank," Mr. Batchlett said, "but you just ride that fry pan till we get some grub around here. I want to make it into the corrals before nightfall."

The old man started back toward the wagon, but he'd only gone a couple of yards when he turned and hollered, "Boy, wrastle me up some firewood; you ain't did nothin' to be a-braggin' 'bout, and we ain't got all day to . . ." Then without finishing, he turned and stumped away. He rolled from side to side as he walked, and was so bowlegged that a fat hog could have run between his knees without touching either one.

Mr. Batchlett winked at me, and said, "You'll get used to Hank. Never mind the wood; Sid's fetching it." Then he looked up at me quickly, and asked, "Water the mare at The Monument?"

"No, sir," I told him. "She was too warm then."

"Cooled out enough now," he said, pointing toward some willows half a mile to the north. "Better give her a couple of swallows; it's a dry run from here to the home ranch."

I got a pretty fair look at the herd when I was riding Lady to water, but I was a lot more interested in the other two cowhands than in the cows—and I couldn't help remembering what the storekeeper at Castle Rock had said. I wasn't close enough to see what either man's face looked like, but they certainly looked funny in the saddle. The one who was dragging wood to the wagon didn't look to be any bigger than I, and was mounted on a tall piebald horse that looked like a short-necked giraffe.

The other rider was just the opposite. From where I was he looked to be seven feet tall, and was mounted on a mule that wasn't much bigger than a burro. His stirrups were so short he looked as if he were sitting in a chair, and he rode hunched over—as if he had a bellyache. I'd have had one if I'd been riding that mule. It was going round and round the herd at a steady dogtrot that would have shaken the teeth out of a garden rake. And, over the bellowing of the herd, he was calling out to the cows, in a voice as monotonous as the mule's trot, "hup . . . yaaa, hup . . . yaaa." It sounded like a gramophone record that was stuck and saying the same words over every time it went around.

The tall man was still riding around the herd when I'd watered Lady and was heading back to the chuckwagon. From behind it a thin line of blue smoke was rising, and the little cowhand was loosening his saddle cinches. When I rode in,

Mr. Batchlett was washing at the water barrel beside the chuck-wagon. He looked around and said, "Sid, this is Little Britches; he's going to ride with us this summer."

Sid's face lit up as if I were an old friend. He grinned and said, "Ain't he the one rode ag'in Le Beau in the matched race, last Fourth o' July? Ain't he the one as done trick-ridin' with Hi Beckman in the Littleton roundup?"

"Yep, that's him," was all Mr. Batchlett said.

"I ought to knowed it was him when I seen him hightailin' off to the water hole," Sid chirped in a high voice. "I ought to knowed by the way he hauls his knees up and hunkers over the neck of a horse." He came hurrying toward me with his hand out. "Yessirree, Little Britches! Yessirree! We're right proud to have you in the outfit. Make yourself right to home. Hank, he'll have the chuck ready in two shakes of a latigo."

I'd never known I pulled my knees up and leaned over a horse's neck when I rode, but I suppose it was because I'd done most of my riding bareback, and had to hold on tight or fall off. When I took Sid's hand his grip was like the closing of a vise, and the palm was as horny as a piece of sun-dried leather. I must have flinched, because he loosened his grip, looked down at his hand, then grinned and said, "That calf-brandin' sure puts bark on 'em, don't it? Been workin' roundup down La Junta way. Never did wear no gloves; cheaper to grow hide than buy it."

Even in his high-heeled boots, Sid Faulker was only about three inches taller than I. He might have been thirty, but it's hard to tell about those red-headed, freckled-faced fellows. His eyes were that kind of blue that can be as warm as June or as cold as January. I knew we were going to be friends.

I had just given Lady some oats, and was washing my face and hands when Hank yelled, loud enough to have been heard in Colorado Springs, *"Come an' git it, ya lazy mav'ricks!"*

After I'd dried my face I looked around the front of the wagon to see if the man on the mule was coming in, but he was still riding round and round the herd, so I asked Sid, "Is the tall man deaf?"

"Shucks, no," Sid chuckled, "old Zeb, he can hear a calf bat its eyes at half a mile. He's got to stay with them ornery critters till I get out there. Leave 'em ten minutes, and they'd be scattered from here to La Junta."

I looked around as far as I could see, and asked, "Then who's Hank calling in?"

"Ain't callin' nobody. Old Hank, he don't never do nothin' by the halves; never did—to hear him tell it. We best to light into that chuck 'fore it gets burnt to cinders."

When we went to eat I found out what Sid meant. Hank had a fire big enough to barbecue a beef, and was holding one arm up to shield his face from the heat as he fished burned biscuits out of an iron pot. Both frying pans were smoking like volcanoes, and the coffee pot was shooting up geysers of steam and grounds. As we filled our plates and cups, Hank kept shouting at Sid, "By dogies, Sid, look what you done to the grub! Ain't nobody never learnt you to fetch in firewood that ain't drier'n gun powder? Look at them biscuits! Frizzled to a . . ."

Hank didn't have to tell us to look at the biscuits; it was hard to look anywhere else. I'd thought I was nearly starved, but I could hardly stuff the chuck down. The canned beans had stuck to the pan and burned, the bacon was hacked half an inch thick, and was blacker than the biscuits. Mr. Batchlett winked at me and said, "Ought to make it to the ranch for supper. Reckon you can hold out? Jenny'll be over to help Helen with the grub, and she's right handy with a skillet."

I didn't think Hank had heard, but he blurted out, "By dogies, give me a parcel o' good dry prairie chips, 'stead o' this here greasewood tinder, and I'll show you who's handy with a skillet. Why, I recollect when . . ."

If Mr. Batchlett heard him, he didn't let on. He looked over at Sid and said, "Going to be a bit tricky getting this herd in to the ranch tonight. It's scrub oak all the way, and some of them old sisters are pretty well wore down. Not being herd broke, they'll try to scatter, mostly back to the north. Little Britches can take the south, I'll ride point and let Zeb bring up the drag; he's right good with a bull whip."

He glanced around at Lady, and asked me, "Reckon the mare can stand up to it? South side shouldn't be too bad."

"Sure she can," I told him. "I've been graining her for two weeks, and she's in good shape."

Mr. Batchlett didn't seem to be listening to me. While I was still talking he got up and went to his horse. As he put the bridle on and tightened the cinches, he told Hank, "We'll start lining 'em out. Soon's Zeb has had his grub, you haul the chuckwagon into the gulch beyond this next hill. Unharness, turn the black loose, and saddle the bay. Give the boys a hand wherever they need it; you can come back for the wagon tomorrow." Then he swung into the saddle and jogged away toward the herd with Sid.

It didn't take me two minutes to get on my boots, spurs, and chaps, and to have my saddle cinched onto Lady. I was anxious to get started on my new job, and caught up to Sid and Mr. Batchlett before they were half way to the herd. "Take it easy! Take it easy!" Mr. Batchlett told me as I pulled up beside him. "You ain't working mustangs, but milk cows! Didn't Hi or your paw learn you better'n that? Slow and easy does it; you watch old Zeb and that mule!"

Mr. Batchlett's voice wasn't rough, but he'd given me a scolding, and I'd had it coming. Both Father and Hi Beckman had taught me to handle cattle as quietly as possible, but we weren't close enough to frighten the herd. And besides, I didn't really think of tame milk cows as being cattle. Of course, I couldn't explain all that, so I just said, "Yes, sir, they did. I guess I forgot."

Mr. Batchlett just nodded, waved to Zeb to come in, and said, "Spread out; we'll start 'em moving."

Before an hour was passed I knew what the storekeeper meant when he told me it would be as easy to herd the Ladies'

Missionary Society as a bunch of milk cows. Steers and range cattle will hold together in a herd, and each herd usually has one leader that does all the thinking. But every one of those milk cows had a mind of her own, and each one wanted to do something different.

Most of them had been petted or spoiled by the people who owned them during the winter, and I began to think that maybe they'd grown to be like those people. Some were docile and some were cranky, some were clever and some were dumb; some were fat and lazy, and others were nervous and skinny. Some bellowed as if they were angry, some lowed in a lonesome way, and some just moaned as if they were sorry for themselves.

It was twelve miles from the Colorado Springs highroad to Mr. Batchlett's ranch at the foot of the mountains. A narrow road led to it, winding through scrub oak, gulches, dry creek beds, and over hills that grew higher as they neared the mountains. It would have been easy to put a big herd of beef cattle over that road. They'd have strung out for a mile or so, and would have trailed along behind each other like elephants in a parade, but those milk cows had no more idea of trailing than so many jack rabbits.

Sid might have had the toughest side of the herd, but Lady and I had every bit we could do on our side—and just a little bit more. Lady was as good a horse as anyone could want on the road, and she was all right for ordinary herding, but she wasn't used to brush country. She couldn't turn short enough to thread her way quickly between the clumps of scrub oak, but those cows could dodge through them like cottontails.

There was hardly a minute, all the way to the ranch, when I didn't have to fight back cows that were trying to leave the herd on my side. I spurred and jerked Lady around until I was ashamed of myself, but quite a few times ten or a dozen cows dodged past us, and I really needed help. The brush was so thick I couldn't see the other riders, and I didn't holler for any help, but each time I got into bad trouble Mr. Batchlett showed up from nowhere. He was never a bit excited, and he didn't seem to be trying very hard, but within two or three minutes he'd have my stragglers all back in the herd. He didn't scold me for letting the cows get away, but once he said, "Take it easy! Don't fight 'em so hard! You're getting your mare wore down."

Hank could pick the wrong times to help me just as well as Mr. Batchlett could pick the right ones. I'd have three or four stragglers all rounded up and on their way back to the herd when he'd come galloping out of the brush in front of us. Every time he scattered the bunch all over again, and every time he blamed me for letting them get away. "By dogies," he'd holler, "why'n't you watch what you're doin'? Don't let 'em dodge past you! Git around 'em! Git around 'em, boy! Head 'em off! By dogies, I recollect when I was your . . ."

About the sixth time Hank scattered a bunch of cows for me I was so mad that I rode back to the herd and left him to round them up alone. It was an hour before I heard his voice again. He was way over on Sid's side of the herd then, and I never saw anything more of him till we got to the ranch.

I was so busy that afternoon that I lost all track of time or moving ahead until the sun went down. Then I noticed that the front range of the mountains was just above us. It was deep twilight when we topped the next hill, and three or four yellow sparks of light showed in the valley below. Those lights must have looked as good to the cows as they did to me. There was a change in the sound of their lowing, and they didn't try to scatter any more. Even the fattest and laziest raised their heads and quickened their pace.

It wasn't until the last cow was in the corral and the gate closed that I realized how tired I was. And I'd worked Lady so hard she stood with her legs spraddled and her head down. We'd done the best we could, but I knew it hadn't been very good. I was thinking about it as I climbed out of the saddle and began loosening the cinch. Then I heard Hank shout, "By dogies, Batch, that there kid you got ain't worth a tinker! Left a whole parcel o' critters get a-past him, then run off and left me to round 'em up alone. Like to never got 'em fetched back. By dogies, when I was . . ."

"Yeah, I noticed," was all Mr. Batchlett said.

He came past when I was pulling the saddle off Lady, gave me a slap on the seat of the pants, and said, "You done all right for your first time in brush country. Put your mare in the horse corral over there; there's feed in the rack. Grub'll be ready by the time you get washed up; bunkhouse is yonder."

I went to the bunkhouse as soon as I'd taken care of Lady, but I didn't wash up, or even take off my spurs and chaps. I was so tired I was seeing double and was a bit dizzy, so I thought I'd lie down on an empty bunk for a few minutes before I washed. When I woke up it was morning.

3

I Seen You Before

THE SUN had just risen and was streaming in through the bunkhouse doorway when I woke up that first morning at Batchlett's home ranch. For a minute I didn't know where I was, then I saw Sid and remembered, but thought I must still be dreaming. He was wearing a white shirt, creased pants and new boots, and was shaving at a washstand in the corner.

I knew it was Sunday morning, and thought Sid must be getting ready for church, but I couldn't understand where he'd got his good clothes. He wasn't lugging anything when we left the chuckwagon the afternoon before.

I was lying there trying to figure it out when Sid spied me in the mirror, and sang out, "By jiggers, Little Britches, you sure ripped off a heap of shingles last night! Hope you don't snore that-a-way 'ceptin' when you're plumb beat out. Sounded like a lost hooty owl in a blizzard. Jenny Wren's got the flapjacks comin' up; you'd best to rise and shine."

I swung my feet out onto the floor, sat up, and asked, "You going to church this morning?"

"Shucks, no!" he said. "Ain't no church closer'n Castle Rock or The Springs—and there's plenty room for worshipin' right close to home. Ain't a man got a right to get slicked up without he's goin' to church?"

None of the cowhands I'd ever worked with got dressed up unless they were going to town, but I was more interested in how Sid got dressed up than why. "Sure, he's got a right to," I said, "but what I can't figure out is how you brought your good clothes and razor along. I didn't see any saddle bags on your rig when we left the chuckwagon."

"Come to think about it, there wasn't," he said.

"Then how did you get your things out here?" I asked.

"Oh, a little bird flowed out here with my war sack bright and early this mornin'."

"Hmm, you couldn't have had much sleep," I said. "It must be twenty miles to where we left the wagon and back."

"Didn't reckon a man could sleep in late with you takin' on like a sick calf, did you? If you knowed as much about this here layout as what I do, you'd shake a leg and get slicked up a mite 'fore we go to the chuckhouse for flapjacks. Jenny Wren ain't the only bird in this bush."

I couldn't do much about getting slicked up, but I took off my chaps and spurs, washed my face and hands, and combed my hair. Before we'd been in the chuckhouse five minutes, I began to understand why Sid had ridden all the way to the chuckwagon to get his good clothes and why he told me I'd get slicked up if I knew as much about the layout as he did.

On the Y-B and most of the other big ranches, the chuckhouse was a separate building, with its own kitchen and a man cook, but it wasn't that way at Batchlett's ranch. Our chuckhouse was a good-sized log room, built onto the back of the house. It had a big fireplace, with three easy chairs and a couple of card tables around it. Down the middle of the room there was an oilcloth-covered table, long enough for twenty or more places, with chairs instead of benches. Opposite the fireplace there was a doorway that connected with the main kitchen of the house.

When Sid and I came in there were eight or ten men, in bib

overalls and blue jumpers, sitting at the end of the table nearest us. Separated from them, at the end nearest the kitchen, were Mr. Batchlett, Zeb, Hank, three men I hadn't seen before, and a boy. "Here he is now!" Mr. Batchlett called out. "Come on over here, Little Britches, and meet the folks! By dang, you sure hit the bunk in a hurry last night. How you makin' it? 'Bout ready for some chuck?"

"Fine," I said, as I walked around the table to him. "I didn't know how tired I was until we got here last night, and I didn't know how hungry I was till right now."

"Betcha my life you're hungry," a big man across the table laughed. "I tried eatin' some of Hank Bevin's chuck a couple of years back. Sit in! Sit in! Grub's on the fire."

"By dogies, Watt," Hank shouted, "give me a parcel o' good dry prairie chips an' . . ."

Mr. Batchlett didn't let him get any further. "This is Watt Bendt," he said; "he's ranch boss. And next is Kenny and Ned and Tom. The boys down yonder are the dairymen."

Ned and Tom were just ordinary cowhands, in their early thirties, but Kenny looked to be about five years old. He was sitting up as straight as a prairie dog beside his father, and watching me with bright blue eyes. "I seen you before," he chirped as soon as Mr. Batchlett had finished. "Hazel cut your pi'cure out of the paper."

I knew it must have been the picture that was in the Denver paper, the time Hi Beckman and I won the trick-riding contest at the Littleton roundup. It wasn't a very good one, because my hat shaded my face so much it was mostly black. I was just going to tell Kenny so when a voice from the kitchen doorway snapped, "I did not either! It just happened to be on the back of an old ad I cut out."

I had to look around Mr. Batchlett to see who was talking, and then I wasn't too sure. Four girls were standing in the doorway, and all but one of them were looking right at me. That one was nearly as tall as I, had long reddish braids that hung down in front of her shoulders, a snubby nose, and a million freckles. The others ran down in stair steps, to one who looked to be about three.

"Well," I said, "it wasn't a very good picture anyway."

"I don't know! I didn't hardly look at it!" the tallest one said sharply.

"You did too, Hazel!" the next tallest squealed. "You stuck it up on . . ."

"I did not!" Hazel snapped, and ducked back into the kitchen without ever looking at me.

I was just turning back to the table when I heard a crisp, "Toot-toot! Gangway!" from the kitchen. When I looked around again, one of the prettiest girls I ever saw was coming through the doorway. She must have been about twenty or twenty-one, and not more than five feet tall, with eyes just like Kenny's, and honey-colored wavy hair piled high on her head. She was wearing high-heeled shoes, with a little white apron over a pink calico dress, and carrying a big plate of steaming flapjacks. Every move she made was quick and perky—like a sparrow's.

As I watched her, Sid sang out, "Hi, Jenny Wren!"

"Hi, everybody," she said as she put the plate of flapjacks down. "You'd better light right into these while they're hot; there's another batch on the stove." Then she looked at me and said, "So you're Little Britches?"

"That's what they call me, Miss Wren," I said, "but my name's Ralph Moody."

Everybody started laughing, even Jenny. Then she hugged her arm around my neck for half a second, and said, "Well, it's only this runty little redhead that calls me Jenny Wren. My name's Jenny Warren, and I teach school at Castle Rock. I saw you ride in the Littleton roundup last summer and the year before. You haven't grown an inch, have you?"

"Yes, Miss Warren," I said, "I've grown nearly two inches."

"I'm Miss Warren only in school," she told me, "and school's out until after Labor Day. Here, I'm Jenny."

That first plate of flapjacks didn't last more than five minutes, and it was Mrs. Bendt who brought in the next plateful. She was Jenny's sister, but they didn't look or act very much alike. She was quite a little older, taller, thinner, and had straight ash-colored hair, with sort of faded blue eyes. She looked tired, and her voice was kind of sharp.

When she set the plate down, Mr. Batchlett said, "Helen, this is Little Britches, the boy I was tellin' you about."

Mrs. Bendt looked at me without a word, then said, "Batch, you ain't goin' to take that little boy out with the trading crews, are you? Why, he can't be no older'n Hazel!"

Mr. Batchlett winked at me and said, "He's older'n you think. He's worked cattle a couple of summers; he'll make out all right."

"Well, I'd never let him do it if he was a boy of mine! Thank the Lord I had mostly girls, or Watt would be trying to make cowhands out of 'em a'ready."

I poured more syrup on my flapjacks and thanked the Lord that I wasn't a boy of hers. Mother was scary enough about my working around horses and cattle, but she'd never said I couldn't do it.

After the flapjacks, Jenny brought in a big platter of fried eggs, and sausage cakes, and fried potatoes, and hot biscuits. I ate until I was ready to pop, and Kenny ate almost as much as I did. Only his head and shoulders came above the top of the table, but he was trying as hard as he could to be a man. He'd pound his knife handle on the table and snap out: "Pass the spuds! Pass the bread! Pass the meat!" Once he looked over at me and said, "Betcha my life my burro can do more tricks than your old mare."

"Lady can't do many tricks," I told him. "My trick horse was a blue roan, named Sky High. He didn't belong to me, but to the Y-B ranch where I used to work."

"Betcha my life my burro could beat him! Betcha my life you can't ride Jack!"

Hank was telling some long-winded story about the way he used to ride horses, but Mr. Batchlett pushed his chair back and said, "Well, it's time we was gettin' at it. Watt, how 'bout you and me riding out to look over the cow stuff while the boys round up the saddle stock? I want them that's going to be working cattle to pick their summer string today, then we'll put the rest of the bunch up on the mountain ranch. Need to save all the grass on the home place for cows."

He looked around at the men and went on, "I want every man to have a fair shake at the horses, so Watt and I'll pick right along with you. We'll pick in go-rounds; no changing your minds after you've made your pick. Hank, you and Zeb can go haul in the chuckwagon. Sid, you and Little Britches can go along with Ned and Tom to round up the saddle stock."

All through breakfast Sid had been trying to get Jenny to talk to him. She hadn't paid any more attention than if he'd been a chipmunk chattering, but once she made his face redder than a thornberry when she asked me, "Does this other little boy go to school with you?"

Zeb and Hank saddled up to go for the chuckwagon when we left the chuckhouse, but Sid had to go and change into his working clothes. I went to the bunkhouse with him, to get my chaps and spurs. He was a little bit grumpy, and grumbled at me, "Daggone you, Little Britches! You didn't have to let on to Jenny Wren that I hightailed down to the chuckwagon to get my glad rags this mornin'. You put in your time gettin' Hazel to hug you 'round the neck; that little Jenny Wren's too growed-up for you."

I hadn't liked it too well when Jenny hugged me right there at the table, and I didn't like Sid's joshing me about Hazel. I guess I was as grumpy as he, and said, "I didn't come out here to get hugged; I came to work cattle." Then I strapped on my spurs and went to saddle Lady, so I could look around a little before we went to bring in the remuda.

Lady was as well rested as I when I tossed my saddle onto her that Sunday morning, but she wasn't any more used than I to the kind of riding we were going to be doing. We'd always worked in prairie country where she could take and hold a steady gait, and we could see where we were going. It wasn't that way at Batchlett's ranch. The home place was tucked right up against the front range of the Rockies, and it seemed as if they had pushed the land out and crumpled it up into knolls, gulches, arroyos and mesas. There was hardly a place where a horse could get a straight run of a quarter mile. On the high ground clumps of scrub oak stood so thick we could seldom see a hundred yards ahead, and along the creek beds the trails wound through thickets of willow and alder. It made perfect summer shade and winter shelter for cattle, but it made the work of a prairie horse and cowhand a nightmare.

It wasn't only in the lay of the land that Batchlett's home ranch was different from others. At the Y-B, or any of the prairie ranches where I'd worked before, the buildings—except for the house, where the help never went—didn't amount to much. There was just a bunkhouse, chuckhouse, a few corrals, and a barn that was mostly saddle shop and forge. Beef cattle were born, grazed, branded, and doctored if they needed to be, on the open range. Only in the worst blizzards a few dogie calves were brought in to the corrals of the home place. Steers were trailed from the range to the railroad for shipping to market, and fences were hated worse than wolves and rattlesnakes.

Ranching at Batchlett's was just the opposite. It was half stock-raising and half dairy-farming, and the two halves didn't mix any more than horses and cattle do. The outbuildings at the home ranch were a regular village, and the dairy part of it was entirely separate from the stock-raising and handling. No cowhand would think of milking a cow or feeding a calf or hog, and no dairyhand ever rode a horse. We even slept in separate bunkhouses. I don't know what the dairymen thought about the cowhands, but the fellows in our crew didn't have much use for dairyhands.

Milk cows that were going to be traded to families in Denver couldn't be branded and turned loose on the range, to raise their calves as beef cattle did. It would have spoiled them for milkers, and they'd have grown too wild. Because many of them were not branded they had to be kept inside of fences. And they had to be brought in to the corrals often enough to keep them used to being handled. As soon as calves were born, they and their mothers were brought in and turned over to the dairy crew. There they were separated. The mothers were put into the dairy herd, and the calves were raised by hand until they were old enough to be put out to graze in the calf pasture.

4

Blueboy

As I RODE around the outbuildings and looked the place over, I kept an eye on the horse corral. And when I saw the others go to saddle up I brought Lady back there. Sid was cinching the saddle onto his giraffe horse, and when he straightened up, the horn stood six inches above the crown of his hat. He was all over his grumpiness, and didn't get a bit peeved when Tom called out to ask if he wanted a ladder for mounting.

"Nope! Got me a sky hook!" Sid called back, hopped, caught the shoulder-high stirrup with his toe, and flipped into the saddle.

Mr. Batchlett and Mr. Bendt had already mounted, and were turning their horses onto a trail that led off toward the mountains when Hazel came running from the house. "I don't have to go to Sunday School today, do I, Paw?" she called from fifty yards away.

"Don't know no reason why not," he said, and turned his horse half back.

"Well, I can't, Paw," Hazel panted, as she ran up to him. "Jenny wants to go, and . . . and I'll have to stay to home to mind the baby."

"Jenny say so?"

"Well . . . I know she wants to go, to . . . to wear her new . . ."

From where I sat on Lady I saw Mr. Bendt wink at Mr. Batchlett, then he asked, "Sure you ain't frettin' 'bout the horse-pickin', 'stead of Jenny?"

Hazel was standing so close that her father's stirrup nearly touched her shoulder. She turned her face up to him, and there were almost tears in her voice when she said, "I got to be here, Paw! I just got to be here!"

Mr. Bendt leaned down toward her, and his voice was real gentle when he said, "You run on now, gal, and help your maw with the dishes. I reckon we might be able to hold off the horse pickin' till you womenfolks get back from church. What you think, Batch?"

"I reckon," Mr. Batchlett said with a grin.

"Promise?" Hazel asked.

Mr. Batchlett nodded, and said, "Promise!" Then Hazel ran back toward the house without ever looking around at the rest of us.

Tom and Ned seemed to know just where we'd find the horse herd. They took a well-worn cattle trail that led northward along the foot of the mountains, forking off like branches of a river at the mouth of each canyon.

Winding in and out through the brush, we'd followed the trail four or five miles when we topped a high bench. Below us, in a little green valley, there was a bunch of forty or fifty horses grazing. Suddenly, one of them threw up his head, pointing his ears toward us, whinnied shrilly, and raced away toward a canyon mouth. In a moment the whole bunch was racing behind him.

"Blueboy!" Tom rapped out angrily. "Mighta knowed he'd wind us 'fore we could get around 'em! You and the kid cut acrost the butte and try to head 'em, Ned! Sid and me'll work around to the far side."

I'd seen a lot of beautiful horses, but never one that caught my eye the way Blueboy did. From up there on the bench, with the horse band half a mile below us in the valley, he was the most beautiful sight I had ever seen. The sun glinted off his racing back the way it glints off ripples in a deep mountain lake. His white-stockinged legs flashed like driving pistons, and his long white mane and tail streamed out like silken flags. He ran with his muzzle high, swinging his white-blazed head from side to side. As I watched, he circled to the back of the band, snaking his head out and raking his teeth at the laggards.

I was so busy watching Blueboy that I didn't notice Tom and Sid drop down over the edge of the bench, or that Ned was spurring away toward the mountains. I pressed my spurs against Lady's flanks and went racing after him. As I caught up, I shouted, "Is Blueboy the stallion?"

"No, gelding since he was a three-year-old, but he don't know it," Ned called back. "Crazy maverick! Out of a blooded mare, by a wild stud."

The canyon into which Blueboy had driven the horse herd wound in an S shape back between two low mountains. By cutting around one of them, and sliding down a shale bank, Ned and I reached the bottom of the canyon just as the horses rounded the last bend. At sight of us, they wheeled and started back, but Blueboy was behind them, slashing and kicking. For a couple of minutes I thought he'd drive the whole band past us. If they'd been unbroken range horses, he would have, but they were mostly saddle stock, and had too much respect for flying ropes. A shifty little claybank dodged back past him, and the rest of the band followed.

I could hardly believe that Blueboy wasn't a stallion. The remuda at Batchlett's ranch was made up of almost every type of stock horse. There were young ones and old ones, mares with colts running at their sides, yearlings, a few unbroken three-year-olds, and geldings that showed the white saddle marks of many hard seasons, but Blueboy handled them all as if they were his harem.

Tom and Sid were waiting at the far end of the canyon to

turn the remuda onto the trail for the corrals, but Blueboy
wouldn't have it. Racing with his head low and his nostrils
wide, squealing, wheeling, and slashing with his yellow teeth,
he charged the lead mares time and again, turning them away
from the trail and driving them into the brush.

"Why in blazes Batch keeps that crazy mav'rick's more'n I
know!" Tom shouted, as we spurred to head the band back
toward the south. "I'd have throwed lead into him when he
was foaled if I'd owned the mare."

"Worthless half-breed!" Ned shouted back. "I'd throw lead
into him now if I was packin' a six-gun."

"Better not leave Batch catch you at it," Tom called, and
spurred away, yelling and swearing at Blueboy.

Time after time we got the horse band headed back onto the
trail, and the older ones would have followed it, but each time
Blueboy raced to the lead and turned them aside.

Sid tried to cut him away from the herd and drive him up
the canyon alone, but his piebald was no match for Blueboy's
speed. He'd circle, with his head and tail high, and race back
to turn the band again. Tom and Ned tried to corner him in a
gulch and get a throw rope on him, but they didn't have any
better luck than Sid. Bounding up the side of the steep, rocky
gulch, Blueboy whirled at the top, snorted at them, and came
tearing back to the herd.

It shouldn't have taken us more than two hours to round up
the remuda and bring it in to the corral, but it was well past
noon before we got it there. And the only way we did it at all
was by the other three fighting Blueboy away while I pushed
the herd along the trail. He never gave up his fight for a second,
and he wouldn't give up his band. At the last moment he broke
through the whirling catch ropes, raced up, and led the remuda
into the horse corral.

Mr. Batchlett and Mr. Bendt were still out looking over
the cattle, Hank and Zeb hadn't come in with the chuckwagon,
and Mrs. Bendt and the children weren't home from church
when we brought the remuda in. There was nothing to do after

we'd unsaddled, so we sat on the top rail of the corral, looking at the horses and talking.

Tom and Ned had been on the home ranch the summer before, and knew every horse in the bunch, but there was no sense in asking them any questions. They'd know which horses they wanted for their own strings, and they'd tell us almost anything to keep us from finding out which ones they were. Sid was sitting beside me, watching half a dozen different horses as they milled and turned, but there was only one I could watch for more than a minute.

Blueboy was never still an instant, and kept himself between us and the rest of the remuda, as though he were protecting it. With his head high, his eyes bright, and his ears pointing, he seemed to be trying to watch everything at once. He was neither fat nor thin, and the hide rippled over the muscles of his rump and shoulders like oil over running water. I had a feeling that, at any moment, he might race at the high pole fence and sail over it without touching. Ned was sitting next beyond Sid, and I asked him, "Has anybody ever ridden Blueboy?"

"Half a dozen, I reckon. Why?"

"I just wondered," I said. "I'll bet it would take a real buster to stay with him ten seconds."

"Pi'tcher horse! Crowhopper!" Ned said, without looking away from the milling remuda. "Takes brains to make a good twister; that mav'rick's loco."

I'd seen plenty of horses that had been poisoned on locoweed. They acted half-drunk, stupid, and crazy, but Blueboy wasn't that kind of horse. He'd proved all morning that he was smarter than any one of us. I began to think that maybe both Ned and Tom wanted him for themselves, and that they'd been running him down so that neither Sid nor I would pick him.

I was still watching Blueboy and wishing I owned him when Sid leaned in front of me and asked Tom, "How come the boss holds onto the blue? Wouldn't a circus pay good money for a showy lookin' horse the likes of that?"

Tom nodded, "Sure would, but Batch, he won't give up on

him. Got him in his blood, I reckon. I've heard tell he had the old stallion in his blood so strong he could taste it. Put in three summers tryin' to lay rope on that wild stud when him and Beckman first come up from Texas. Run him clean down into the Sangre de Cristos and back half a dozen times. Spent the price of forty good stock horses on him."

"Catch him or give up?" Sid asked.

"Reckon you don't know Batch very good," Tom said, as he and Ned climbed down from the fence. "He don't give up his chips till the last card's down. Couldn't lay rope on the stud, but he had a thoroughbred mare shipped in here. Turned her loose in the mountains. Daggone shame he couldn't'a got nothin' better'n that blue devil for a colt!"

I'd been interested in Tom's story, but it was what Ned had told me that made up my mind. I'd ridden some pretty good bucking horses at the Y-B and the fair-grounds, though I'd never ridden any real twisters, and was a little out of practice. But when Ned said Blueboy was only a crowhopper, I made up my mind that I was going to pick him for my string, no matter what anybody thought about him.

Sid and I sat without saying anything for quite a few minutes after Tom and Ned had left, then I asked, "Made your pick yet?"

"Well, yes and no," Sid answered. "I been keepin' an eye on that sorrel gelding yonder, and aim to dab my rope on him if I can. If he don't bust it and throw me cattiwumpus, and if he can turn on a dollar and a half, I might think about him. For this brush country, I like a horse tall enough to histe a man up, so's he can see where he's headed for. You got an eye peeled yet?"

"Mmm-hmm," I told him, "if he doesn't histe me over the fence on his first pitch. I haven't tried to ride a rough one for nearly a year."

"Ground'll always catch you! Never heard tell of it lettin' nobody through! Which one you aimin' to go after?"

"Blueboy," I told him.

"Blueboy! What you aimin' to do, start up a circus?" Sid asked sharply. "Ain't you the one that claims he come out here to work cattle?"

"That's what I am here for," I told him, "and I'm going to do it with Blueboy. If he can handle cattle the way he handles horses, I guess we'll make out all right."

"Take it easy! You ain't workin' mustangs, but milk cows!" Sid said—and he said it in exactly the same voice Mr. Batchlett had used when he'd told me the same thing the day before. Sid pointed to a sleek-looking seal-brown mare, and went on, "You forget about that Blueboy; he's too much horse for you! How 'bout that little mare with the star in her forehead? I been watchin' her, and she's handy and clever; make you a mighty fine trail horse."

Zeb and Hank drove in with the chuckwagon just then, so I didn't have to argue with Sid any more. Mrs. Bendt and the children were right behind them with the buckboard. Before we had the teams unharnessed and watered, Mr. Batchlett and Mr. Bendt rode in. And Jenny rang the dinner bell as soon as she saw them.

The day the horse strings are picked in the spring is one of the biggest days on cattle ranches. In working cattle, a cowhand and his horse have to be partners, and understand and trust each other. If a man picks the wrong horses in the spring, there isn't much understanding, and even less trust. A man may be a top hand, but if he gets a poor string of horses he can't do a very good job. Or a man can be only a fair rider and, with a good string, do the job of a top hand.

Picking our horses in go-rounds, as Mr. Batchlett had said we would, no one could be sure of getting the horses he wanted, and most of the men were nervous and jumpy when we sat down at the dinner table. Nobody joked, and Sid didn't even try to get Jenny to talk to him. First one man would tell about some smart horse he used to ride, then another would brag about one he'd had that was smarter. But no one mentioned the horse-picking until we'd nearly finished eating. Then Kenny piped up, "If Batch would leave me have my pickin's, I know what ones I'd take. I'd take . . ."

"Never you mind which ones you'd take" his father told him. "Them of us that's been around here and knows 'em ought to have claim to a little edge. Who's goin' to get the first pick, Batch?"

I hadn't seen Mrs. Bendt or the girls since they drove in from church, but when the talk of horse-picking began they crowded into the kitchen doorway. Mr. Batchlett turned toward them and asked, "How about writin' eight numbers, folding 'em, and putting 'em in a hat for us, Hazel?"

I think Hazel had the numbers all written out and folded ahead of time, and that she knew right where each one was in the hat. Anyway, she was only gone two minutes, and when she passed the hat to Mr. Batchlett, her father, and me, she kept twisting and turning it. Mr. Batchlett shut his eyes, reached in real slowly, and picked out the number one slip. Mr. Bendt and I just looked and grabbed. He got number six and I got five.

As soon as we'd all drawn our numbers, Mr. Batchlett pushed his chair back, and said, "Let's get at it! You all know how it works: go-rounds; each man picks one horse in his turn. You'll have three chances with the rope—what you get on it is your pick, like it or not. With the help of your partner you'll saddle it, and ride it to a count of ten. Miss either way and you'll lose your turn till the go-rounds are over. That goes for all of you!" Then he looked around at me and added, "but Watt'll give you a hand if you want it, Little Britches."

If we'd been alone I'm sure I'd have thanked him and told him I'd be glad to have Mr. Bendt help me. But with all the men, even the dairyhands, and Mrs. Bendt and Jenny and Hazel there, I didn't like to be singled out. I'd come out there at a man's wages to do a man's job, and I didn't want anybody to think I couldn't do it, so I looked over at Mr. Bendt, and said, "Thank you just the same, but I'd rather take my chances along with the rest of the cowhands."

5

Picking a String

IN A GOOD many ways, horse-picking day on the big cattle
ranches was like a Fourth of July roundup. Horses that had
been out on the range or pasture all winter would usually
buck when they were saddled for the first time in the spring.
The good ones might never buck again all summer, but on that
first shake-down they'd pitch and twist like fury. The older
ones—the smartest—were often the hardest to catch and ride.
From years of handling cattle they'd learned every trick of the
trade—and some that were all their own. They knew just as
well as the men did that if they could keep from being roped,
or could dump their rider, they'd be turned back to pasture
for the summer.

A horse string wasn't all that was chosen at the spring picking. Cowhands almost always worked in pairs, and that was the
time when the new men chose their partners. One man didn't
say to another, "Will you be my partner?" He waited until the
man he wanted to team up with had ridden into the big corral
and roped his first horse. Then he rode into the breaking-pen
to open the gate, help with the saddling, and stand by as
pickup man. Picking the wrong partner could be even worse
than picking the wrong horse.

45

By the time we were all saddled up, and Mr. Batchlett was ready to ride in for his number one pick, everybody on the ranch, except the baby, was crowded around the big pole horse corral. The dairyhands were perched along the top rail of the breaking pen like a row of magpies. Mrs. Bendt, Jenny, and the smaller girls were peeking through the bars, and Hazel and Kenny were on the top rail of the horse corral, with their arms and legs wrapped around the high gateposts like a pair of teddy bears.

Those of us who were going to do the picking sat on our horses outside the gate, and my heart was pounding like the hoofs of a stampeding herd. I knew how much I was going to need good horses that summer, and I knew I'd made a bad mistake in telling Mr. Bendt I didn't want his help. I was determined to get Blueboy, but didn't have any more idea than a goose what other horses to pick.

I think everyone was holding his breath when Mr. Batchlett rode into the corral. The second he unlimbered his rope and started it swinging, the horses began to mill and dodge. Before I had any idea which one he was after, his line whistled out and the loop settled around the neck of the seal-brown mare Sid had pointed out to me. She seemed to have known she was going to be chosen, and came out of the milling bunch without ever tightening the rope. When Mr. Batchlett turned her toward the breaking pen, Mr. Bendt was there to open the gate. "Easy, Starlight," was all he said as the mare crowded past him.

Starlight bucked hard, quick, and for only five or six seconds. Anyone who knew anything about horses could see that she and Mr. Batchlett understood each other perfectly—and that one was having as much fun as the other. He never left the saddle far enough that a piece of paper could have been slipped under him, and when he led the mare out through the gate she nuzzled his shoulder.

Hank had drawn number two, and was barely inside the corral when he spurred straight at a high-headed bay gelding.

It looked to be an easy catch, but the bay bolted away as the loop flew. So did the rest of the bunch, with Blueboy in the lead and Hank spurring close behind—swearing at the bay and gathering his rope back in. He let his second loop fly before it was half built, and it closed before it reached the bay. His third loop was nearly as big as a circus tent. It fell short of the bay and snagged an old black mare. Everyone knew she wouldn't buck, and no one went into the breaking pen to help Hank saddle her. Mr. Batchlett hardly excited the bunch at all when he took Starlight out, but Hank had driven them half crazy.

Sid's turn followed Hank's, and I knew he'd go for the tall sorrel, but I was worried about who would go in to open the bucking-pen gate for him. I wanted to do it myself, but it would have taken a lot of nerve for a boy to pick himself as a man's partner. I didn't even look toward Sid when he started to ride in for his first pick, but just sat on Lady, looking at the excited horses in the corral. As he rode past me there was a sharp sting on my hip pocket. When I jumped and looked around, Sid grinned and jerked his head toward the breaking pen. I couldn't have been happier if somebody had given me a thousand dollars.

Sid didn't make much work of getting his rope on the sorrel, and led it toward the bucking pen by the time I was there to open the gate. It bucked hard and fast, but Sid was a fine rider and stuck like a burr.

Zeb had drawn number four, but didn't even bother to ride his mule into the corral. Blueboy was driving the remuda in a racing merry-go-round, but Zeb slouched into the corral as unconcerned as if he'd been going to the well for a bucket of water. He stood with his loop dangling at his side, and when the horse he wanted passed him he flipped the rope over its neck. The horse was the smallest in the corral, and he didn't show a bit of fight, but Hank was at the breaking pen gate, pushing it open and shouting, "Hold him, Zeb! Hold him! Head him this-a-way, so's I can give you a hand!"

My turn was next, and I was so busy thinking about the way

I'd try to handle Blueboy that I didn't notice Hazel until Sid came to open the gate for me. She was still sitting on the top rail and had her arm wrapped around the gatepost just above my head. I was starting to shake a loop in my catch rope when she reached out a toe and just touched me on my shoulder. When I looked up, she whispered, "If I thought you could ride good enough, I'd tell you to pick Clay."

"Maybe I'll pick him on second go-round," I whispered back. "I've already got one all . . ."

"Hmff!" she sniffed, "a little boy like you prob'ly couldn't handle Clay anyways. He's mighty quick."

If she'd been grown-up I wouldn't have flown mad so quick about her calling me a little boy, but, with her, I couldn't help it. "Which one is he?" I snapped at her. "We'll see if I'm good enough to handle him!"

Hazel didn't look at me, and she didn't look at the horses, but off toward the dairy barn, and her lips hardly moved as she said, "The little claybank—with the black stripe down his back."

I'd been nervous when I was sitting there on Lady, waiting to go in and make my try for Blueboy. But if my hands were shaking when Sid opened the corral gate for me, it was because I was so mad I couldn't hold them still. I crowded Lady right in before the gate was open more than a yard, shook out my loop, and looked to see where the little claybank was. I'd no-ticed him that morning when he dodged back past Blueboy and led the remuda out of the S canyon. But all I remembered about him was that he ran with the slow bunch, had a short, hoppity-hop gait, saddle scars on his back, and carried his head low. I didn't want him at all, but I wasn't going to let Hazel think I couldn't handle him.

The bunch was still excited and jumpy, and I didn't help things any by spurring Lady into the corral so fast. The first thing I knew, I had a merry-go-round going, and the claybank was right in the center—sort of dog-hopping along, with his

head low and tight against the rump of a big bay. If I'd been
on his back, I couldn't have got a rope around his neck.

I was sure I hadn't made any move that would let the claybank know I was after him, but he watched me like a gopher.
I let the bunch make three or four circles, while I just sat there
with my rope swinging easy. Then I spurred Lady hard and
straight into the merry-go-round. As the horses wheeled away,
the claybank's head came loose from the bay, and I whanged
my loop down at it. It was one of the best throws I'd ever
made, but the claybank ducked his head, and my loop slithered
across his mane. It had barely touched the ground when I heard
Mr. Bendt shout, "Hazel, you get down off'n that fence! Get
on over with your maw where you belong!"

It must have been nearly ten minutes before I got another
chance to make a throw at the claybank. Of course, after my
first throw, he and everybody else knew I was after him, and
he kept his head tucked up against some other horse so tight I
couldn't shake him loose. Hank kept shouting orders at me,
and I think it was his shouting that made me miss my second
throw; I let the loop go when I didn't have more than half a
chance.

When I gathered in my rope I was so nervous that it came
up wiggling like a snake. My mouth was dry and there was a
lump in my throat that was half choking me. I knew I was
doing a little-boy sort of a job, right out there in front of everybody, and that Hazel was probably snickering at me. I had to
sit there for a minute or two, trying not to hear what Hank was
yelling, and trying to make up my mind whether or not to dab
my loop onto the first horse that would make me an easy catch.
One more miss and I'd lose my turn altogether.

As I sat there I built a new loop, and was swinging it sort of
lazy-like when Hazel yelled, "Now! Now!"

I woke up as if I'd been dreaming, and the first thing I saw
was the little claybank dog-hopping past me. He had his head
turned my way, and was looking at me as much as to ask if I'd

given up. Without even thinking, I whipped my loop just over Lady's ears and yanked it down. It came tight around the clay-bank's neck.

Sid was grinning like a jack-o'-lantern when he opened the breaking pen gate and let us through. As I passed him the catch rope, he asked, "Know what one you got?"

"Sure," I said, "the one I went in after."

"Dogged if you didn't," he chirped, "but I'll bet a hat you don't know what one it is."

"I ought to," I told him, "I had a hard enough time getting a loop on him." And then I added, ". . . with Hazel's help."

"Bet she gets her biscuits warmed," he chuckled. "This here is her old man's prize cuttin' horse. Watt's been chewin' on his knuckles ever since the picking begun—scairt somebody'd dab a rope on 'fore his turn come up."

"Then I'm going to turn him back," I said. "I didn't know he was any special horse."

"No, you ain't neither!" Sid snapped. "Watt, he wouldn't let you—Batch neither! Now you get on outside and haul that saddle off; you still got a job o' riding to do 'fore you got a claim to this little devil."

I did a lot of thinking as I took off my spurs, uncinched my saddle, and pulled it off Lady. In the first place, it wasn't very fair for Hazel to have told me about picking Clay. And in the second place, I'd be in a bad way if I had Mr. Bendt sore at me. By the time I got back to the breaking pen I had my mind made up about what I was going to do. If the claybank bucked hard enough to give me any excuse at all, I'd use one of the tricks I'd learned for the Littleton roundup: I'd flip out of the saddle, somersault, and land sitting down. I could do it without being hurt, and it would be hard for anybody to see that I hadn't been thrown. After what Hazel had said about my not being good enough to handle Clay, I didn't like to be the first one tossed, but it seemed to be my only way out of a lot of trouble.

I must have buttoned my lips tight when I made up my

mind. When I was climbing the fence with my saddle, Sid snapped, "Get that look off'n your pan, and them idees out of your head! You wouldn't be foolin' nobody if you took a flopperoo, and you wouldn't be doin' yourself no good. Histe that saddle over here, and haul your belt up tight."

Clay didn't make a move when the cinches were pulled tight or when I eased into the saddle. I didn't think he was going to buck at all, but before Sid turned him loose, he half-whispered, "Watch out for him! He ain't goin' high, but he'll be a side-windin' son-of-a-gun, and quicker'n scat. Hold your hat in your hand and keep it up high; you'll need all the balance you can get out of it."

I didn't have time to do much thinking, and I couldn't have flipped out of the saddle on purpose to save my neck. It was only what Sid had told me about holding my hat high that saved me a dozen times. Clay never went more than a foot off the ground, and he didn't bog his head enough to even give me a light line to hold. He didn't sunfish, and he didn't swap ends, but he did every double-shuffle, fence row, and zigzag in the book—and some that weren't.

I don't think the seat of my pants was square in that saddle for a tenth of a second after Clay's first side-slip. Twice I was so far off balance that I could see the ground between my own legs. But, both times, just when I thought I was a goner for sure, Clay changed direction and snapped the saddle back under me. I don't suppose he put on more than a ten-second show—nobody could really have called it bucking—but it seemed to me like an hour. When he swung around to the gate and stopped, he turned his head and looked at me as if he were saying, "Well, you made it, didn't you, kid?"

Everybody, even the dairyhands, were crowded around the breaking pen when Sid opened it and let me ride Clay out. Hazel was hopping up and down, and half a dozen were talking at the same time, but I was only listening for Mr. Bendt. "Reckon you know what you done to me," he said, with a laugh that didn't have any music in it. "Dang near put me afoot, that's what you done! Figgered I had a chance right up to the last hop. You wasn't on by more'n a boot heel." Then he slapped Mr. Batchlett on the back, and hooted, "By dog, did you take note of all the air he beat with that Stetson? Looked like a dadgummed hawk fightin' a coyote with one busted wing."

Anyone could have seen how badly Mr. Bendt felt, and that he was just trying to cover up by hooting and making a joke. I didn't feel a bit good myself. Even though I'd stayed on Clay, I'd only proved that Hazel was right when she said I probably couldn't handle him. I hadn't wanted the horse in the first place, and wished I could find some way of turning him over to Mr. Bendt.

I was sitting there on the claybank with my head down, thinking, when Mr. Batchlett slapped me on the leg, and said, "Get your feathers up, boy! Between you and Hazel, you earned him fair and square. He'll dump you plenty of times, but you'll prob'ly learn to ride him." He'd started away, then turned back, and said, quiet enough that no one else could hear, "You understand, Little Britches, that by pickin' this horse you've picked yourself one of the toughest jobs in the outfit—and there won't be nobody comin' to help you."

"Yes, sir," I said, "I know it." I really didn't, until that minute, but I couldn't say so.

I rode Clay around a little after Mr. Batchlett talked to me, and he was as easy to handle as Lady. I was so excited about having him that I didn't pay too much attention to the picking and shaking-down until it was almost my turn for the second go-round. All I'd noticed was that no one had picked Blueboy. Everyone ahead of me had used his first-pick horse to go in after his second. When Zeb went in, I rode Clay up to wait for my turn. I was sitting on him, just outside the corral gate, thinking just how I'd catch Blueboy, when I saw Hazel run to her father. He leaned down, and she seemed to be whispering to him for a minute, then she came running over to me. When I leaned down she whispered, "Take Pinch!"

"If I don't take Blueboy this time, somebody else will get him," I whispered back.

That time Hazel looked right up into my eyes. She shook her head hard, and said, "Uh-uh! You take Pinch; you'll need him!"

After Hazel's having picked Clay for me, and especially after her having helped me catch him, I couldn't tell her to mind her own business, so I said, "All right. Which one is he?"

"Well," she said, "he's bay, and he's a little bit jugheaded, and not very pretty, but he's . . . there he goes! Right behind that silver-tip!"

I'd seen plenty of Pinch when I'd been trying to catch Clay, and had told myself he'd be the last horse in the remuda I'd ever pick. He looked old and bony and homely and lazy, and was about the meanest gelding I'd ever seen. He kept his ears pinned down tight, and every time another horse got in front of him he'd snake his neck out and bite it on the rump.

The remuda was running in a merry-go-round, and I took Clay into the corral real slowly, planning to make a flip catch the first time Pinch passed me. But he didn't go past. He dropped out of the circle and nipped his way into a bunch that was jammed in the far corner. I'd hardy looked toward Pinch, and don't know how in the world he knew I was after him, but he did—and so did Clay. Both of them knew a lot more about the whole business than I did.

Pinch turned to face us squarely as I rode toward the corner. One after another, the other horses dashed away, but he didn't move a muscle, and Clay never once turned his head toward the others. He slowed his gait and, under me, felt the way a cat looks when it's creeping up on a ground squirrel. I couldn't very well make a flip catch with Pinch facing right at me, so I began to whirl my loop slowly—and must have glanced up at it. In that split moment Pinch dodged to get away, and quicker than the pop of a whip, Clay dived to stop him. If I hadn't grabbed for the saddle horn faster than I could think, he'd have spilled me. As it was, I dropped my coil and the loop fell dead. I'd have lost my catch rope altogether if the end of it hadn't been tied to the saddle horn.

I was even more ashamed of myself for grabbing the horn than for wasting a throw and dropping my rope. Neither horse

moved until I had the rope coiled again and had begun to swing my loop. As it came forward on the fourth swing, I yanked it down hard at Pinch's head. But his head wasn't there —and I came awfully near not being there either. In the split fraction of a second it took that loop to strike, Pinch had snaked his head away and dodged to one side. Clay dodged right with him, and I had to grab for the saddle horn again.

I don't think Pinch ever moved his hind feet, but he kept feinting and dodging with his front ones, and Clay feinted and dodged a little quicker. He didn't pay any more attention to me than if I'd been a sack of rags—and that's just about the way I rode him. More than half the time I was half out of the saddle, and the only way I could stay in it at all was by keeping a death grip on the horn. Hank was yelling orders at me, I could hear the men hooting and laughing, but the two horses kept feinting so fast I couldn't get my balance long enough to coil in my rope.

I must have slid back and forth across my saddle a thousand times before I had sense enough to pull Clay away from that corner, so he'd stand still long enough for me to think. I knew I'd lost my head in trying to handle Pinch, and I guess that's what made me think of Hi Beckman. At the Y-B ranch he was always telling me, "A man that loses his head loses his horse. Don't never tackle a horse till you've watched him and know his quirks."

When I'd sat still and thought a couple of minutes, I was sure I knew how to catch Pinch—and it worked just the way I'd thought it would. I whirled my rope, drove him out of the corner and into the merry-go-round, then crowded him until he caught up to the slowest runners. He did what I knew he'd do; snaked his head out to nip the horse in front of him on the rump. My loop caught him when he was looking where he was going to nip.

Pinch behaved all right when I led him to the breaking pen, but Sid didn't. When I was swinging out of my saddle, he fanned my behind with his hat, as if he thought I'd burned it when I was sliding around on Clay. He didn't say a word, but he didn't have to: the men howled and hollered like a pack of moon-struck coyotes.

I didn't look at anybody when I rode Clay out and stripped off my saddle, and I was halfway back to the breaking pen with it when Mr. Batchlett called, "Hey! How about them spurs! Better leave 'em on the outside!"

With everybody laughing at me—and having to go back to take off my spurs—I was a little careless about the way I saddled old Pinch. He blew his belly up like a balloon when Sid was passing the cinch under him, and I didn't notice that he was still holding his breath when I yanked the cinch tight and set my knot. "Better hold off a minute and tighten that cinch again!" Sid told me, as I started up the poles to mount, "he's still as swole up as a bloated calf!"

I'd fussed around and been laughed at enough, and I wasn't going to wait and let people think I was afraid to get on Pinch. Besides, I didn't think the old horse would any more than crow-hop. "He's just hay-bellied, that's all!" I said, balanced on the top rail, and eased myself down into the saddle.

I found out how hay-bellied Pinch was in less than two seconds after Sid turned him loose—and I found out what kind of crow-hopping he did. That old horse went at the job of unloading me the same way a man would go at chopping wood —except that he made a quarter turn between every down stroke. He didn't move either forward or back, each jump was just like the one before it, and he didn't hurry. With a tight saddle, any man—if he had a stout enough neck and backbone —could have ridden him all day without being thrown, but I didn't have any of them.

Pinch let out a big groan and a barrelful of air on his first jump, and from there on, the saddle rolled around on him like the skin on a cat. With every thud and turn, it slipped farther forward and to one side, and I got dizzier and dizzier.

It would have been a disgrace to grab the saddle horn, but I couldn't even do that. It was way around where my right knee should have been, and I'd had to kick my feet out of the stirrups. I don't remember much of anything after the first half-dozen jumps, but, when Pinch stopped, I had a death grip on his mane with both hands, and my legs were clamped in front of his shoulders like a collar.

At first, there wasn't a sound outside the breaking pen, but the men started laughing again when Sid picked me off. And I heard Mr. Bendt hoot, "By diggity, I'll say he's a trick rider! That kid's sure got a ridin' style all his own!"

The lump came back into my throat, and I was sure I'd made such a fool of myself that I'd always be a joke around the place. But Mr. Batchlett was waiting when I led Pinch out of the pen. He put his hand on the back of my neck and rubbed it around a couple of times, good and hard. Then he said, "I could'a told you what would happen before you climbed aboard, but I reckoned it was best to let the horse learn you. Now you'll remember to double-check your gear before you step foot in a stirrup. You ought to do all right this summer if you can learn to ride 'em; you got two right smart horses."

I still didn't think much of old Pinch, but I nodded and said, "Yes, sir—and I think I'll remember."

When my turn was coming up for the third go-round, I kneed the last breath of air out of Pinch and hauled my cinch strap as tight as I could get it. Blueboy still hadn't been picked, and I didn't want to take a chance with a slipping saddle when I went in after him.

Hazel hadn't come near me since I'd made that terrible ride on Pinch's neck, but she came walking over when we were waiting outside the corral gate. She didn't mention the ride, or the way I'd slipped and slid around on Clay, but asked, "Which one you goin' to pick this time?"

"Blueboy," I told her.

"Fiddle-tee-dee!" she said, with her nose wrinkled up. "He ain't got any more sense than y . . . , than a jack rabbit. Look at him! 'Four white feet and a white nose; haul off his hide and feed him to the crows.' Why don't you pick Juno?"

"Because I want Blueboy," I told her.

"Why?"

"Because I like him," I said. "Isn't that enough?"

"Hmff! 'Tis for you, I reckon!" she snapped, and started away toward her mother. Then she flung back over her shoulder, "but you'll be sorry to the very longest day you live."

"If I'm sorry, it'll be because I got this crabby old jughead," I snapped back. But when I rode into the corral I wasn't as sure as I had been that I wanted Blueboy. He'd been getting more and more excited as the picking went on, and was no longer running with the bunch, but dashing this way and that—ripping at the other horses and driving them out of his way. If I hadn't had that little tiff with Hazel, I'd have tossed my rope onto a neat-looking pinto mare that had caught my eye. But if I'd done it, everybody would have known I was letting Hazel boss me around. I just about had to take Blueboy, whether I still wanted him or not.

If cow horses aren't mind readers, they come awfully close to it. I'd hardly made up my mind that I had to take Blueboy before Pinch knew it. He didn't pay the least bit of attention to any other horse in the corral—and he surprised me half out of my skin. I'd just set my loop whirling when Blueboy made a wild dash past us. The cantle of my saddle came up and spanked me across the seat of my pants, then it snapped to the side. I don't suppose it took me a tenth of a second to catch my balance, or I'd have gone flying. But in that split instant old Pinch had pulled the throttle wide open. He was racing stride for stride with Blueboy, and holding him in against the pole fence at my right. All I had to do was to let my loop drop over his head; I could have made the catch just as easy with a barrel hoop.

Every other horse had cooled right down when it felt the rope around its neck, but Blueboy went wild. He reared, struck with his fore hoofs, then whirled and charged away. Pinch whirled to face him and half squatted—almost like a dog sitting down. The rope whizzed out like a whip lash, and Blueboy was.

the cracker when he reached the end of it. Pinch didn't budge
an inch when the rope twanged tight against the knot on the
saddle horn, but Blueboy did a flying somersault and landed on
his back. He was still groggy when he lurched to his feet and
let me lead him to the breaking pen.

I think all the men had expected another show when I rode
in to make my third pick. And I don't believe one of them expected me to take Blueboy. I guess it happened so fast that it
took everybody as much by surprise as it did me. As Sid
swung the bucking pen gate open, he yapped, "What in the
blazin' . . . ?"

But Mr. Batchlett came up to the fence and called, "Watch
that horse, Sid! He's treacherous!"

"Ain't it best I turn him back?" Sid asked.

"He picked him; leave him learn his lesson!" Mr. Batchlett
said in a hard dry voice. "But watch out when you saddle up!
And hang in close for a pick-up when the kid mounts!"

Blueboy was still acting half stunned, and hardly made a
move when Sid hauled the cinch tight. Sid had his mouth
clamped as tight as he pulled the cinch, and he didn't open it
until I was balanced on the top rail, ready to ease into the saddle. He'd taken the hackamore from his own rig, put it on
Blueboy, and let the nose band out until it was only a couple
of inches above the nostrils. As he passed me the hold-rope, he
said, "See them scars acrost this blue devil's muzzle? Them's
hackamore scars; he's got a tender nose bone. Keep your hold-
rope hauled up tight, so's he can't neither bog or h'ist his
head. Don't try to grab a-holt of nothin' when you get throwed!"

Then I eased into the saddle, found the stirrups, and Sid
drew his horse away to turn us loose.

Blueboy went up like a geyser, and came down running and
crowhopping. He didn't twist or side-jump, and I'd ridden
yearling calves that were harder to stay on. After three crow-
hopping, bouncing turns around the breaking pen, he settled
into a fairly even gait.

I was sitting in the saddle sort of loose-jointed—thinking

what I was going to say to Hazel—when Blueboy suddenly busted wide open. He caught me when I wasn't ready, and I didn't have a chance. From the instant of his first side-jump, I bounced around in my saddle like a pea in a gourd. I forgot what Sid had told me about keeping the hackamore tight, and couldn't even hold an arm out for balance. Both arms and both legs were flailing and I was flying in mid-air when Sid's arm looped around me and pulled me across his horse's neck. I don't think Blueboy even missed me; he kept right on pitching as if he were trying to throw the saddle over the moon.

The wind was knocked out of me so much I couldn't talk when Sid gathered me in—but he could. He spluttered at me like an old setting hen, wanting to know why in the world I'd picked Blueboy in the first place, why I hadn't been watching out for tricks, and why I didn't take a dive when he caught me napping. There weren't any good answers, and I didn't try to give any. It seemed as if I'd made a monkey of myself with everything I'd tried to do all afternoon, and I didn't feel very happy when Sid let me slide down at the gate. If I could have slipped away, climbed onto Lady, and headed for home, I think I'd have done it.

Blueboy was still kicking and bucking, and Mr. Batchlett looked pretty sore when he opened the gate and came in. "Well, young fellah," he said, "you picked yourself a big handful, didn't you? What you goin' to do with him now you've got him?"

"I haven't got him," I said. "He had me thrown clear when Sid grabbed me."

"Rode out your ten count, didn't you?"

"Yes, sir," I said, "but then he wasn't bucking like . . ."

"Then he's yours! You going to ride him or ruin him?"

For a second it seemed as if the bottom had dropped out of my stomach, and my mouth went dry as powder. The first thought that crossed my mind was that Mr. Batchlett was sore at me for having picked Blueboy, and that he wanted me to get hurt.

I hadn't been so scared since the first time I was dumped off a horse—and I think that's what saved me.

That first tumble came back to me in a flash. It had been when I was eight years old. Father had picked me up, caught the horse, and told me to get back on. "Unless you show him who's boss right now, it will ruin you both," he'd told me. "He'll lose respect for you, and you'll lose respect for yourself." When I'd hung back and told him I was afraid, he'd said, "You don't have to be ashamed of that. Every man who ever did a brave thing was afraid. It doesn't take courage to do the things you're not afraid of."

It almost seemed as if I could hear Father's voice again. I looked up at Mr. Batchlett, and said, "I'll ride him now . . . and thank you."

He slapped me on the shoulder, and called, "Get a rope on that blue devil, Sid! We got a bronc-twister comin' up."

There wasn't any real bronc-twisting to my second ride on Blueboy. He'd nearly bucked himself out in trying to unload the saddle. I kept the hackamore rope pulled tight, and he only made about ten straightforward pitches before he came to a stand.

Even Hazel came over to the gate to meet us when I rode Blueboy out of the breaking pen, but she was still snippy. The first chance she got, she turned up her nose at me and said, "Well, you got him, Smarty, but you'll be sorry."

When Mr. Bendt was in the corral for his third pick, Mr. Batchlett came and stood beside me. "You've got more horse there than a boy of your age ought to have," he told me, "and I reckon I'm out of my head to let you keep him. He's headstrong as a mule, tougher'n bull beef, and can't be trusted. Don't you go tryin' to ride him without there's one another of us close by."

I just nodded my head—we stood there for a couple of minutes, watching Mr. Bendt catch Juno—the neat pinto mare I'd had my eye on, and the one Hazel had told me to pick. Then Mr. Batchlett squeezed my shoulder a quick little grab, and said, "I know how you feel about him, Little Britches. Felt the same way 'bout his old man when I was younger— greatest wild horse ever I laid eyes on!" He rubbed a hand along Blueboy's sweaty neck, smiled, and said, "Reckon maybe that's why I ain't give up on this worthless son-of-a-gun."

It was so late when we finished the horse-picking that Mr. Batchlett decided not to send the rest of the remuda to the mountain ranch till morning, and I was glad of it. I hadn't really been hurt at all, but I'd been thumped and twisted around until I ached all over. As soon as we'd had supper, I made a beeline for my bunk.

6

A Yella Ribbon

O N BATCHLETT'S home ranch part of the cowhands' job was to keep the fences up and, as a day could be spared, posts were cut and hauled from the mountains. When we'd finished breakfast Monday morning, Mr. Batchlett pushed his chair back and said, "Don't aim to start tradin' trips till next week, but once we're at it there won't be no time for side work. How about you boys wrastlin' in a few loads of fence posts? That'll give you an hour or two, morning and night, to get your horse strings worked in easy."

Then, as we left the table, he took hold of my arm, and said, "Ain't much of an axe arm, is it? You little devils had best to split up for this go-round. You ain't got weight enough between you to wrastle a good-sized post. Supposin' you team up with Zeb, and Sid can go along with Ned. Tom, you and Hank can take the spare horses up to the mountain ranch." Then he turned to Ned and said, "Take the posts out of that fir stand in the bend of Bootheel Canyon. It's only fifteen miles up there, and they're easy to get at."

I didn't mind going to cut fence posts as much as the others seemed to, but I didn't like the idea of going with Zeb very well. In the two days I'd been with the outfit he hadn't said two words to me—and not many more to anyone else. He didn't go with us when we left the chuckhouse to work out our horses, but slouched off toward the forge.

Pinch and Clay didn't worry me very much, but I knew I'd have to do a lot of work with Blueboy before I had him steadied down enough for handling cattle. I was lucky in catching him with my first throw, and he didn't fight when I drew him in and tied him to a corral post. But when Sid was helping me saddle him he side-jumped, bobbed his head, and lashed his tail like a mad tomcat. Sid wouldn't let me get on until he had his horse saddled and was mounted alongside.

Blueboy didn't buck until we were outside the corral, then he geysered and came down running and pitching toward the wagon road. Half a dozen times I was nearly thrown, but grabbed the horn, clamped my legs tight, and managed to stay with him. He started down the roadway in hard crowhops, then stretched his head out like a wild goose in flight, lowered his back, and turned on the steam. From far behind I heard Sid shout, "Yank that hackamore! Bust his nose!" But with Blueboy's head stuck out the way it was, the nose band had slipped half way up to his eyes, and I had no more control of him than if he'd been a runaway railroad engine.

The roadway ran straight across the valley for a quarter mile, then twisted up a steep hill to the east. At the first turn Blueboy left it and drove straight up the hill, trying to rake me off against scrub-oak clumps. I could have dived into one of them and got out with nothing more than a few scratches, but I knew that if I did I'd never be able to ride him again. I had to find some way to control him, and my chances were growing less with every second I waited.

There was only one thing I could think of to do, and I did it. Suddenly letting the hackamore rope go slack, I snapped it, the way I'd have thrown a running noose. As the nose-band bounced forward across the tender cartilage, I made a quick turn of the rope-end around the saddle horn, kicked a foot high, and whanged my heel down on the slack rope.

The jolt nearly threw me out of the saddle, but Blueboy's nose came down as if a boulder had been dropped on it. Before he could raise it again, I'd hauled in the slack and taken another turn around the saddle horn. With his chin pulled tight against his chest, and with his breathing half cut off by the band across his nose, some of the fight went out of him. When Sid caught up to us, Blueboy and I were both trembling like aspens, but not for the same reason. He was madder than a wildcat in a trap, and I was as happy as if I'd just got him for a Christmas present.

Sid jawed and rowed at me all the way back to the corral, telling me I was a fool for trying to ride Blueboy, that he'd kill me, and that I'd better turn him in with the horses being taken to the mountain ranch. Blueboy fought the tight hackamore and me all the way, side-jumping, lashing his tail, and rearing. But I was so proud of being able to handle him at all that I wouldn't listen to Sid.

When we were riding up the straight piece of road toward the corral, I saw Mr. Batchlett standing by the gate watching us. He just nodded to me as we rode up, and said, "Cool him out a bit before you leave him!" then walked away.

By the time I'd led Blueboy around enough to cool him out, Zeb had a team of work horses hitched to a wagon and was waiting for me. Ned and Sid had already driven off to the mountains, but Zeb didn't seem to be in any hurry. He was sprawled out on the wagon seat like a rag doll, and when I climbed up he shifted one leg just enough to make room for me. He didn't make a sound, and I didn't see him move the reins, but the team started off at a slow walk.

"That blue horse has sure got a mind of his own," I said, just trying to make talk, but Zeb only nodded. He seemed to be looking off toward Pikes Peak, where the morning sun gleamed on the snowy summit as if it had been a diamond set in the necklace of white clouds that surrounded it.

The wheel tracks twisted in and out of gulches, and the team plodded on, but the only move Zeb made was to keep his face turned toward Pikes Peak. I didn't like sitting there like a frog on a log, so I asked Zeb if he liked the horses he'd picked, and if he didn't think the grub at Batchlett's was good. All the answer I got was a nod, so I began thinking of things I could do to make Blueboy into a good cow horse— and wondering why Hazel had tricked me into picking her father's prize cutting horse. I was still thinking about it when the wheel ruts turned in between high canyon walls. Then I almost jumped off the seat. There hadn't been a sound except the chuckle of the wheel hubs on the axles and the clump of horses' feet, when Zeb suddenly sang out, "*She wore a yella ribbon around her neck.*"

It was more hollered than sung. Zeb's voice was high and through his nose, and it went up and down like the braying of a mule, but the canyon walls caught it, and echoed, "*Neck . . . neck . . . neck . . . neck . . .*" until it died away to a whisper. Zeb sat with an ear cocked, listening until the echo died away, then slumped back with his eyes half-closed.

An hour later we'd left the canyon floor and climbed rough wheel tracks that led over the spur of a low mountain. Neither of us had made a sound since Zeb sang, and I'd gone back to thinking. At the top of the rise, Zeb stopped the team, and sat up with his back toward me, looking off to the south. "I cal'clate this here is jist about the die-rection he was a-lookin' in when first he seen her," he said slowly.

"When who first saw who?" I asked.

"Zebulon Montgomery Pike," Zeb said, almost reverently. "Who else but Injuns ever seen her afore him?"

"I don't know," I said, "because I don't know who she is."

"The peak! The peak!" he half whispered. "The silver-haired queen o' the Rockies."

The clouds had moved away, and the mantle of snow on the summit of Pikes Peak did look like a head of silvery, wavy hair. "It's a beautiful mountain, isn't it?" I said.

"The queen! The queen!" he said in a sort of hushed voice. "And she's a-settin' there holdin' her pot o' gold in her lap. Ain't no man never goin' to dig deep enough to rob it afore the day o' jedgment."

I'd heard people say there was probably more gold left inside Pikes Peak than had ever been mined from it, but I'd never heard anyone call the mountain a queen. I was sitting there thinking of it when Zeb clucked to the horses and we moved on. He didn't speak again until we'd pulled up below a stand of tall firs in Bootheel Canyon.

Ned and Sid were hacking away to beat the band when we reached the canyon, and already had eight or ten posts on their wagon. I wanted to hurry and catch up with them, but there was no hurrying Zeb. He sat looking over the firs for nearly ten minutes before he pulled the wagon in below them. I had one horse unharnessed, hobbled, and turned out to graze before he had the buckles undone on the other. But when I took the axes out of the wagon, I could see he hadn't been loafing while I was having my fight with Blueboy. They were ground and stoned almost to razor edges, and each head was carefully wrapped in a gunny sack.

I'd only felled a few small trees in my life, but had chopped plenty of railroad ties for firewood. Father had been brought up in the woods of Maine, and could really make chips fly. He'd made me a small axe a couple of years before he died, had taught me to swing it, and always made me keep the edge honed sharp. I thought that felling a really big tree would be a lot of fun, so I grabbed the lightest axe, and started for the tallest fir at the lower edge of the stand. It was nearly twenty inches through the butt, and I went at the uphill side of it as fast as I could swing the axe. When I had to stop for breath, I looked up to see Zeb leaning on his axe handle and watching me. "Cabin or bridge log?" he asked.

I felt pretty silly as I watched Zeb climb slowly up the hill beyond me, but I'd already ruined the tree, and there was nothing to do but go on and fell it. But when I went to do that, I found that I hadn't run out of breath soon enough; I'd cut so far into the uphill side of the tree that it was going to fall that way. It did, but not all the way. It tangled with some other trees, and hung swaying—as if it were just waiting for someone foolish enough to walk under it.

While I was standing there, a tall, slim tree came whistling down a little way beyond me. The slender trunk curved as it cut through between a couple of larger trees, and the top fell within a few feet of the wagon. I climbed a little way up the leaning trunk of the big tree I'd cut, and jounced up and down, but wasn't heavy enough to shake it loose.

After I'd jounced a few more times, I went down and began chopping the limbs off the tree Zeb had felled. By the time I'd finished, he had a couple of others, just like it, stretched out with their tops lying close to the wagon. He hadn't said a word, but when I stopped for breath, I could hear him making some kind of a noise as he chopped. It sounded like a string of slow grunts, connected by high-pitched whispers. When I listened real sharply I could hear that he was singing, "She WORE a yella RIBbon aROUND her NECK. She WORE a yella RIBbon aROUND her NECK." He was grunting every other sound as the axe came down, and with every slow stroke a chip, nearly as big as my head, flew.

I didn't stop for breath any oftener than I had to, and Zeb didn't hurry a bit, but he had a couple of dozen trees felled before I had six limbed out. Every one of them was just the right size for fence posts, and every top was within fifteen feet of the wagon. I guess he thought he was far enough ahead of me by that time. When I stopped to look up again, he was fitting his shoulder under the trunk of the tree I'd left hanging. He heaved up and against it, then jumped back, as quick as a cat, and the tree came crashing down.

I kept my axe swinging, but watched Zeb. Working in his lazy, loose-jointed way, he lopped off the branches of the big tree, and topped it where it was about four inches through. Measuring with his eye, he notched the trunk every seven feet as he came back down the steep hill. Then he cut half way through at each notch, rolled the log over, and finished the cuts.

Zeb was beginning his last cut when I stopped for a breather. When I looked up again he was nowhere in sight. I'd limbed out two more trees before he came back, carrying half a dozen chips of granite, each a little larger than his hands. Using them for wedges, he went to work, splitting the logs he'd cut from the big tree. Sparks flew from the granite each time the back of his axe head hit it.

I wanted to stand and watch him, but was ashamed to, and half afraid he'd say something rough to me for being fool enough to cut so big a tree. I was chopping limbs as fast as I could go when he came walking down the hill past me. He carried two of the quartered sections of the biggest log, and each of them must have weighed nearly double what I did. He shouldered them squarely across the wagon, spit a thin streak of tobacco juice, and said, "Make right nice corner posts, them will. Ain't it time we et?"

Through the early afternoon, Zeb kept going in that lazy, loose-jointed way of his, but it made the sweat run down my back to limb trees as fast as he felled, cut them into post lengths, and carried them to the wagon. The sun was still high when we had our wagon loaded, but I hadn't done a quarter of the work. Sid and Ned had been chopping steadily, but they still had a couple of hours' work to do when we pulled away for the home ranch.

I'd thought we were pretty slow in coming out that morning, but we were twice as slow going back. Once in a while Zeb would sing a few words of "Yella Ribbon," half under his breath, but most of the time he just sat sprawled there on top of the posts with his eyes partly shut. And every half mile or so, he let the horses stop for a long rest.

By the time we left the canyon floor and climbed the spur, the sun was dipping down toward the top of the high range of mountains to the west. We had just reached the top when

Pikes Peak came into sight beyond a low mountain to the south, and the sinking sun reflected from its summit in a soft orange glow. Zeb lifted the reins just a trifle and stopped the team. "Cal'clated to git here 'bout this hour," he said, looking off at the peak. "This here's the time o' day she takes the lid off'n her pot o' gold an' lets it shine on her hair."

"She's beautiful, isn't she," I said.

"Yep. A queen . . . every inch of her . . . and there ain't no man can harm her."

We must have sat there twenty minutes, as the sunlight played on the snow fields of the summit. Zeb didn't speak again, and I didn't either. When you're looking at something beautiful and grand and sort of peaceful, it always seems nicer to be with someone who doesn't talk.

After the glow had faded a little, Zeb handed me the reins, climbed down, and stuck a post between the spokes of the hind wheels. With the steel wagon tires squealing and sliding over the rocks, I took the horses down the grade as carefully as I could. Zeb followed at the side with a heavy post over his shoulder, ready to trig the wheels if the load should crowd too hard on the horses.

Even with the early start we'd got from Bootheel Canyon, Sid and Ned caught up to us as we were pulling out between the hogbacks that stand in front of the mountains. Twilight was deepening, and the lights of the home ranch showed like fireflies through the clumps of scrub oak. Neither Zeb nor I had said a word since we were at the top of the spur, but as the lights came into sight Sid ya-hooed from the wagon behind, and I ya-hooed back. As if it had wakened Zeb from a dream, he drew the reins up, and crooned, "*She wore a yella ribbon around her neck.*" A minute later he said, "They's days it ain't half bad to be a-livin'." Then, without another word, he drove on to the home place.

The rest of the hands went to the bunkhouse right after supper, but I wanted to see how Lady and my new horses were doing. There was a full moon just rising, and the horses stood in little groups, with one hip dropped and their heads drooping lazily. Zeb's mule was off in a far corner, and Sid's pinto and Lady stood head-to-rump near by. She came trotting over when I whistled, and took the piece of biscuit I'd brought her. I was scratching her forehead, and didn't notice Mr. Batchlett till he leaned his arms on the gate beside me.

He didn't say anything for a few minutes, and I didn't know what to say, so I kept still. Then he asked, "How'd you make out today? I see you got a pretty good load."

"Fine," I said, "but Zeb did most of the work."

"Mmmm-hmmm," he said, "you could learn a lot from Zeb."

"Well, not by his talking," I told him.

"Kind of an off-ox old critter," Mr. Batchlett said, "but a plumb good one. Looked at Pikes Peak at sundown, didn't you?"

"Yes, sir," I said, "but how did you know?"

"I know Zebulon Pike Montgomery," he answered.

"You mean Zebulon Montgomery Pike, don't you?" I asked.

"No, Zebulon Pike Montgomery. That's old Zeb's name. His paw named him, near as he could, after the man that found that mountain, and he worships both the man and the mountain he found. Old critter won't work no place where he can't keep an eye on it, night and mornin'."

"He calls it, 'her'," I said; "the queen of the Rockies."

"Tell you about the pot o' gold she's holdin' in her lap?"

"Yes, sir," I said, "and about the way it glows on her hair at sunset."

"Then you and him will get along all right. Old Zeb, he don't open up much about her hair less'n he likes you."

"Then we're even," I said; "I like him, too."

"Mmm-hmmm. Them as really knows him does. You better run on now and turn in; sunup comes mighty early in the mornin' this time o' year."

Mr. Batchlett was still standing there, looking off toward Pikes Peak, when I went to the bunkhouse.

7

Long-tailed Wildcats

POST-CUTTING went better for me the second day than the first, but it was rough for Sid. We took three wagons and Tom teamed up with Ned, so Sid had to work with Hank. At breakfast Mr. Batchlett told us to make an early start because he'd have some work for us when we got back.

When we reached Bootheel I didn't bother with any felling, but waited for Zeb to drop a tree, then went right to work on the trimming. The practice I'd had the day before helped, and I was able to keep up with him as he felled, cut the trees into posts, and loaded them. We were working a couple of hundred yards from the others, but all morning I could hear Hank rowing and hollering at Sid. By noon we had our wagon piled high, Tom and Ned were about half loaded, but Hank and Sid didn't have more than a dozen posts on theirs.

After we'd eaten, Zeb helped Hank and Sid, so I went to work with Tom and Ned. With what Father had taught me, and what I'd learned from watching Zeb, I could make a tree fall fairly near where I wanted it to. As soon as Tom and Ned found it out, they let me do the felling and cut the posts, while they did the trimming and loading. It worked out pretty well, and I was kind of proud that I'd found something I could do better than most full-grown cowhands.

The sun was still high when we reached the home ranch, but I didn't do anything to be proud of after we got there.

As soon as we had the teams unharnessed Mr. Batchlett called, "You boys can leave the unloading till morning and saddle up; we got fifty head of stock to cut and sort this afternoon. Better toss your saddle on Clay, Little Britches, and work the kinks out of him."

I don't think I worked many kinks out of Clay, but he worked plenty of them into me. Having the only cutting horse on the place in my string, it was my job to separate each animal from the herd as Mr. Batchlett called for it. I'd seen plenty of cattle cutting, but had never been the one to do it, or paid much attention to the way it was done.

As soon as Mr. Batchlett pointed out the first calf he wanted, I rode Clay straight at it, planning to guide him around it and drive it out of the herd. Until he found which calf we were after I was the boss, but from there on I was lucky to stay in the saddle. Clay could sense an animal's move before I could see it, and regardless of which way I tried to guide him, he'd dodge with the calf. He did it so lightning fast that before I could set myself, the saddle would be jerked out from under me. Twice I got spilled completely, and had to pick myself up while Clay took the right calf out of the herd alone. After the second tumble, Mr. Batchlett called, "You're trying too hard! Leave him have his head as soon as he knows which one you want! And keep aholt of the horn. He don't need help from nobody!"

I'd always thought it was a disgrace to grab the horn, or to let a horse do whatever he wanted to. But it was sure that Clay didn't need any help from me, and just as sure that I'd have to hang onto the horn if I was going to stay with him. After that I didn't fall all the way off again, but I was close to it forty times, and had a lot of trouble making Clay take the right calf out of the herd. Hank kept yelling at me all afternoon, and three or four times Mr. Batchlett called, "Take it easy! Take it easy! Don't try to rush him!" By the tone of his voice I knew he thought I was just about hopeless. When the job was finally done I was so ashamed of myself that I wanted to crawl off and hide, and I felt as if I'd been run through a thrashing machine.

Being ashamed of the bad job I'd done riding Clay got me into plenty of trouble. Right in the middle of supper, Hank began to make fun of me for the way I'd fallen off a tame old cow pony, and telling how he used to catch and ride wild broncos when he was my age. If I hadn't been so tired and ashamed of myself, it wouldn't have bothered me, but that night I couldn't help boiling over. "Why don't you brag about your post-hacking?" I snapped at him. "I'll bet I can cut twice as many posts as you can any day!"

"You didn't cut no posts!" Hank shouted. "Zeb cut 'em! By dogies, if I ain't cut two posts to your one I'll . . . why when I was . . ."

Mr. Batchlett thumped the table hard, and said, "That's enough! You team up with Zeb tomorrow, Sid, and let these two wildcats find out who's got the longest tail."

Next morning I was up before the sun, took my axe to the forge, ground the cutting edge to a long slim bevel, and honed it carefully. Then I wrapped it in a gunny sack so it wouldn't get nicked, and put it in Hank's wagon. He was the last to come in for breakfast, and was bent over with one hand on the small of his back. "By dogies," he sort of whined, "they's a cloudburst o' rain a-comin' on 'fore noontime. The way this here misery gits into my backbone, I can always tell it. Don't reckon we dast venture into them mountains till it's over. Water'll come a-roarin' down them canyons forty foot deep."

"A few clouds drifting in from the north," Mr. Batchlett said, "but I don't reckon we'll get more'n a drizzle of rain."

"By dogies, not the way my back's a-feelin'!" Hank groaned. "This here's cloudburst misery I got! Couldn't no more swing an axe or lift a post today than I could fly."

Mr. Batchlett didn't look up, but said, "That's enough belly-achin'! You're going to cut posts with the kid, like it or not! If you want to limber up while the boys unload, you can take the turn-back yearlings out to the calf pasture."

"Way my back's a-kickin' up, I don't know if I can make it or not, but I'll do the best I can," Hank whined.

He was still at the table when the rest of us went out, and we were pretty well started on the unloading when he hobbled to the corral, caught a horse, and saddled it. He was still walking bent over, and made three tries before he pulled himself up into the saddle. But the horse he'd caught was one of his new string. It took half a dozen crowhops as soon as Hank was in the saddle, and he rode them out with his back as limber as a buggy whip. Then he saw us watching him, and began to cuss and rub his back as he rode out of sight.

Hank hadn't come back from the pasture when the other two teams drove off to the mountains, so I went to the corrals and was scratching Lady's forehead when Hazel and Kenny rode up to the gate. She was on a nice little pinto and he was bareback on a sleepy looking old donkey. Ever since Sunday I'd been wanting to see Hazel and ask her why she'd tricked me into picking Clay, but she didn't give me a chance. Before I could open my mouth, she taunted, "Well, Smarty, didn't I tell you you'd be sorry for picking Blueboy? I seen you when he run away with you Monday morning. You looked like he was goin' to dump you off again every minute."

I didn't like that "again" business, and besides, I didn't want her to think she could act as if I was just a little boy, so I said, "Well, I haven't seen anything to be sorry about yet! And if you saw him running away, you must have seen me bring him back. I didn't look very much as if I was falling off then, did I?"

Before she could answer, Kenny piped up, "Betcha my life you can't ride Jack."

"That old jackass?" I asked him.

"Betcha my life you can't ride him like he is."

It was bad enough to have Hazel picking on me, and Kenny made me kind of peeved. "I don't care how he is," I told him, "I'll bet I could ride him backwards from here to Castle Rock."

Both of them began snickering, and Kenny slid off and passed me the reins. I didn't even bother to put them around the donkey's neck, but hopped and swung a leg over, so I was sitting on him backwards. I expected him to make a few crow-hops, but he didn't. He just stood still, trying to kick the clouds out of the sky—and I began to slip.

As far as Jack's kicking was concerned, any little girl could have ridden him, but he'd shed his winter fur, and his back was as slippery as a wet bottle. With every kick I slipped a few inches farther, and it wasn't long before my behind was almost down to his ears. Then all he had to do was twist his neck and lay me on the ground. That's where I was when Mr. Batchlett came to the corner of the corral and called, "Better saddle up and go see where Hank's at! Take the north trail along the foothills and you can't miss him."

I was glad of any excuse to get away from Hazel and Kenny, but it was only by luck that I found Hank. I'd ridden nearly to the north end of the ranch when I saw a wisp of smoke rise from a plum thicket, and Hank and his horse were hidden inside it. He was sitting cross-legged on the ground, smoking his pipe and whittling. When I surprised him he said his back hurt so much he'd had to stop to rest, and couldn't get back into the saddle without help.

Hank moaned and groaned all the way back to the corral, but he didn't do much of it after we got there. Mr. Batchlett was waiting by the gate, and as soon as Hank let out one groan, he snapped, "That'll be enough! You've ducked this kid all you're goin' to! Now get on that wagon and head for the mountains! If you're not back with a full load of posts by sundown I won't keep you around here."

Hank climbed down as spry as a spider, pulled off his saddle, and hurried away toward the wagon, calling back,

"Don't you have no fear, Batch! Me and the kid'll fetch in all the horses can haul!"

As I started to follow, Mr. Batchlett caught me by the shoulder, and said, "Now don't go swingin' an axe like you're killing snakes, and don't bust a gut liftin'! You got plenty of time between now and sundown." Then he turned away and went in to catch up his horse.

If anybody had heard me scolded the way Hank had been I could hardly have looked at him, but it didn't seem to bother Hank a bit. All the way to the mountains he talked like a magpie with a split tongue, bragging about the things he'd done when he was my age. After the first mile I began thinking about Zeb and Pikes Peak and Blueboy and Clay, and only heard Hank as I'd have heard a flock of geese gabbling.

With all his talking and bragging, I think Hank was worried about getting a load of posts back to the home ranch by sunset. He didn't let the horses stop for a single breather, and kept them trotting whenever the hills weren't too steep.

At the lower end of the Bootheel, a narrow side canyon led off to the north. There was no roadway up it, but the dry creek bed was fairly wide and cobbled with stones the size of muskmelons. Each time we'd passed it, I'd noticed the thick stand of tall firs along the canyon walls.

I was half dreaming when we reached the mouth of the side canyon, and nearly fell off the seat when Hank suddenly turned into it. "By dogies," he shouted, "I'm a-goin' to show 'em how to fetch out a load o' posts quicker'n you can say scat my cat! Ain't no sense a-goin' up Bootheel where the good trees is all took out. I know this here country like I know the palm o' my own hand, and I know where the best post trees is at. Why, when I was your . . ."

"Mr. Batchlett told Ned we were to take them out of Bootheel," I said, "and I don't think he'd like it if we . . ."

"You leave me do the thinkin', kid!" Hank shouted. "You'll have both hands full and your little britches to hold up jest a-doin' your end o' the post-hackin'!"

There was no sense in my trying to change his mind, and I wasn't big enough to make him do anything he didn't want to, so I kept my mouth shut. The canyon twisted and wound around in the shape of a great question mark, and the farther we went the narrower and rougher the creek bed grew. The first good stand of firs was above a high ledge, the second on a mountainside too steep to climb, and the third behind an aspen thicket. I think we'd driven about five miles before we came to any good post trees that could be gotten out.

"There, by dogies! How's them for post trees?" Hank shouted, and passed the reins to me. "You turn the wagon about while I go to knockin' some of 'em down."

The wagon was hard to turn in the narrow creek bed, and before I had it around Hank had stripped off his jumper, grabbed an axe, and was hacking at a big tree about a hundred feet up the mountain side. "Leave 'em be! Leave 'em be!" he yelled when I started to unhitch. "We ain't got time to mess with no horses! Ain't no grass for 'em nohow!"

I should have had sense enough to move the team farther down the creek bed, and to unhook the traces, but I lost my temper when Hank began yelling at me. "Then you'd better quit hacking at this side of that tree!" I yelled back. "It'll nearly hit 'em if it falls this way."

"You leave me do the thinkin'!" Hank hollered, but moved around and began hacking at the uphill side of the tree.

Then, when I went to get my axe I found that he'd taken it and left me his dull one. I grabbed it up, jumped off the wagon, and shouted, "You've got my axe! It was wrapped in a gunny sack."

"You ain't got no axe!" he yelled back. "The both of 'em belongs to Batch, don't they? Now get on up here and go to limbin' out! I got this here tree almost down a'ready."

I'd never stopped to think that all the axes belonged to Mr. Batchlett, and that I didn't have any more claim to one than to another. If I had, I'd have been grinding the other axe instead of being kicked off by Kenny's burro. I was standing thinking about it when there was a crash above me, and I looked up to see Hank's tree topple sideways and hang in the branches of the tree next to it.

The axe Hank had left me was too dull to work with, and had four big nicks in the edge, so I ground it into half-decent shape on a smooth stone beside the wagon. When I'd finished Hank had hacked off four more trees, and they'd all fallen part way down, crisscrossing each other. I'd stopped to look at the mess when he yelled at me, "Don't stand there a-gawkin'! Get them trees limbed out and cut to post lengths! Can't you see I'm way out ahead o' you?"

"Yes, I can see," I told him, "but I'll cut my own posts and you can cut yours." Then I went farther along the stand, found some trees the right size for posts, took off my jumper and went to work. I tried to do it as near the way Zeb did as I could. Before I cut into a tree I planned just where I wanted it to fall, and when it was down I trimmed it, cut it into posts, and carried them to the wagon. As I worked, I heard several more crashes, ring after ring of an axe against stone, and a lot of cussing up where Hank was working.

I had my fourth tree down and was cutting it into post lengths when, from right behind me, Hank shouted, "Gittin' pretty dad-gummed big for them little britches o' yourn, ain't you? Git on over there and go to trimmin' out them trees I chopped down 'fore I have to lay a hand on you!"

I knew Hank was bluffing, and he didn't scare me a bit. "I'm not going to help you, and you're not going to lay a hand on me," I told him. "You took the best axe and now you can cut your own posts; this is supposed to be a race."

Hank went grumbling back, and though I could hear him cussing once in a while, he didn't bother me again for three or four hours. He hadn't taken a single post down to the wagon, and each time I took mine down I glanced up to see how he was doing. He was still hacking away at standing trees, but every one he'd cut had fallen crossways and hung up in the branches. I could have gone up and showed him how to make them fall the right way, but I was still peeved about his taking my sharp axe and wouldn't do it.

Though we hadn't stopped to eat, and the sky was so overcast I couldn't tell the time, I guessed it to be about four o'clock when I started to fell the tree that would finish my half of the load. As it toppled straight out toward the creek bed I jumped back, and found Hank standing behind me. "By dogies, didn't I tell Batch?" he shouted. "We're a-goin' to get the dadgumdest cloudburst ever you seen! Look how them clouds is a-settin' in! We'd best to hightail out'n here 'fore we get catched in a flood and drownded."

I stood my axe down and stepped out where I could see the sky better. The clouds had become dark, and I was pretty sure we'd get rain, but not a cloudburst, so I said, "It's all right to go if you want to, but Mr. Batchlett will know by the axe marks that I cut every post on the load."

"Reckon we might as leave stick it out a while longer," Hank said, and started back with an axe over his shoulder. When I went to pick up mine, I found that he'd traded with me again. He'd left me the one I'd ground so carefully that morning, but the edge was nicked and scalloped till it looked like the crust on a piece of pumpkin pie. There was no sense in trying to make Hank trade back, or in trying to use the ruined axe, so I went over to grind it on the rock beside the wagon.

I might have been sitting there fifteen minutes when the horses suddenly snorted and plunged away, with the wagon bouncing, slewing, and spilling off all the posts I'd loaded. A moment later the top of a tree whipped down where the wagon had stood.

As the team raced away down the creek bed Hank came yelling at me, blaming me for scaring the horses. I knew he'd found out, from watching me, how to drop a tree where he wanted it, and had purposely felled that one so it would frighten the horses. When I yelled back and told him so, he quieted down and said pleasantly, "Ain't no sense of us a-squabblin' 'bout it. I reckon we'd best cut acrost the ridge and get home 'fore that cloudburst sets in. I know these here mountains like the palm of my own hand. 'Tain't more'n seven, eight miles the way the crow flies."

"Isn't it best to go back the way we came?" I asked. "If we found the team we could finish out the load by sunset."

"No, by dogies!" Hank shouted. "I don't aim to get catched in no dad-burned canyon in a cloudburst! And I don't aim to get catched in these here mountains after dark without no gun! There's a mess o' bears hereabouts, and there ain't no tellin' when a mountain lion'll spring out on you."

There was nothing for me to do but pick up my jumper and axe, and follow him as he led off up the mountainside.

8

Lost

HANK led off up the ridge we'd been working on, quartering along below the trees. With the whole sky clouded over I couldn't be sure of the direction, but if the canyon had looped around the way I thought it had, we'd be heading north. I knew the home ranch was just a little south of straight east, so I asked, "Aren't we going the wrong way, Hank?"

"Just a dite," he said, "to get around these here trees."

I kept still for another half hour, but was sure we should have gone up the ridge on the other side of the canyon. After Hank turned up a rocky ridge to our left, I asked again, "Are you sure we're going the right way?"

"Got the mountain fever a'ready?" he laughed. "By dogies, I seen prairie men get so fuddled up in these here mountains they didn't know straight up from Sunday. Now you take . . . Why, afore I was your age . . ."

"I didn't say you were wrong," I told him. "I just thought we should have gone up the other side of the canyon."

"Go fer enough that-a-way and you'd land plumb in the Great Salt Lake. You just keep your britches drug up till we fetch the top of this here ridge, and I'll point you out the dome of Pikes Peak. I know these here mountains like I know the palm of my own right hand."

The ridge was a lot higher than it looked to be, and it took us nearly two hours to reach the top. When we got there Hank couldn't point out Pikes Peak or anything else. By that time it was drizzling, and the clouds hung so low we could barely see the next ridge. There was a deep canyon to cross before we reached it, the drizzle had turned into a steady rain, and it was growing dark and cold. I couldn't keep my teeth from chattering; was so hungry my stomach squealed, and was beginning to worry when Hank sang out, "By dogies, I reckon I missed a beeline by a hair! This here'll fetch us out to the calf pasture—just t'other side that low ridge."

I was so mixed up that all the ridges looked alike, but I did remember a low one to the west of the calf pasture, so I said, "Oh, yes, I remember it now! I guess we'd better hurry before it gets darker or Mr. Batchlett begins to worry."

"Batch, he ain't got no worries—'ceptin' that team a-gettin' drownded in the cloudburst. Way this here rain's a-pickin' up, it won't be long afore it hits. You hang close on my trail so's you don't get lost when dark comes on."

I hung close on Hank's trail, but don't know if we ever got to the top of the ridge he was talking about. Before we were halfway down the one we were on, it was so dark we had to feel for each step before we took it. And the rain was getting colder with every step. Once I slipped and fell, and my axe went rattling and sliding down the mountain. There was a second or so when it didn't make a sound, then it rang against a rock—way below us.

Ever since twilight I'd been afraid a bear or mountain lion would spring out on us, but that didn't frighten me any more. I was too afraid that I might step off a cliff, and that my own head might land on a rock the way the axe had. Hank was either as scared as I, or his teeth chattered worse. When he tried to scold me for dropping the axe his words sounded as if he were chewing them when he let them go.

I chewed right back, and told him I thought we'd better stay where we were till daylight, but he wouldn't do it. He said we'd be in the calf pasture in half an hour, and all I had to do was to watch my step and keep close behind him. I couldn't watch my step, and when I tried to keep close I bumped into him. He yapped and scolded me, but didn't try to go any farther down the mountain. We quartered across the face of it for what seemed an hour, then climbed again. I think it was the climbing that saved us. We'd only gone a little way, crawling on our hands and knees, when we came to a solid wall of rock—and there were dry fir needles at the foot of it.

I don't know whether I slept or not, but I dug down into the needles and raked them over me as if they were a blanket. I only remember being cold and scared for a long time, and that I ached all over. When the first light of morning came, white fog filled the canyons, and low-hanging gray clouds sliced off the tops of all the peaks and ridges. Hank was half-buried in the needles, lying on his back and snoring with his mouth open. As I watched him, he jumped in his sleep and mumbled something I couldn't understand, but I could tell that he was afraid. For the first time, I knew we were nowhere near the calf pasture, and that Hank was completely lost.

I'd heard plenty of stories about people being lost in the mountains and wandering in circles until they died of cold or starvation. I was already so hungry I felt weak, and was sure we'd just wander around until we dropped in our tracks. Then I remembered that we'd have been at the home ranch before dark if Hank had followed back the way we'd come, instead of being so cocksure about making the shortcut.

The more I thought of it the sorrier I was for myself, and began thinking I hated Hank for always bragging and acting as if he knew more than anybody else. I don't know why, but that started me remembering things I'd done since I'd come away from home—and I wasn't a bit proud of them.

Mr. Batchlett had had to scold me a dozen times for tearing into things before I'd stopped to think. I'd picked Blueboy

when I knew he was too much horse for me and that nobody
wanted me to take him. And, only because Hazel had called
me a little boy, I'd picked Clay and made a monkey of myself
every time I'd used him. I'd made an even bigger monkey of
myself when I'd climbed on Kenny's donkey backwards. And
I couldn't be very proud of bragging because I could cut posts
better than Hank; or of sharpening the axe I'd thought I was
going to use, and leaving his dull—or of not showing him
how to fell trees after knowing I had beat him anyway.

I'd never stopped to think of it before, but, ever since I
could remember, I'd wanted to do something real big, so
people wouldn't call me Little Britches and treat me like a
boy. But more than half the time I'd tried to do things that
were too big, and had only made myself look silly.

As I lay there thinking about it Hank mumbled again, and
struck out in his sleep. My first thought was that he'd struck
out just as blindly when he tried to make the shortcut. And
then I was ashamed of myself. I couldn't help thinking he and
I were a good deal alike. Maybe he was trying to do things
too big for him so people wouldn't call him an old man.
Maybe he bragged about things he used to do because he
couldn't do them any more, and because he wanted the same
thing I did: to have other people think he was as smart and
able to do things as they were.

As the daylight strengthened I forgot about being afraid
—and about being sorry for myself. I'd thought I hated Hank,
but I knew I didn't, and that he was the one to be sorry for.
All I had to do was to use my head a little to know that I
wasn't in very much trouble. We couldn't be too badly lost,
because we hadn't gone very far, and knew the home ranch
was just east of the mountains—certainly not more than ten
or fifteen miles away. In June there would be no blizzards or
hard cold that low in the mountains, and the sky was almost
never clouded over for more than one or two days at a time.
Just as soon as we could see the sun and find our direction,
it would be easy to find our way out.

And when we did get out nobody would blame me for

getting lost, and I'd have all the rest of my life to do something really big enough to be proud of. But Hank was an old man. He'd probably never be able to do anything big enough to make people respect him. Beside that, Mr. Batchlett had told him he wouldn't keep him unless he was back with a load of posts by sunset. Then, too, after all his bragging about knowing the mountains, the men would josh him forever about getting lost. I didn't believe there was much sense in trying to go any farther until the sun came out, so pushed more dry needles up over Hank and went back to thinking until he woke up.

Hank came out of the needles as if he'd been stung, grabbed his axe, and swung it above his head. Then he jerked around and shouted, "Where'd he go? Where'd . . . by dogies, I don't know what Batch is a-thinkin' 'bout, a-sendin' men off to these mountains without no gun!"

"I guess you were having a bad dream," I told him. "Nothing has stirred around here since daylight."

Hank rubbed a hand across his eyes, and said, "By dogies, I must'a dozed off. What time o' day is it?"

"About six," I said. "It's been light for about an hour."

Hank climbed stiffly to his feet, and didn't have to do any acting for me to know he had a bad backache. He didn't put his hands on it, but stood as if he were carrying a heavy log on his shoulders. "Dadgummed weather!" he grumbled. "A man can't scarcely see a landmark no place. Was the sky lighter one way or t'other at sunup? Why didn't you rouse me?"

"It wouldn't have done any good," I said, "and I thought you needed the rest. Daylight came so slow that . . ."

"You leave me do the thinkin'!" he hollered. "If you'd'a roused me as daylight come on, we'd been out o' these here mountains 'fore now. I reckon the calf pasture lies right over that ridge yonder, and I don't aim to have nobody . . ."

Hank didn't finish, but picked up his axe and hobbled away down the mountainside. I stumbled along behind him with my teeth chattering. It had stopped raining, but our clothes were still wet from the night before. Under the dry fir needles, I hadn't noticed it much, but, as soon as the cold morning air got through them, I felt as if I'd been dipped in an ice pond.

The wet rocks were as slippery as soap, and drops of water hung on every bush and twig. By the time we were down as far as the fog, we'd both fallen a dozen times, and were as wet as if we'd been in pouring rain. With each fall Hank moved slower and rowed at me as if I'd made him fall. With every step, the fog grew thicker, until we couldn't see ten yards ahead, and it seemed to me that Hank was bearing off to our right. When I asked him about it, he chattered, "Don't tell me where I'm a-goin'! Don't you think I know? I aim to follow this here canyon down to where it comes out right to west'ard of the buildin's. Ain't no sense in us a-headin' for the calf pasture!" There was nothing for me to do but keep my mouth shut and follow where he led me.

As near as I could guess, it was about noon when the fog began to lift. Little by little, it rose until we could see nearly a mile ahead, and there the canyon ended—with mountains rising around it in a solid wall. Hank was too tired and discouraged to even swear. He slumped down on a rock, with his face buried in his hands, and for a minute or two I thought he was crying. Then he mumbled, "Dadgummed fog must'a twisted me abouts; this here's the wrong way. We got to get out! We got to get out whilst we still got the strength!"

I don't want to remember much about that afternoon. A cold drizzling rain came on again as soon as we'd started back, and Hank was so worn out he could take only a dozen or so steps without stopping to rest. At first I tried to help him, but was as weak as a wet robin, and glad enough to rest whenever he had to. All afternoon he kept telling me the mouth of the canyon was only a couple of miles ahead, but I knew he was just talking to keep me from being afraid. Well before dark I'd given up any hope of ever getting out alive, and the only thing I could think of was getting back to the dry fir needles under the overhanging cliff.

Hank must have given up hope at about the same time. He didn't try to lead the way any more, he didn't talk, and I don't think he knew I was trying to find the cliff again. It was almost dark when I saw it, high up the mountainside. Hank had to make the last part of the climb on his hands and knees, then flopped down as if he were dead. I pushed as many needles as I could over him, scraped out a nest, and covered myself over.

I was sure that was the end of me, and tried to pray, and to think about Mother and the other children at home, but it was sort of warm under the dry needles and I kept falling half asleep. Once, when it was as black as pitch, I heard a scream that made shivers run up and down my back. Hank mumbled, "Mountain lion," but I wasn't frightened, and the next thing I knew the sun was shining.

Hank was still asleep, and it was cold under our cliff, but across the canyon the sun looked warm and yellow against the mountain. For a little while I was too lazy to move, but I knew then that we'd be able to find our way back to the home ranch, and it was kind of nice just to lie there and know it.

After a while I called to Hank, but he only groaned. And when I got up and shook him he didn't wake. I was sure he was dying, and I guess I lost my head. I was shaking the liver out of him when he mumbled, "Ain't no sense a-hollerin'. Save your strength to get out, kid. Go towards the sunrise!" Then he flopped back and went to sleep again, and wouldn't even try to wake up when I shook him.

Before I started to skirt the cliff and climb towards the sun, I scooped out a deep nest, rolled Hank into it, and covered him good and deep with the dry needles. Then I took off my jumper and spread it over the top.

My legs were about as wobbly as a new colt's, but by taking it easy and resting often I got to the top of the ridge. I wasn't any longer afraid of not getting out, but I was afraid of not being able to find my way back to where I'd left Hank. Before

I started down the far side, I stopped long enough to fix every mountain and ridge and canyon in my memory.

I had thought that once I reached the top of the ridge, the going down would be easy, but it wasn't. From just holding myself back, my legs got so shaky I had to keep sitting down to rest them. I'd nearly reached the bottom, and was sitting on a rock, trembling, when I heard the sweetest music I ever hope to hear. It was faint and far away, and came echoing up from the canyon in front of me, "*She wore a yella ribbon around her neck.*" The echo of the "*neck*" whispered over and over again as it died away.

I wanted to laugh and cry at the same time, and went running down the mountain, yelling, "ZEB! ZEB!" as loud as I could. Then my legs went all to jelly, and I fell, tumbling and rolling like a stick in a spring flood. I must have bumped my head, because when I woke up, Zeb was holding me as if I were a baby, and was splashing cold water from a creek onto my face.

I tried to tell Zeb I was all right, and that I'd wait right there while he went to get Hank, but he wouldn't do it. He just shook his head, and said, "Covered over warm, the way you say, that old rooster'd hold out a week if he had to. Batch and the boys is somewheres hereabouts; I'll fetch him after I get you took care of."

"Then we weren't very far from the home ranch?" I asked.

" 'Bout twenty odd miles due west, I'd say."

"Then how did you know where to look for us?" I asked.

"Cal'clated old Hank might head for Californy. Most men goes the wrong way when they get scairt. Don't stop to take note of signs around 'em. You set there till I let off a blast to call the boys in."

I hadn't noticed till then that Zeb was carrying a six-shooter. He pointed it at the sky and emptied it—two and two and two. Then he picked me up, hung me over his shoulders like a shawl, and slouched away down the canyon. He didn't seem

to hurry, or pay much attention to where he stepped, but his
loose-jointed stride would have kept me trotting. And he wound
through boulders and brush without breaking a twig or rolling
a stone.

9

Goin' to Make Out

WHEN Zeb brought me out of the side canyon, Mr. Batchlett and Sid were waiting. They both came running, and Mr. Batchlett called out, "Is he all right, Zeb? Where'd you find him?"

"Didn't find him no place!" Zeb called back. "Little varmint found me! He's got Hank wropped in cotton wool atop a ridge back yonder."

By that time I was rested enough to have ridden alone, but Mr. Batchlett wouldn't let me. He took me back to the home ranch—wrapped in blankets like a papoose—and Mrs. Bendt had him put me to bed in the house. But all she'd let me have to eat was about half a cup of chicken soup.

I wasn't really sick from being out in the mountains, but I'd fallen down so many times I was scratched and black and blue all over, and was as weak as a brand new kitten. I don't think I'd been in bed five minutes before I was sound asleep. When I woke up, Hank was in another bed in the same room, and was really sick. Mrs. Bendt was sitting by his bed, trying to spoon medicine into his mouth. I could hear it gurgle in

his throat as he groaned and mumbled. Then he flailed out one
arm, and, shouted, "Go towards the sunrise!"

That first day Hank thought he was still up in the mountains,
and that something was after him. Mrs. Bendt hardly left
his bedside, but couldn't do much with him, because he'd yank
away and strike out at her. It was Mr. Batchlett who finally
got him quieted down and asleep, but at first I thought he was
being pretty rough. He cuffed Hank, scolded him, and forced
his mouth open while he spooned in some whiskey. But after
Hank went to sleep Mr. Batchlett tucked the covers up around
his shoulders, told Mrs. Bendt to keep bottles of hot water
around him, and said, "Poor old maverick! Ought to had better
sense than to crowd him. Ought to knew he'd try to bull his
way out when he seen he was bested."

Mr. Batchlett wasn't talking to me, but I didn't want Hank
to get blamed too much, or fired for not having brought in
a load of posts, so I said, "We had the wagon half-loaded
when the team ran away, and I didn't have Hank bested. He'd
cut a lot more trees than I had."

Mr. Batchlett looked around at me, and said, "So I seen
when I went up there. Traded axes with you too, didn't he?
Lucky thing he didn't drop that tree right atop the team!
Might as well try stoppin' a cyclone as old Hank when he's
got the bit in his teeth."

I hadn't said a word about our post-cutting, but Mr.
Batchlett seemed to know the whole story, so I just said,
"Yes, sir, I know it." Then he told me I needed to get some
more sleep and went out.

By that time I wasn't half as much interested in sleeping as
eating. After more than two days without a bite, I felt as if I
could eat a whole steer, but they wouldn't give me anything
but soup. As soon as Hank went to sleep, Jenny started being
our nurse. She kept bringing bottles of hot water to lay around
Hank, and once in a while she'd bring me a cup of chicken
soup. But it wasn't until supper time that she let me have a
cracker to go with it.

I liked Mrs. Bendt fine, and she was real good to me, but I liked Jenny a lot better for a nurse. Every time Mrs. Bendt came in she called me a poor little boy, and said it was a shame I'd had to go through any such a hardship, but Jenny never said a word about it. Each time she came in to see Hank she'd sit on my bed and talk a few minutes, or make some kind of joke. But she always talked about things that had happened at her school, or let me tell her things that had happened at home.

After supper all the men came in, but they tiptoed as if they'd been walking up a church aisle in the middle of a sermon. Then, after they'd whispered a few words, asking me how I felt, they looked at Hank and tiptoed out. I really didn't feel sick at all—just a little weak and awfully hungry—but I liked having them come in to see me, and maybe I acted a little bit sicker than I was.

During the night Hank went out of his head again, thought we were still lost, and kept mumbling for me to go toward the sunrise. Mr. Batchlett came in and stayed with him most of the night, and soon after daylight Sid brought the doctor from Castle Rock. He was a gruff old man, but I liked him. After he'd put his ear horn on Hank for about two minutes, he said, "Shock and exposure! Heart's as steady as an eight-day clock! He'll be all right, but he'll need care. Try to get some broth into him—a little whiskey wouldn't hurt. Keep him warm and out of drafts. He'd be better off in a room by himself."

Then he came over and put his ear trumpet all over my chest and stomach. Mr. Batchlett was standing beside him, and said, "His mother's a widow woman in Littleton. Ain't it best I take him home to her?"

There were lots of reasons I didn't want Mr. Batchlett to take me home. In the first place, Mother would worry too much, and in the second place, I knew I couldn't find another job that would pay me a dollar a day. Besides that, I liked Batchlett's ranch and everybody on it, and I wanted to stay right there, so I said, "The only thing the matter with me is that I'm half starved to death."

The doctor shook his head at Mr. Batchlett. "No need to take him home," he said. "The boy's more than half right. These little skinny ones stand the gaff in pretty good shape, but he'd better be kept quiet a few days. Needs to gain his weight and strength back."

"Well, if I could just have something to eat, I'd be all right now," I said.

"Mmmm, hmmm, I wouldn't doubt it," he told me, "but we're not going at it too fast." Then he turned to Mrs. Bendt and said, "I'd move him out of here if I could. Wouldn't hurt to let him have a little solid food now; maybe an egg and a piece of toast. A little something light every couple of hours till supper time, then he'll be ready for meat and potatoes."

"Hadn't I better take him back to town when he's up and around?" Mr. Batchlett asked.

"That's up to you, Batch," the doctor told him. "Might be good for him to be out here, but I wouldn't let him overdo for a week or two. Isn't this the boy who rode your bay in the matched race I saw last summer?"

"That's him. Little Britches, they call him around town."

"Mmmm, hmmm," the doctor said slowly. "No . . . don't believe I'd take him back . . . can't get hurt any more around here than around a race track." Then he put his things back in his bag and went out.

I think Kenny liked me to be sick, because Mrs. Bendt moved me into his room and let him sleep in the bunkhouse —and I think Sid liked it even better. Hank was pretty sick the first few days, but he slept quite a bit, and when he was sleeping Jenny came in to stay with me. There wasn't much for her to do, except to bring me an eggnog once in a while, but she'd sit on my bed and visit, sometimes for an hour or so.

After Hank and I got lost the men didn't cut any more posts, but were getting stock ready for trading trips. That kept them around the corrals most of the time, and Sid came in to see me five or six times a day. He always managed to come when Jenny was visiting me, and I think he came to see her a lot more than to see me. If he did, he might just as well have stayed at the corrals. The minute he'd stick his head in the doorway, he'd sing out, "Hello there, Jenny Wren! How's this little old pardner o' mine makin' out?"

The first couple of times, she said, "Oh, he's getting along fine." Then she shook up my pillows, straightened out the bed clothes, and said she'd better go see if Hank needed anything. I think Jenny had to count Hank's pulse every little while and write it down for the doctor, but she only counted mine when Sid came in. He always told her how pretty she looked, and asked if she'd hold his hand like that if he'd get lost in the mountains. But she'd just say, "Can't you keep quiet a minute? How can I count a pulse with you chattering like a magpie?" About the third time he asked her, she snapped, "Well, run right along and get lost if you want to. I'll have Watt look for you when he goes up after the Christmas tree." Then, when all the men came in after supper, she talked to everybody else, but acted as if she didn't know Sid was there.

Mrs. Bendt didn't let Kenny come in to see me, but Hazel came the second afternoon. She didn't tell me she was sorry we got lost, and she didn't ask me how I was feeling. But she didn't make fun of me for falling off Kenny's donkey, either. When Jenny told me Hazel was coming in, I lay back on the pillow and tried to act a little bit sick, but she just looked at me and said, "Hmmmf! I was sicker'n that when I had chicken pox! You don't look sick enough to me that Jenny has to stay in here with you half the time!"

"Who said I was?" I asked her. "Do you think I'm staying in this bed because I want to?"

"Then why are you tryin' to look so puny? If I was a boy I wouldn't stay in no old bed when I didn't have to!"

If I'd had on anything more than my underdrawers, I'd

have jumped right out to show her I wasn't staying there because I wanted to. But, of course, I couldn't do that, so I
said, "You bring me my clothes, and I'll show you how long
I'll stay in this bed!"

"Betcha my life you wouldn't either!" she sniffed. "Maw
washed 'em, and they're hangin' out on the line, drippin' wet.
By the looks of 'em you must'a been crawlin' 'round in a hog
wallow!"

I think her mother heard her being snippy, because she
called, "That's enough, Hazel! You come and tend the baby
while I get supper ready!"

All the time Hazel had been talking to me, she'd been holding a little grape basket filled with milkweed silk. Just before
she left, she set it down on the bed beside me, and said,
"You can have these! I don't want 'em no more!" After she'd
gone, I took the silk out, real carefully, and there were
seventeen birds' eggs hidden in it—every one different.

There was no reason why I couldn't have been up after
two days of just eating and resting and sleeping, but Jenny
wouldn't let me. And every time Sid came in she'd fuss around,
counting my pulse and taking my temperature, as if I were
really sick. After those first two days he didn't ask if she'd
count his pulse, but he kept on calling her Jenny Wren, and
watched—sort of calf-eyed—every move she made. Then,
when I was all well, he asked if she didn't think I'd better
stay in bed till the doctor came to see Hank again. She said
she didn't think anything of the kind, but that's what she made
me do.

Either girls and women are a lot alike, or Hazel was trying
to copy Jenny. She came in to see me every day, but she was
just as snippy with me as Jenny was with Sid. When I tried
to thank her for the birds' eggs, she turned down the corners
of her mouth, and said, "Hmfff, I didn't want 'em any more.
I'm getting too big to be playin' with birds' eggs. Throw 'em
away if you don't want 'em!"

I didn't really want the eggs, and didn't know what I'd

do with them around the bunkhouse. Besides, I was older than Hazel anyhow. But I couldn't just throw them away after she'd given them to me. Sometimes I looked them over while Jenny wasn't there—they were the prettiest ones I'd ever seen —but I always put the basket under the bed before she came back. And when the doctor finally came and let me up, Hazel said she'd keep them in the house, just as a favor.

Mr. Batchlett was as fussy with me as Jenny had been. In a couple of days he and Sid were going for a trading trip into the mountains, and Zeb and Tom were going along the foothills south of Pueblo. More than a hundred cattle had to be gotten ready for the trips, and I wanted to help with the work, but Mr. Batchlett wouldn't let me. He'd only let me exercise Lady and Pinch an hour a day, and I couldn't go near Blueboy or get on Clay. But on the third morning he let me get up at sunrise, to help with starting the trading herds away.

I'd almost have given an arm to go on the trip with Mr. Batchlett, but I don't think Sid wanted to go at all. When Zeb was lashing his camp gear onto the pack saddle, he noticed that Tom had forgotten the coffee pot, and asked me to get it from the chuckhouse. Sid was coming out just as I got there, and looked as if his best friend had died.

"What's the matter?" I asked. "Is Hank worse this morning?"

"Worse!" he snapped. "Wisht I was that worse off! Wisht I knowed what I done to get that little Jenny Wren so daggoned down on me! Reckon she figures I'm the most no-account cowpoke this side the Divide." Then he snatched up his grub sack and walked off fast toward the corrals.

When I came into the chuckhouse, Jenny was standing at one of the little windows by the fireplace, looking out toward the corrals. She stepped away from it quickly when I opened the door, and said, "Well, how's my patient this morning?"

"Fine," I said, "but Tom forgot to take a coffee pot, and Zeb sent me to get one."

"Didn't you just come across one that was boiling over?"

I shook my head, and must have looked dumb, because she laughed, and said, "A little pot with a red top?"

"No, ma'am," I said, "all I saw was Sid and his grub sack, but he didn't drop any coffee pot."

She laughed again, and said, "I thought I heard steam blowing off just before you came in. I must have been mistaken."

"I guess so," I told her, "because I didn't hear any. But I've got to hurry; Zeb's waiting for the coffee pot."

Zeb and Tom got away from the home ranch first, and when Mr. Batchlett and Sid went I rode a few miles with them. They both seemed glum, and Sid didn't want to talk, but Mr. Batchlett had me ride beside him. "Reckon I let old Doc Gann talk me into a tangle," he said. "I ought to took you home when you got up and about. Promised your maw I'd keep an eye on you, and I ain't done a very good job of it."

"Well, you'd have had to be an eagle to keep an eye on me when Hank and I got lost," I told him.

"Not if I'd went along on the post-hackin', and not if I'd kept Hank with Zeb and the others. And I ain't proud about goin' off and leaving you run loose for the next couple of weeks. You're too like to go raring into things you hadn't ought to and get your neck broke."

Mr. Batchlett had been riding along, watching the cattle as he talked, but he whirled toward me and said, real sharp, "I don't want you tryin' to ride Blueboy till I get back here! You hear me? You ain't got the strength to handle that much horse no time; he'd kill you, weak as you are now."

"You won't have to worry," I told him. "I think I learned quite a lot while Hank and I were up in the mountains. One time when I thought we'd never get out alive, I started to hate him, and then I remembered that sometimes I rare into things just the same way he does."

Mr. Batchlett stopped his horse and looked at me as if he were puzzled, then he said, "Well, dang me! Maybe you ain't been hurt as much as I figured on. If that old maverick has learned you that much he might still be worth keepin' around."

I knew from the way he said it that he'd planned to let Hank go as soon as he was well, so I said, "It was more my fault than his that we got lost. If I hadn't bragged about being able to cut more posts than he could, we'd have gone with the other teams."

Mr. Batchlett reached over and slapped me real hard on the leg. "By dang, Little Britches," he said, "I been thinkin' I was a fool to bring a headstrong kid like you along, but you're goin' to make out after all. Now you get back to the home ranch; you've rode far enough. And listen, Watt's your boss while I'm away. Watch him and you'll learn a lot. If he says you done good and didn't risk your neck too often, and if you've gained your weight back, I'll take you with me on my next trip."

10

Betcha My Life

WHEN I got back from seeing Mr. Batchlett off, Mr. Bendt was at the horse corral, saddling Hazel's pinto, and she was with him. She didn't act as if she knew I'd ridden up, and her father didn't look around until he'd tightened the cinch. When he'd finished, I said, "Mr. Batchlett says you'll be my boss while he's away; do you have a job for me?"

"You betcha my life!" he sang out. "Goin' to be awful short-handed with Tom away! Reckon you could scout around the brush and root out the cows that's had calves?"

"Sure!" I said. "Where'll I put 'em?"

Hazel was still standing with her back to me. She didn't look around, but said, "Hmmfff! He wouldn't even know where to start lookin', and he'd prob'ly get lost agin!"

I knew she was really talking to me instead of her father, and I didn't like what she'd said, so I snapped, "I suppose you'd . . ." but Mr. Bendt cut me off.

"That's enough!" he said. "If you kids want to fight we'll get some gloves! And now, my gal, you've talked yourself into a job o' work! We'll leave you show him where to root 'em out, and where to bring 'em in to! Go tell your maw you're goin'!"

I didn't like having a girl sent to help me, but there wasn't much I could say, and I did need help. The home ranch stretched eight or nine miles along the foot of the mountains, there were a million places for cattle to hide, and I didn't know a single one of them. Any kind of cattle are hard to find in scrub oak country, like the home ranch, but milk cows are the worst of all—especially when they've just had calves.

When Hazel went to the house I could see that Mrs. Bendt didn't like having her go to find the cows with me. She called Mr. Bendt to the chuckhouse steps, and though I couldn't hear what she was saying, her voice sounded sharp. I didn't want to seem to be listening, so I rode Lady out beyond the corrals, and had to wait quite a while before Hazel came back.

"Well, come on if you're comin'!" was all Hazel said, as she spurred the pinto past me and headed him onto the trail. She followed it north for about three miles, then turned off along a creek bottom, pulled up, and said, "Let's clean out this here creek bottom first. You take that side and I'll take this one. Bring 'em out where we turned off the main trail. Betcha my life I find more'n you do."

"Your life wouldn't do me any good," I told her, "but I'll bet you a nickel."

"Cash?"

"Yes, cash," I said, and pulled Lady toward the creek.

The fall I'd worked at the Y-B roundup, we'd ridden into the mountain canyons to hunt out strays. They were beef cattle, and pretty wild, so I was sure I wouldn't have any trouble finding tame old milk cows. I took Lady through the creek at a splashing run, and cantered toward the head of the valley. Before I got there I was sure Hazel had tricked me out of a nickel. If she hadn't known there'd be cows in that bottom she wouldn't have made the bet, and I didn't see a single one on my side of the creek. It seemed to me that it was kind of a dirty trick for her to pick the only good side —and then fool me into making a money bet.

When I turned back, I'd made up my mind that I'd run Lady spraddle-legged again if I had to, but I'd find every single cow and calf on my side of the creek. The valley was only about a mile long and half a mile wide, but I must have run Lady ten miles before we found our first cow with a calf. Willows and alders grew thick along the sides of the creek, and the whole valley was dotted with chokecherry and wild plum thickets. They were all too high to see over, so I had to keep riding back and forth between them as if I'd been in an obstacle race.

When I did find the one lone cow and calf I was in worse trouble than I had been before. The minute I'd leave them to look for some more, they'd disappear, and I had to waste a lot of time finding them again. Before I was anywhere near the end of the valley, Hazel ya-hooed from the main trail. And when I answered, she called back, "Are you lost agin?"

I knew I was going to lose my nickel, but I wasn't going to let her think I cared, so I snaked that old cow out of the valley as fast as the calf could trot.

I'd expected Hazel to have two or three cows with calves, but when I reached the trail she was grinning like a coyote, and had seven of them rounded up in a little herd. "Is that the best you could do?" she sniffed. "I thought you was supposed to be a cowhand."

"I am a cowhand," I told her, "but I'm not a magician. I can't find cows in places where there aren't any."

"Want to bet there ain't?" she taunted.

I wasn't going to let Hazel wangle me into another foolish bet, and I hadn't hunted over the lower end of the valley, so I said, "Well, there might be one or two in this end, but I'll bet you there aren't any farther up."

"Give me a penny apiece for every one I find between the middle of the valley and the hogback?"

"A penny!" I said. "I'll give you a nickel apiece, and I'll eat my shirt if you find more than two."

"Good thing Maw washed it! Give me a hand at putting these critters down to the creek so's they won't scatter."

"Why?" I asked. "They can scatter from down there just as easy as from up here, can't they?"

"Hmfff! That's all you know about cattle, is it? Why would they scatter when there's grass and water handy, and plenty of places to hide their calves?"

Hazel didn't hurry her pinto a bit as we rode up the valley. She just let him mope along, and seemed to be killing all the time she could. When I'd gone up there I'd found a good cattle trail along the creek, but she didn't follow it. Instead she let her horse wander around among the chokecherry thickets like a lost dogie calf. Most of the time she acted as if she didn't know I was along, but once she showed me a meadow lark's nest. Another time she said she'd bet me her life there were baby magpies in a nest in a high cottonwood tree. Then, when we were riding through a little open place, she said, "How do you do that . . ."

"That what?" I asked.

"Oh, never mind; you're too puny now. I was just wonderin' something." Then I couldn't get another word out of her.

We were skirting a plum thicket near the head of the valley when Hazel slid out of her saddle and dropped the reins. Then she looked up at me and said, "It's nickels instead of pennies, ain't it?"

When I nodded, she bent and went into the plum thicket. When she came out she was driving a skinny red cow with a spotted calf that couldn't have been more than a few hours old. The minute the cow saw Lady and me she turned toward us, hooked her head and bawled.

I knew the cow and calf had been in that thicket all morning, and that I'd ridden within a dozen yards of them. To have Hazel find her so easy made me feel sort of silly. I had to say something, and I couldn't tell her she was smarter than I, so I said, "Don't worry, Mrs. Meine, I'm not going to hurt your Villiam."

Hazel looked up, puzzled, and asked, "What did you say?"

"Oh, nothing! The old cow just reminded me of a woman in Littleton, that's all."

"Who?"

"Oh, just a woman that lives across from the schoolhouse and has a spoiled little kid. She's always shaking her fist at us, and hollering, 'Go 'vay, bad kids! Don't you hurt my Villiam!' "

That was the first time that Hazel acted as if she thought I had a lick of sense. She snickered, and said, "Well, I guess it fits her—him, too; it's a bull calf. You keep 'em movin' while I take a look at the alder island."

Mrs. Meine kept trying to dodge back into thickets where I couldn't ride Lady, and I had to get down two or three times to drive her out on foot. I was so busy I didn't think any more about Hazel till she came driving in another cow and calf. That one was a big fat Durham with thick shoulders and a heavy brisket. She didn't pay any attention to me, but kept turning toward her calf, sort of murmuring to it. "This is Mrs. Spivak," Hazel called out. "She looks just like Pete's wife over at the cream station. I found her in them—in those alders where the creek goes around the island."

"Then I'm not going to give you a nickel for her," I called back. "If she was on an island, she was just as much on your side of the creek as on mine."

"What do I care about your old nickel; I got to name her, didn't I?"

"Sure," I told her, "but I don't know if it fits or not."

"Well, you will when you see Pete's wife."

Of course, I couldn't argue about it any more, and I didn't care anyway. What worried me was Hazel's finding cows I'd missed. And I didn't think it was very fair of her to leave me watching that Mrs. Meine and Mrs. Spivak didn't sneak away while she went to hunt more cows.

It wasn't ten minutes before Hazel called from off to my right, "Here comes another one; it's your turn to name her!"

A tall slab-sided Holstein came out between two clumps of bushes. When she saw me she stopped, raised her head high, and stood staring, as if she was daring me to make a move.

"That's Mrs. Tompkins," I called back to Hazel. "She acts just like the substitute teacher we had last spring."

"Well, you can't squeal out of paying me a nickel for her; she was way over on your side. You keep movin' 'em along; I'm going to look in this plum thicket."

"Oh, no you don't!" I said. "I had to spend half of my time keeping track of the cow I found. I'm not going to watch yours and let you gyp me out of any more nickels."

"All right then, don't!" she said, and drove the Holstein in with the others, "but you'd better get some nickels ready. I'll betcha my life there's a cow and calf in that plum thicket over there."

"Oh, bet your small change first!" I told her. "I'll bet another nickel there isn't."

I lost my nickel, but Hazel didn't lose a single cow while she went poking into the thicket. As soon as she took over the driving, the cows plodded along like oxen. She didn't seem to pay a bit of attention to them, or to her horse either. She let him poke along as if he were half asleep, but whenever a cow tried to turn aside he was always in the right place to keep her from it. "Just stay back out of the way and don't spook 'em!" Hazel told me; "I got plenty to do without you gettin' 'em scairt!"

I stayed back, but watched Hazel like a fox. She didn't seem to be doing a bit of hunting, but turned the pinto aside, slid off, and brought another cow and calf out of a little thicket. It didn't look any different to me than forty other thickets we'd passed, but Hazel went to it as straight as if it had a sign on it. "How did you know there'd be a cow in there?" I asked her. "Why did you look in that one when you didn't look in the others we've passed?"

"Because it had a hole in the middle. Couldn't you see the light through the top branches?"

The sky did show a little through the top branches of that thicket, and it didn't through the others, but I would never have thought of its meaning there was a hole in the middle. "Well, even if there was a hole in it, how did you know there'd be a cow in there?" I asked.

Hazel stopped her horse, put both hands on her hips, and looked at me as if I were hopeless. "Well," she said, "if you was a cow and was goin' to have a calf, could you find any better place than that to hide in?"

I didn't like having Hazel act as if she thought I was just plain stupid, and snapped at her, "Well, I'm not a cow, and I'm not going to have a calf, and I'm not so much like a cow that I can think like one."

"Hmfff! You'd better get to be if you don't want to go on losin' nickels!" she snapped back.

That nickel business was worrying me a lot. I only had sixty cents, Hazel had already won half of it, and it was still a long way to the middle of the valley. It seemed to me that I'd better not fight with her, because she might win more money than I had, and I'd have to be in debt to her. I'd been going to say I didn't care how many nickels she won, but instead, I said, "I'll drive the cows for you. With this many, you'd have a terrible time if they got scattered."

"You stay back and leave 'em alone if you want to help me!" she said. "Why would they scatter if they ain't hurried or scairt half out of their wits?"

It wouldn't have been so bad if I could have kept busy, but just to trail along behind gave me too much time to worry about the nickels. And Hazel brought in four more cows and calves before we reached the middle of the valley. After that, she drove the little herd and let me do the hunting. I poked into a lot of thickets that didn't have a cow in them, but I looked in four that did, and Hazel told me I'd done pretty well for a greenhorn.

By that time Hazel had stopped acting as if she thought I was stupid, and we picked names for every one of the cows as we drove them slowly toward the main trail. I wanted to name a pretty little Jersey with her first calf, Jenny Wren, but Hazel wouldn't let me. She said that cows with calves were all married, and that they had to be named Mrs. Somebody. I had to give in and name the little Jersey for Mrs. Hazlett, my Sunday School teacher in Littleton.

I was so glad Hazel hadn't won more than all the money I had, that I didn't mind having lost half a dollar. Then I began feeling cheap about saying I wouldn't pay her for the cow she found on the island, so I said, "I was thinking about Mrs. Spivak. That island where you found her was as much on my side of the creek as it was on yours, so that's fifty-five cents I owe you. I'll give it to you when we get back to the bunkhouse."

"I don't want your old money!" she told me. "All I wanted was to show that a girl is just as good a cowpoke as a boy— even if your name is Little Britches and you rode in the roundup and got your pi'ture in the paper."

"My name isn't Little Britches," I said, "it's Ralph. And I didn't have anything to do with my picture getting in the paper. And besides, it doesn't take cowpokes to do trick riding; it takes smart horses and a good teacher, and that's what I had."

Hazel looked around at me as if she couldn't believe what she heard me say. For half a minute her eyes looked as if she might cry. Then she looked back at the cows, and after another minute, she repeated my name, "Ralph," as though she'd never heard it before.

I couldn't think of anything more to say, so we just rode along behind the cows for a while. Then Hazel said, "This mornin' I was goin' to ask you how you done that somerset trick Jenny seen you do at the roundup, but now I ain't goin' to. You got to promise you won't show me till you gain back to what you was before Hank got you lost. Paw says you can't do no hard ridin' till you gain your weight back."

I could tell by the sun that it was already past noon, and

I was hungry enough to eat a horse; so I said, "Well, I'll promise, but I'll never gain my weight back without eating. Hadn't we better round up those first cows you found and start back toward the corrals?"

Hazel shook her head. "Wouldn't be no sense in that!" she said. "It would take a couple of hours, and Jenny put us up some picnic grub—if the milk ain't all shook to butter. I know a good place to eat, soon's we get these critters throwed in with the others."

11

The Secret Spring

HAZEL had been right when she told me the cows wouldn't scatter. There wasn't one of her first bunch in sight when we took the named ones down to the creek, but they were all there—hidden away in the willows, chewing their cud or feeding their calves. The only one missing was the one I'd brought in, and Hazel didn't have to tell me why she was gone: I'd driven her too hard and frightened her. She'd probably taken her calf a mile away to hide it.

Anyone who didn't know Batchlett's home ranch might have thought it was nothing except a brush-covered wilderness. But Hazel knew every inch of it the way I knew the streets of Littleton, and she knew spots that were prettier than any in the Denver City Park. She took me to one of them to eat our picnic grub, and told me it was her own secret place, and that nobody else knew about it.

It was in a little pocket, back behind the row of red rocks that stand like a broken fence in front of the foothills—the same row that makes the Garden of the Gods near Colorado Springs. Where the walls of the pocket rose like organ pipes around a pulpit, a cold spring bubbled from under the rocks and trickled away through a thick grove of aspens. The bottom of the canyon was covered with clover, and violets and columbine grew at the edge of the grove. To the west, the mountain rose in staggered cliffs, and high above them the green of firs looked like dark rumpled velvet against the blue sky. All around the spring the rocks were lined with moss, and peppery watercress grew at the rim of the little basin that caught the overflow.

Nearly a quarter of a mile from the spring we unsaddled the horses and hobbled them so they could graze. Then Hazel led the way through a gap in the fence of red rocks, along the edge of the little canyon, and into the grove of aspens. We were hardly among the trees when she put a finger to her lips, and whispered, "Betcha my life we see a deer, Ralph. Least ways, there'll be a rabbit, or maybe a skunk. This time o' day they'll be comin' in for water. Sundown's best in the spring; that's when swallows swoop in to get mud for their nests."

Hazel made me stay behind her, and we crept up toward the head of the little canyon like Indians. When we were within fifty yards of the spring, she stopped and motioned me to come up beside her. "Ain't no deer," she whispered, "but there's rabbits. See 'em?" and she pointed. "Doe and her litter."

Through the trunks of the aspens I could see half a dozen jack rabbits feeding and playing on the little patch of clover. The half-grown ones seemed to be having a picnic of their own, scampering around and chasing one another, but the old doe was nervous. There didn't seem to be a breath of air moving, but I was sure she had scented us. She'd nibble a few mouthfuls of clover, then stand high on her haunches and look around in every direction.

Hazel and I stood for nearly ten minutes, watching the rabbits play. Then a sudden flash of brown shot out from the mountainside. I'd hardly seen the brown streak before a squeal, so sharp it made my ears ring, filled the canyon. It was all over in a second. There was a whirl of gray and brown. Then the other rabbits were gone, and the one that had squealed lay twitching, with what looked to be a slim-bodied, hump-backed cat standing over it.

"Darned weasel!" Hazel shouted, and ran, dodging through the trees, toward the clearing. By the time we got there the weasel had gone and the rabbit lay perfectly still. Hazel dropped to her knees, picked up the limp body, and turned it so the red trickle of blood at its throat showed. "Darned weasel!" she said again. "Bit his windpipe clean through—poor little critter!" For a minute I thought she was going to cry, but she didn't. She pinched her mouth up tight, and said, "Oh, well, it's only a rabbit, and I s'pose rabbits was made for other critters to eat . . . but I hate a sneaky weasel!"

If I'd been alone I wouldn't have thought of burying the little rabbit, but thinking it might make Hazel feel better, I said, "Shall I dig a grave so we can bury him?"

"Uh-huh, I guess we'd better. If we don't the darned old weasel will come back and get him . . . or he'd stink and spoil the nice smell of the spring. I'll show you where the graveyard's at; I a'ready got a lark and two sparrows buried in it, one sparrow last year and the other two the year before."

Hazel led me to where three separate little piles of rock stood in a row among the aspens. "I'll fetch rocks while you dig the hole," she told me. "Dig it deep, and we'll have to pile on some heavy rocks or a pesky coyote might dig him up. I never seen one around here, but there's plenty of tracks where they come to the basin to drink."

"I'll bring the rocks," I told her. "Why don't you pick some leaves to line the grave with?"

Hazel stood thinking for a minute, then she said, "There wouldn't be no sense in that. He's dead now, and it wouldn't help none to wrap him up in leaves . . . but it wouldn't be right to let him get dug up. I'll fetch light rocks; you can help with the heavy ones."

After we'd buried the rabbit, we washed at the brook below the spring, and Hazel laid out our grub on the cloth it was wrapped in. There were sandwiches and cake, a pint jar of

chicken stew, and a quart of milk. We didn't say a word while
we ate the first sandwich and drank a dipper of milk. Then
Hazel looked up and said, "There ain't no sense bein' so glum
'cause we seen a bunny-rabbit get killed. We wouldn't be
havin' no stew if a hen hadn't got her head chopped off. I
guess it got planned that way right from the beginning: some
things just has to get killed so other things can live . . . even
darned old weasels. Why don't you ever tell me anything about
your brothers and sisters?"

I spent nearly a whole hour telling Hazel about the other
children at home, and some of the things we'd done. And
she told me she was going to Castle Rock in the fall, to live
with Jenny and go to school in town. But she said she wasn't
going to be a school teacher when she grew up, because they
turned out to be old maids too often. What she was going to
do was to marry a rancher who had a big ranch like Batchlett's
home place, with mountains right behind it and lots of cattle
and shelter for them.

"Then you'll have to marry an old man," I told her. "Men
don't get big ranches like this, and lots of cattle, till they've
been in business a long time and saved their money."

"Oh, well," she said, "he wouldn't have to have it when I
married him, but I'd have to know he was a good cow man
. . . and didn't waste his money bettin' on things he couldn't
win. Then I'd help him, and we'd keep all our heifer calves
every year, and I'd have lots of children—all boys—and then
we wouldn't have to hire no—any cowpokes."

I don't remember just what I told Hazel, but it was some
of the things I'd been thinking the night I rode to catch up
with Mr. Batchlett—and I do remember telling her that I'd
want some of my children to be girls.

I forgot all about the time until the shadow of the mountain
cut off the sunshine. Even then, I had to remind myself that
I was being paid a dollar a day, and that I hadn't done much
in the past week to earn it. I don't know just what it was, but
there was something about the little pocket in the canyon that

made me feel lazy and restful. Maybe it was the spring and the sound of the trickling water, or maybe it was just the feel and smell of the little green clearing. It's funny, but the nicest smell about it wasn't from the flowers or the clover, but the odor of skunk. Not the kind that makes your eyes smart and your nose wrinkle, but just the faint, musky kind that smells almost like perfume—and makes you remember places you thought you'd forgotten.

"You don't need to come," I told Hazel, "but I'd better get back to work. I've only found five cows and calves all day, and that isn't worth a day's pay."

"That's why we come here, 'stead of eating where we left the cows," Hazel said with a grin. "You don't think I'd wasted all this time, exceptin' Paw said you couldn't do much till you got your strength back. You ought to eat more sandwiches; you do look kind of puny."

"There's nothing puny about me," I said, as I picked up the saddle bag, "and I'll bet I didn't lose two pounds."

"Nickel?"

"No," I said, "I'm all over betting on things I couldn't win; maybe I might have lost three pounds."

"Nickel?"

"No! Not a penny!"

"Then eat another sandwich, and we'll get back after them —those cows. Like as not we'll have to hunt some of 'em, and it'll be supper time 'fore we get 'em fetched in to the corrals."

Instead of trying to make me look silly after we went back to work, Hazel showed me as much as she could about finding, handling, and driving cows in the brush. If her pinto could have taught Lady the way Hazel taught me, we'd have got along fine, but of course he couldn't. I had to rein her for every move she made, and she couldn't stop and turn quick enough to head off a dodging cow. It was supper time before we got the cattle to the corrals, and I knew I hadn't done a very good job, but all Hazel said was, "You'd have better luck if you took Pinch tomorrow. Cows don't dodge past old Pinch more'n about once."

After that first day I don't think Mrs. Bendt minded Hazel's working with me—and I didn't either. Pinch was one of the best horses with milk cows that I ever saw, and his name fitted him exactly. If a cow hung back or tried to dodge away, he'd be behind her in a rush, and nip her on the butt of her tail. He never bit harder than a pinch, but two lessons were enough for any cow. Even though we had different cows every day, it almost seemed that they were getting used to us and learning to behave. Hazel said it was I who was learning, but most of the credit really belonged to Pinch.

Each day we took our grub sack to the secret spring at noon, but we didn't loaf around again the way we had the first day. And we didn't talk any more about the kind of a ranch, or number of children we'd have when we grew up. Once we stopped in the aspens to watch a deer drinking at the basin, and another time we saw a raccoon dipping something in the water before he ate it. But we never saw the weasel again, and we didn't find any rabbits that he'd killed.

Jenny always packed enough grub for three men, and Hazel kept pestering me till I'd eaten most of it. I knew she was doing it so I'd gain my weight back in a hurry and could show her the somersault trick I'd done at the Littleton roundup. It sort of worried me, because it was a real tricky stunt, and I hadn't tried it for nearly a year.

To do the trick I had to have a horse going at a dead run, then dive out of the saddle, turn a somersault in the air, and come down on my feet. But doing it right depended as much on the horse as it did on me. He had to set his feet and be sliding to a stop the instant I made a move to leave the saddle. That would throw me forward, and if I ducked my head and shoulders just right, I couldn't help turning all the way over in the air. Then, when I landed on my feet, I'd be standing right beside the horse's head. But if the horse didn't stop quick enough it was pretty hard to go all the way over, and sometimes I'd land on the seat of my pants.

I'd made a monkey of myself in front of Hazel times enough.

The fourth day I worked with her I decided that, before I let her see me try that stunt, I'd practice it until I was nearly perfect. There was a bright moon that night, and it seemed a good time to begin practicing. I didn't know Pinch well enough to trust my neck to him, and Lady wasn't good at quick stops. But, after everybody was asleep, I took her to a little spongy meadow I'd picked out, about three miles from the buildings. I knew I'd land falling or sitting down a few times before we got the knack of the trick again, and wanted as soft a landing place as I could find.

Lady and I had done the trick together dozens of times, but she seemed to have forgotten all about it. I used to make a little hissing sound the moment before I left the saddle, and she'd stop pretty well when she heard it. But for a while that night it didn't mean a thing to her. Over and over again, I had to hiss and jerk the reins at the same time before she learned again that the hiss meant for her to set her feet. Then I tried my first somersault, but I was awkward, Lady didn't stop fast enough, and that spongy meadow felt as hard to my bottom as if it had been solid rock.

We didn't go back to the buildings until we'd tried the stunt at least twenty times—and until I was so sore and lame I could hardly sit in the saddle. Sometimes it almost worked, but I never did come all the way over and up onto my feet, and sometimes Lady forgot to stop when I hissed.

All the next day Hazel kept telling me, "Sit back in the saddle; you act like you had a bur in your britches!" or, "By jiminy, you look punier today than you did when Batch fetched you back from the mountains! If you don't start to eating more, you ain't never goin' to gain your weight back." I couldn't tell her that I felt punier than I looked, and that I thought I'd beaten at least five pounds of weight off my behind. And she never guessed that I'd been up half the night, or that I'd taken any falls.

I'd made up my mind that no matter how banged-up I felt, I was going to practice again that night, but I didn't. When we brought in the cows at supper time, Lady was lame in both front legs. The sogginess of the meadow hadn't softened my falls much, but had let her hoofs cut deep, and thrown a terrible strain on her legs. I knew they'd have to be doctored, or they'd swell and stiffen.

As soon as Ned was snoring that night I got up, built a fire in the forge, and put a bucket of water on to heat. Then I stripped a couple of gunny sacks into long bandages, the way I'd seen Father do it, got them boiling hot, and wrapped both of Lady's fore legs from pastern to elbow. Even though it was a warm night, the bandages cooled off fast, and way before moonset my hands were so swollen and parboiled they looked like two bunches of red bananas. But just before sunrise, when I took off the last bandages, the swelling was pretty well gone from Lady's knees.

The next day I really felt puny from lack of sleep, but I felt worse about having abused Lady, and because we wouldn't be able to practice for a long time. I was thinking about it when Hazel and I were riding over to the secret spring to eat our noon grub, and wasn't paying much attention to Pinch or the way we were going. Then too, my bottom was still so bruised and lame that I wasn't sitting square in the saddle, but kind of scrooched over to one side.

We were cantering along at a pretty fair clip, side by side, when a pheasant flushed out of a little bush, right in front of Pinch. I was sitting loose in the saddle, and he set his feet so fast I didn't have a chance to catch myself. It must have been my thinking about the stunt that made me duck my head and shoulders when the quick stop threw me forward. I flipped all the way over in the air, and when I landed, I was standing on my feet at Pinch's head.

Hazel's pinto had stopped nearly as fast as Pinch, so she came pretty near getting spilled too, but as soon as she caught her balance, she yapped at me, "You dirty promise-breaker! You said you wouldn't try that till you gained your weight back, and you're punier this mornin' than you been any day yet! And besides, you done it so quick I couldn't see how it worked!"

"I didn't promise I wouldn't try it," I told her. "I only promised not to show you till I got my weight back, and if you didn't see how I did it, then I didn't show you."

"Hmmfff! Show-off!"

"No," I said again, "it wasn't that either! It just happened all by itself when Pinch stopped so quick. When I try to show off I always make a monkey of myself."

Hazel put both hands on her hips and squinted at me as if I'd been a weasel. "You ain't tryin' to tell me you done it without meanin' to? Do I look like a darn dodo?"

"Well, if you did, I wouldn't tell you so," I snapped, "but sometimes you talk like one. If you knew anything about that trick you'd know there's nothing to it except timing and letting yourself go loose enough, and the timing worked all by itself."

For a minute Hazel sat there with her eyes squinnied up, but she didn't look as if she hated me. And I knew she was trying to figure out for herself just what made the trick work. Suddenly she said, "Show me how . . . no! No! This time you got to promise you won't even . . ."

I could tell from the look on Hazel's face that she'd made up her mind to try the trick by herself, and I was afraid she'd break her neck, so I cut in, "If there's going to be any promising, you're going to do your share. Before I'll promise you anything, you'll have to promise me you won't try that trick till your father says you can."

"Did your father say you could the first time you done it?"

"No," I said, "because he didn't know anything about it till he saw me do it at the roundup."

"Then I ain't goin' to promise! If it was fair for you to do it without your paw knowin', it's fair for me."

"It was different with me," I told her. "I learned to do it from Hi Beckman, and he's a champion trick-rider."

"Then it ain't no different with me," she snapped. "You

won the prize at the roundup, didn't you?"

"Only because I was riding with Hi," I said. "I couldn't have done it by myself."

"That don't make no never-minds! If you won the prize you're a champion, and Paw don't need to know."

I could see I wasn't going to get anywhere by arguing, and I was afraid of her being hurt if I didn't get some kind of a promise, so I said, "I'll promise not to try it again till I'm back to seventy-two pounds, if you'll promise not to try it till I say you can."

"Ain't no sense in that, you'd never say it."

"Yes, I will too!" I said. "I'll say it just as soon as I think you and a horse are trained well enough that you could do it without getting hurt. Do you promise?"

Hazel sat studying me for a minute with her mouth pinched up tight, then she swiped an X across her shirt with one finger, and said, "Cross my heart!"

I wasn't too much worried about Pinch, after the way we'd done the trick almost by accident. But he needed to learn to make those quick stops without having to wait for a pheasant to fly up in his face. And long before I'd ever let Hazel try it, her pinto would have to be dead positive on his stops. "All right," I told her, "it's a promise, but I won't teach you to do it till you can get Pinto to stop on a postage stamp without a touch of a line."

That afternoon we started training Pinto and Pinch. By time to take the cows in, they had learned that a hiss meant for them to stop, but Pinto was too slow and came down too hard on his front feet. Pinch was a lot better at it, because he'd been trained as a rope horse, and had learned to save his knees by throwing all his weight on his hind legs.

12

A Man Owes It to His Horse

WITH most of the men away, I thought I might have trouble finding anything to do on Sunday, but I didn't. Hazel helped Jenny bring the breakfast into the chuckhouse, and when we were nearly through eating, she said to her father, "You didn't ride fence this week, did you, Paw?"

"Nope," he said. "Didn't have no time. Prob'ly won't get none this next week neither. Got to round up the whole shebang and cut out the tradin' stock for next trip."

He'd barely finished when Hazel said, "Ralph and me could ride fence for you this mornin'. Maw said I didn't have to go to Sunday School."

Mr. Bendt looked up, scowled, and asked, "You and who?"

I didn't think Hazel could ever get flustered, but her face went as red as a sunrise, and she sort of stammered, "Me and . . . me and Little Britches."

The dairyhands began laughing, and Mr. Bendt chuckled, "Put a new handle on him, did you? Well, I don't see no . . ."

"Oh, no you don't!" Jenny sang out. "Helen said you could stay home from Sunday School if you'd mind the baby and help with the dishes."

"Well, I'll do the dishes first—all by myself," Hazel told her, "and Martha said she'd mind the baby."

"What did you bribe her with, your birds' eggs?"

"Ain't got no birds' eggs!"

"Haven't any!" Jenny corrected her.

"Well, haven't any, then! But Martha said she'd mind the baby."

Mr. Bendt looked up at Hazel as if he were puzzled, and asked, "What you rarin' to ride fence for, gal? Didn't you kids get enough ridin' this past week?"

"Well, we . . . we know where there's a magpie's nest, and we think there's some young ones in it that's about ready to fly, and we want to get one and teach it to talk."

If we wanted anything like that, it was new to me, but when Mr. Bendt looked over, I nodded.

"You ain't goin' to have much time for learnin' magpies to talk," he told me. "You got the cuttin' horse in your string, and we got plenty cuttin' to do 'fore Batch gets back here."

I was in sort of a mess. I didn't want to teach a magpie to talk, and I did want to try cutting cattle with Clay. Besides, I'd have to get a good report from Mr. Bendt if I was to go on the next trip with Mr. Batchlett. But, after Hazel's having taught me to find and handle cows, I couldn't go back on her, either, so I said, "Well, I don't know how to teach magpies to talk. I'm just going to help Hazel get one so she can teach it—if it's all right with you."

"Hmmm," he said, "wouldn't hurt none to get the fences rode, but I reckon there's a possum in the woodpile." Then he looked back at Hazel, and asked, "What you want a magpie for?"

"Martha wants it. I told her we'd try to get one for her. Can we, Paw?"

"Sounds to me like one of your two-way deals, gal; gettin' out of Sunday School to mind the baby, and gettin' out of minding the baby by puttin' it up to Martha that she wants a

magpie. Reckon you'd best go along to Sunday School; there'll
be plenty time for magpies after you get home."

It was easy to see that Hazel knew better than to argue.
She didn't act sulky or peeved, but just shrugged her shoulders
the least bit, as much as to say, "Well, I tried," then picked
up some dishes and went out.

When we were leaving the chuckhouse, Mr. Bendt asked me,
"Want to give me a hand hookin' up the buckboard?" Then,
as we walked toward the carriage shed, he said, "If you're
rarin' to ride, it might not be a bad notion to give Clay a work-
out. You ain't quite got the hang of him yet."

I'd felt guilty about picking Clay ever since Sid told me
he was Mr. Bendt's prize cutting horse. And I'd felt worse
since the day I'd made a monkey of myself when I tried to use
him. It seemed to me it would be better all around if I could
give him back. So I said, "I know I haven't got the hang of
him, and maybe I never will. But if I'm going on trips with
Mr. Batchlett I won't have much use for him, and you'll need
him here on the home ranch. Wouldn't it be better if I traded
him for a trail horse out of your string?"

We were walking along side by side, and I watched Mr.
Bendt's face when I asked him. For a second or two it lighted
up, then it sobered again, and he said, "No! No! You picked
him fair and square—with a little help from Hazel—and he's
yours for the season. Fact is, if you'd give him half a chance,
he'd do better with your weight on him than mine. Trouble
is, you rare in too hard, try to rush things too much."

"Yes, sir," I said, "I know it now. I learned it on cows and
calves. Hazel showed me how to do it the slow, easy way."

"Want I should show you on Clay?"

"I'd like it if you would," I said. "I guess I never paid
enough attention when a good cutting horse was being ridden."

"Ain't nothin' to it if you take your time, watch you don't
throw your horse off balance, and leave him have his head.
When we get the folks off to church we'll take a try at some
of them cows and calves you and Hazel fetched in. What's all
this magpie business?"

"Well, I guess Hazel just wants to get one for Martha," I said. "She showed me where there was a nest last Monday."

Mr. Bendt didn't say any more till we were hitching the horses to the buckboard. Then he asked, "You kids ain't got a maverick out there you been tryin' to ride, have you? You looked pretty shook-up a couple of days back."

"No, sir," I said. "We haven't seen a horse except the ones we've been riding ourselves."

"Betcha my life Hazel's got somethin' up her sleeve besides magpies and fence ridin'. You ain't been learnin' her none of them trick stunts you done at the roundup?"

It caught me so much by surprise that I was slow in saying, "No, sir." And when it came out it was so low that it sounded like a lie, even if it wasn't, so I had to add, "but we were teaching the horses how to do one of them."

"That how your mare got her fore legs stove up?"

A lump came into my throat, and I felt as if I were talking to my own father again. He had always been able to read every sign, just as Mr. Bendt did, and to know what I'd been doing when I was out of his sight. As soon as I could swallow, I said, "Yes, sir. I stopped her too fast on soggy ground."

"So I took note, but you ought to of put liniment on 'fore you bandaged 'em; there's a bottle in the bunkhouse."

"I used good hot bandages," I told him, "and I don't think her knees are sprung; she was only lame one day."

"No, they ain't," he said, "but you might'a ruined her. Ought to filed her fore hoofs down tender 'fore you started out. That'll learn 'em to dig in with the hind ones on them quick stops; saves their knees."

"I know it," I said. "Hi Beckman taught me that, but I didn't think about it."

"A man owes it to his horse to think about them things 'fore he staves 'em up. Better take the buckboard on up to the house; the women folks is waitin'."

When I drove the buckboard up to the side door, all the children had on their best clothes, and were waiting with Mrs. Bendt and Jenny. They all looked fine, except Hazel. She had on a thin, light pink dress, high buttoned shoes, white stockings, and a straw sailor hat to match her dress—with a little bouquet of artificial flowers on it. Some girls change altogether when they wear their best clothes, but Hazel didn't change a bit. With her freckled face and arms scratched from getting cows out of thickets, and with the end of her snubby nose peeling from sunburn, she looked about as funny in those fancy pink clothes as I would have. But Hazel didn't seem to care.

When I was holding the horses, she called, "You got Barney's check strap too loose; leave it that way and he'll keep his head bobbin' like a woodpecker." As she said it, she came around to me, and whispered, "We'll be back by two. Have Pinto and Pinch saddled up, 'cause if we don't practice 'em good and plenty they'll forget what we learnt 'em yesterday."

Before I could answer, Jenny called, "Hazel, come here and let me get you straightened out! My goodness, you look like a scarecrow! Your hat's on crooked, your dress is hiked up on one side, and your stockings are twisted."

"Well, I'm all covered up, ain't I?" Hazel called back, "and that's what clothes are for." But she went over and let Jenny fix her. Then, as they drove out of the dooryard, she called to me, "Now don't forget what I told you!"

When I went back to the corral, Mr. Bendt was filing one of Pinto's front hoofs. He didn't look up, but said, "Reckon I'd best trim these down tender 'fore you kids bust his knees up. He ain't never been trained for ropin'; ain't learnt to take the strain of hard stops on his hind legs."

"Then it's all right to teach him the tricks?" I asked.

"Don't see no harm, so long as you're halfway careful," he told me. "But if I know my gal, she ain't goin' to let you stop at learnin' tricks to horses."

I waited a minute to see if he was going to say anything more, and asked, "Then it's all right for me to show her a few of the tricks that aren't too dangerous?"

"They're all dangerous, ain't they?" he asked. "If they wasn't they wouldn't be good enough to win at a roundup."

"Well, they're not awfully dangerous if you have your horses trained just right," I said. "They all work by timing, and a lot depends on the horse."

"Always does. Nine-tenths of bein' a good horseman is learnin' a horse what you want of him. Half the other tenth is in leavin' him free to do what you learnt him."

I still didn't know if he meant that I could or couldn't show Hazel how to do any of the tricks, so I said, "What I need to know most is if it will be all right to show Hazel some of the safer stunts. She's been kind of . . ."

"Ain't it kind of hard for a man to tell what he needs to know most?" he asked, without stopping his filing.

"Well, yes, I suppose it is," I said, "but I do need to know if it would be all right for me to teach Hazel."

Mr. Bendt kept on filing until Pinto flinched. Then he dropped the hoof, straightened up, and said, "Guess that'll learn you not to throw too much weight on 'em." He slapped Pinto, turned to me, and said, "Tell Hazel to pull him up easy and take care on her first few stops. He's goin' to raise dust when he pounds them tender hoofs down. She'll get shook up, but if she's mindful she won't get throwed. If I do say so, she ain't a bad little rider—for a girl."

"She's the best I ever saw, but I need to know . . ."

"Yeah, I know! I been studyin' on it. Reckon Helen would raise Old Ned if she knowed what you kids was up to. Reckon I shouldn't ought to put you two workin' together; not after Hazel knowin' 'bout you trick-ridin' in the roundup. Has she ever saw you do one of them stunts?"

"Well," I said, "not on purpose, but I did one by mistake yesterday. A pheasant flew up in front of Pinch, and when he stopped too quick I somersaulted without thinking."

"Land on your feet like Jenny seen you do at the roundup?"

"Yes, sir," I said, "but it was only because the timing happened to work just right."

"The grease is in the fire then," he said, as if he were talking to himself. "She ain't goin' to get bested if she can help it, and she'll get stove up less if she's learnt how to do it the right way." Then he looked right into my eyes, and said, "I don't want you kids divin' off no horses out in the brush. If you want to learn her, you'll have to do it here at the corrals, and when there's one another of us men around to pick her up if she gets hurt. Now ain't it about time we got to work on them calves?"

13

Keeping Time with the Fiddler

SUNDAY wasn't a regular working day on the home ranch, but the day when lots of odd jobs, like separating cows and calves, were done. As soon as he'd finished with Pinto, Mr. Bendt sent me to call Ned, while he called the dairyhands. Until cows and calves were separated they belonged to the cowhands, but then they were turned over to the dairymen.

Hazel and I had been bringing in about fifteen cows a day, and they'd been put with their calves into a fenced pasture behind the dairy barn. As soon as we were saddled up, Ned and I brought a dozen or so cows and their calves into the cutting corral. On one side, gates opened into smaller corrals, and from these, runways led to the milking-herd pasture and the calf sheds. It was our job to put each cow or calf through whichever gate the dairymen opened for it, and then we were done with them until they were turned back to us as pasture calves or dry cows.

When everything was ready and the dairymen were at their gates, Mr. Bendt rode into the cutting corral on Clay. "Don't come in for 'em till I get 'em plumb cut loose," he told us, then

turned Clay's head toward the cattle that were huddled tight
in the far corner of the corral.

No one watching them would have thought they had the
least bit of interest in those cattle. Mr. Bendt sat slouched in
the saddle, with the reins held rather loosely in his left hand.
As the milling cows watched nervously, Clay walked toward
them at a turtle's pace. I was watching every move, but could
barely see Mr. Bendt draw the reins one way or another to
guide him.

With all the cows and calves having to be separated, I'd expected Mr. Bendt to take almost any animal on the outside of
the herd, but he didn't do it. Step by slow step, Clay came to
the edge of the huddle. The cattle didn't break away from the
corner, or seem to be any more nervous than when he first
started toward them. For a minute or two, I thought Mr. Bendt
hadn't made up his mind which animal he wanted to bring out.
He seemed to be slowly stirring the herd around—as if it had
been cold molasses, and Clay had been the spoon.

When it had turned about half way around, I noticed that
Mrs. Tompkins, the slab-sided Holstein I'd named for our substitute teacher, was on the outside. Her black-and-white calf
was close beside her, but toward the inside of the herd. At the
moment I spotted them, Mr. Bendt moved the reins just a
trifle, let them drop loose, and took hold of the saddle horn
with both hands.

From there on there was no question about which animal he
and Clay were after; it was Mrs. Tompkins' calf. But how Clay
knew it, I couldn't figure. He hadn't even been looking at the
calf when Mr. Bendt gave him a free rein, but he began edging
his way toward it, inch by inch. I don't believe Mrs. Tompkins
ever guessed what he was up to until he had her and her calf
edged out three or four feet from the rest of the herd. Then it
was too late.

From being a turtle, Clay changed into a cat playing with a
mouse. When Mrs. Tompkins tried to dodge back past him, he
dodged right with her, to head her off. She whirled and went

the other way, but he was still between her and the herd. After two or three more tries, she threw her head up and stood, seeming to dare him, the way she had me when she first came out of the brush. Clay stood facing her, his weight on his hind legs, and teetering on his front ones, ready to dodge whichever way she did.

Watching Clay, I could almost feel him planning what to do next. Suddenly he made a quick lunge forward. As Mrs. Tompkins sprang out of his way, he cut between her and her calf. Before she missed the calf Clay had it against the corral fence and running toward us. I'd been so busy watching Clay that I forgot my part of the job, but Ned spurred in behind Clay, and ran the calf through the gateway that one of the dairymen had opened.

The moment Ned took the calf, Clay became a turtle again, and turned back slowly toward the herd. It wasn't until then that I realized I hadn't learned a thing about riding a cutting horse from watching Mr. Bendt. From the moment he'd let the reins go loose, I hadn't seen him any more than if Clay had been riderless. I was feeling pretty much ashamed of myself when I noticed that Mr. Bendt had turned Clay toward me. "Catch on?" he asked, as he came alongside.

"No, sir," I said, "I don't believe I learned a thing—except to go into the herd real slow and easy. If you picked that black-and-white calf yourself, I don't know how you let Clay know it. And after he started to crowd Mrs. Tompkins out, I forgot all about watching you."

"Mrs. Who?"

"Oh," I said, "that's just a name Hazel and I put on that Holstein when we found her."

"How come that name?"

"Well," I told him, "she held her head up and stared at Lady just the way she did at Clay, and it kind of reminded me of a substitute teacher we had last spring."

"Better not tell Jenny that," he chuckled. "She was a substitute schoolma'am up to last winter. Now you pay heed while we go in and get Miz Tompkins! You watched the horse work; now take note what I'm doin'."

That time I didn't watch Clay any more than I could help, but kept most of my attention on Mr. Bendt. It helped, too, to know which animal he was after.

Mrs. Tompkins was standing at the edge of the herd, bawling for her calf, when Mr. Bendt turned Clay back to the cutting. As he moved slowly toward her, she stuck out her head and bellowed at him. When he'd covered half the distance she turned and plowed back into the corner. Clay didn't change his creeping gait, and Mr. Bendt didn't make a move of any kind. But I was pretty sure that Clay knew what cow they were after as well as I did. Again he sort of drifted into the herd, mixed with it, and began to edge slowly toward Mrs. Tompkins.

She had her head turned toward him, watching, and jammed her way along the fence. If Mr. Bendt made the slightest move, or drew the lines either way, it was so little I couldn't see it, but Clay moved slowly to head her off. When she saw him coming, she whirled, dropped her head, and hooked her way in the other direction. It was then that I saw Mr. Bendt make his first move, and I would have missed it if I hadn't been watching him like a coyote. He seemed to lean forward an inch or two in the saddle. Then he let the lines go loose, grabbed the horn, and Clay shouldered his way through the cows in front of him.

Before Mrs. Tompkins was more than two lengths up the fence line, Clay had her pinned tight. His shoulder was even with her hip bone, and she could neither turn out nor whirl back. In her panic she raced straight forward, and Clay followed her only until Ned and I were in position to take her through an open gateway.

When I turned Pinch back, Mr. Bendt was waiting for me. "Wasn't nothin' to that one," he said. "Didn't give me no ridin' to do. Want I should bring out another one?"

"I'd like it if you would," I told him. "I think I learned something that time."

"Good! Which one you want me to fetch out?"

I started to say, "Mrs. Spivak," but caught myself, and said, "There's a big Durham in there, with thick shoulders and a heavy brisket, and she's got a lively bull calf with a white face. I'd like to see you get the calf."

"Seen 'em," he said; "he'll be a good one." Then he turned Clay and started back at a slow creep. There was nothing much different from the first time, until the Durham and her calf had been brought to the outside of the herd. But I did notice one thing: when Clay stirred the cows around in the corner, he managed to get fairly close to every one of them. And it was when his head was near the Durham that Mr. Bendt drew the lines just a trifle toward her.

Mrs. Spivak didn't try to dodge back into the herd, but lumbered away with her calf tight at her flank. Clay followed close alongside, and I had my eyes fixed on Mr. Bendt, watching for the slightest signal. When it came, it was so slight and quick I wasn't sure I'd really seen it. Quicker than I could think, Clay charged at the cow and turned her. The calf didn't turn quick enough, and in a split second Clay was between him and his mother. Then the fun began.

That calf of Mrs. Spivak's could run faster than a jack rabbit, turn quicker than a cottontail, and had the determination of a lion. Bawling like a spoiled brat, and with his tail stuck straight up, he was bound to get back to his mother, and did more fancy ducking and dodging than a cork bobber when you've got a big trout on the line. Clay was outguessing him on every dodge, but I missed about half the fun because I had to keep all my attention on Mr. Bendt. He was all of six-foot-two, and weighed over two hundred pounds, but was always in perfect balance. Holding the horn with both hands, he seemed to be as loose as a sack of feathers, but anyone could see that his weight was always with the turn of his horse.

After it was pretty well winded, Clay pinned Mrs. Spivak's calf against the fence, and brought him up for Ned and me to take over. When I turned back from the gate, Mr. Bendt had dismounted and was taking his saddle off Clay. "Switch horses," he called, "if you don't mind me ridin' Pinch."

"Of course, I don't mind," I told him, as I rode up, "but I'll never be able to ride Clay the way you can."

"A man never knows what he can do till he's tried his best," he told me. "Cinch your saddle on tight and go fetch that calf's maw; she'll be an easy one for you."

I'll never be sure whether I guided Clay to that big red cow or not. If I moved the lines it wasn't more than an inch, and if I leaned her way in the saddle it wasn't any farther, but Clay seemed to read my mind. His steps were as slow and sneaky as a cat's when it is creeping up on a bird. If he'd been moving in water, he'd barely have made a ripple, but each step took him closer to the red cow. When I was positive Clay knew which cow we were after, I let the reins fall loose and took the saddle horn in both hands. From there on my only job was to keep from hindering him.

With her calf already taken away, Mrs. Spivak was easy to cut from the herd. Clay pushed her straight out, and, if she hadn't become confused, she'd have waddled straight to the gate where we'd driven out her calf. But when we were only started, another calf bawled from the herd. In an awkward, lunging turn Mrs. Spivak tried to dodge back, but Clay had her cut off before she was half around. My bottom slipped a bit in the saddle, and there was a pull on my arms, but I'd seen Clay's move coming and was able to keep my balance. Mrs. Spivak made one more try to turn back, then trotted, lumberingly, toward the open gateway. As Ned came to meet her, he called out, "What's this one's name?"

"Mrs. Spivak," I called back.

Mr. Bendt, Ned, and all the dairyhands hooted and laughed as though I'd just told them a big joke. "Betcha my life Hazel picked out that name!" Mr. Bendt hooted. "Don't you boys never tell Pete about this or he'll drop the price o' cream ten cents a gallon."

I couldn't be sure whether the men were laughing at me because we'd named the cow, or at the name we'd given her, but

I wanted to get the subject changed, so I asked Mr. Bendt, "Did I do all right that time?"

"Done all right at settin' him on, but don't fight them stirrups so much on the turns; go with the horse."

I didn't know I'd used the stirrups at all, or think I'd slipped enough in the saddle that anybody could say I hadn't gone with the horse. But, of course, I couldn't say so, and asked, "Which one shall I bring out this time?"

"There's a little Jersey in there," he told me. "Try fetchin' her out and leavin' the calf."

I knew he was talking about the little cow I'd named Mrs. Hazlett for my Sunday School teacher in Littleton, and was glad he'd picked me a gentle easy one. Hazel and I hadn't had a bit of trouble with her, she didn't try to sneak away, and always stayed in the middle of the herd. That's where she was when I turned Clay back toward the corner.

We went into the herd real carefully, but I didn't know just what to do when we got there. With the little Jersey right in the middle, there was no use in starting the cows milling to get her on the outside. It seemed better to move Clay in behind her and try pushing her straight out, but at the first step he took in her direction, she began wriggling away. I still wanted to keep behind her, but was a little bit confused about how to do it.

I didn't know I made a move in the saddle or with the lines, but I must have. Anyways, I got Clay confused too, and had a hard time making him understand which cow we were after—and that we wanted her and not the calf. By the time I was ready to let the reins loose I didn't need anybody to tell me that Clay was peeved. He had his ears pinned back tight, and shoved Mrs. Hazlett roughly to the outside of the herd, as if he were trying to show how much better he could do without any help from me.

I thought I'd had plenty of trouble inside the herd, but when we got to the outside I found it had just begun. Mrs. Hazlett didn't turn out to be any gentle, Sunday School teacher kind of cow. As soon as she found she was outside the herd, and that

her calf was still in it, she went crazier than a cat with a salmon
can on its head. She could duck, dodge, and whirl so fast I
couldn't keep track of her, but Clay could outguess her at every
turn. Whirling, racing, doubling back, and sideslipping, he
made his body into a fence between her and the herd, and
never once let his head turn away from her.

With bucking horses, I'd learned to watch their heads, and
to set myself to go whichever way the head turned. With Clay
there was nothing to go by. His head swung back and forth to
face the cow, and I could never guess which way the saddle
would slip out from under me. All I could do was to hang onto
the horn for dear life, and hope I wouldn't fall off before Mr.
Bendt and Ned rode in to take that pesky cow out of the corral.
In some way I managed to stick, but was never square in the
saddle for two seconds at a time.

As soon as Mrs. Hazlett was out through the gateway, I rode
up to Mr. Bendt, and said, "I guess I made a pretty bad mess
of it. I thought I'd learned something from watching you,
but . . ."

"Got the cow, didn't you?" he asked.

"No, sir," I said, "Clay got her. All I did before I gave him his
head was to get him mixed up."

"That's 'cause you was rattled when you started out. Man
lets hisself get rattled, he's bound to rattle his horse. Next time,
you size up what you want to do and stick to it. 'Tain't hard to
set a horse's head, once a man has got his own head set."

"I think I can do better on that part next time," I told him,
"but I don't know if I'll ever be able to ride Clay any good. I'm
not quick enough at figuring out which way he's going to turn,
and I came near being spilled three or four times."

"That's 'cause you're workin' at it too hard," he said. "Just
leave yourself foller along easy—the way your best girl does
when she's dancin' with you."

"I haven't got a best girl," I told him, "and I don't know how
to dance. Maybe that's the trouble."

" 'Tain't the girl that counts, and 'tain't the dancin'. It's more like keepin' time with the fiddler. Lose track of it and you're a goner; stay with it and you can't go wrong—leastwise, not less'n you go to watchin' your own feet. Now you go back and fetch out that little Jersey's calf. He won't give you much trouble."

Mrs. Hazlett's calf didn't give me much trouble, and none of the other cows or calves gave me as much as I expected. Except for making up my mind and sticking to it, I wasn't sure I was doing anything different from what I'd done before Mr. Bendt talked to me. But right from that time Clay began to understand which animal I wanted. And there was something to that "keeping time with the fiddler." Of course, there wasn't any music, and there wasn't any measured time to Clay's moves, but, once I'd found it, there was a rhythm my body would follow if I let it go loose enough. I still slipped around in the saddle a good deal, but only when I lost the rhythm and tried to guess what Clay was going to do next.

When I brought up the last cow, Mr. Bendt called out, "That'll do it, boys! That's enough for today! We'll work the rest of 'em off piecemeal during the week." Then he rode up beside me and said, real quietly, "Betcha my life you'll ride him! Betcha my life! 'Tain't somethin' you'll learn in an hour or a day—nothin' worth while gets learnt easy—but you're commencin' to get the hang of him, and that's what you're goin' to have to do. He's older'n what you are, and he knows more about cow critters. He ain't goin' to learn new ways from you; you got to learn 'em from him."

"Yes, sir, I know it now," I said, "but I've still got an awful lot of things to learn."

"Betcha my life! But you got lots o' years to learn 'em in. Don't go rarin' at 'em like as if tomorrow'd be the day o' jedgment! Reckon we'd best to get unsaddled and washed up for dinner; the folks'll be gettin' home from church directly."

14

Dirty—Squealin'—Pig!

JENNY had a fine dinner ready when Mrs. Bendt and the children came home from church, but Hazel would hardly give me a chance to eat it. She took my plates away before I'd had seconds, and kept making signs for me to hurry.

I was still hungry when I left the table, and a little grumpy when I went out to saddle Pinch and Pinto. Before I'd been at the corrals ten minutes, Hazel came running from the house. She'd changed into overalls and blue shirt, and yapped at me, "What's the matter with you? You're slower'n a blind mule! How can I learn stunt tricks if you're goin' to spend all day gettin' saddled up?"

"If you don't let me finish my dinners you'll never learn!" I yapped back. "How do you think I'll ever gain any weight if you grab my plates away before I'm half full?"

"Jiggers!" she said, "I didn't think about that! Want I should run an' fetch you a hunk o' meat?"

"No," I told her, "but I rode all morning, and could have eaten twice as much."

"Hmfff! Practicin' when I had to go to Sunday School!"

"Yes, on Clay, and I didn't do very well."

"Nobody never does, but Paw!"

"Then why did you tell me to pick him?" I snapped.

"Oh, just because . . ." Hazel smirked. Then she flared at me, "Don't be fiddlin' with them cinches all day! It's close onto three o'clock a'ready."

We'd cantered half a mile up the trail when Hazel looked back, and called, "What did you do to Pinto's fore hoofs? He's dog-hoppin' like they was burnt."

"Nothing," I said, "but your father filed them down so we wouldn't sprain his knees while we're practicing."

Hazel whirled Pinto around fast enough to nearly throw him. Her face was so white under the freckles that it looked like a turkey's egg, and her eyes were squinnied half shut. Then she spit out—as if she wanted each word to hit me right in the face, "You—dirty—squealin'—pig!"

I'd expected Hazel to be mad, but not that mad, and hurried to say, "I guess you don't know your father very well! If you did, you wouldn't have tried to fool him about magpies this morning. He knew you were making that up, and he knew what we were doing out there yesterday just as well as we did. Do you think I'm crazy enough to lie to a man like that when he asks me questions?"

The color came back under Hazel's freckles, and she looked more worried than mad. "What did he say?" she asked.

After her calling me a squealing pig, I wanted to keep her worried for a while, so I said, "That I should have filed Lady's hoofs down before I took a chance on ruining her."

"No, I mean about us."

"Well, he said to tell you to be careful about putting Pinto into quick stops or you'd get shaken up."

"Don't beat about the bush!" she snapped. "What did he say about learnin' me trick stunts?"

"Well, he said I couldn't show you the somersault . . ." then I waited a minute, and added, ". . . out in the brush, but I can teach it to you at the corrals when he or one of the other men is around."

I'd expected Hazel to get excited when I finally told her, but she hung her head, and her voice was almost a whisper. "And I said you was a dirty, squealin' pig." Then she looked up, and said, "But I take it back . . . Ralph. And I'm glad I can, 'cause I hate a squealer worse than anything else in the whole world."

"Worse than a weasel?" I asked her.

"Well, a weasel's a sneak, and so is a squealer, and I hate sneaks."

"Wouldn't it have been a little bit sneaky to let your father think we were going after a magpie when we were coming out here to practice?" I asked.

"Well . . . yes," she said slowly, "I s'pose it would." She seemed to be thinking about it for half a minute. ". . . and sometimes I hate my own self," she added. Then she spurred Pinto, and raced on down the trail.

Hazel led the way to the valley where we'd practiced the day before, but I wasn't happy as I followed her. When we'd talked about my showing her the somersault trick, I'd only worried for fear I'd bobble it, but, after talking to her father, it scared me. If everything worked just right, the trick wasn't too dangerous, but there were a lot of ways for it to go wrong. Hazel could land on her head and break her neck, she could get caught in the saddle gear and be thrown under the horse's feet, or she could leave the saddle too soon and be trampled if he failed to stop.

I'd first learned to do the trick by myself—just from watching Hi Beckman do it once—but I'd taken some pretty bad spills in learning. Some of the worst ones were because I didn't have the horse trained well enough, but most of them were because I got scared and let my muscles tighten up at the last moment before I left the saddle. If that happened, I didn't duck my head and shoulders enough to spin all the way over, or my knees grabbed the saddle and kept me from being thrown clear.

I'd done the trick at least a hundred times when I'd landed

on my feet, and probably a thousand times when I hadn't, but I'd never practiced without doing the somersault. As I rode along behind Hazel, I began to think that maybe the trick could be learned without somersaulting. I couldn't teach her anything while she was spinning in the air. There was no time for thinking while I was doing it myself; the thinking had to be done before I left the saddle.

That was why I'd somersaulted when the pheasant flew up in front of Pinch. I'd been thinking about the trick, and when I was thrown hard and loose enough, my muscles did the right things all by themselves. It seemed to me that I could teach Hazel most of the trick without her ever leaving the saddle. If I could, it wouldn't be very dangerous, and would save her a lot of bad spills.

As soon as we reached the valley we began running the horses and stopping them short. Pinto reared and plunged on the first few stops, but Hazel knew how to handle him, and stuck to the saddle as tight as a bur. When he'd settled down, she snapped, "This ain't learnin' 'em nothin' new! I thought we come out here to learn 'em trick stunts!"

"We did," I told her, "but before we start, there are some things you ought to know about it. It's a real dangerous trick. I nearly broke my neck fifty times before I learned it, but I think I've figured out a way for you to learn without getting hurt. Everything depends on the moment before you leave the saddle. If you and Pinto can learn to get up to that very moment just right, the worst thing that could happen to you would be to land sitting down, but if . . ."

"I ain't scairt about the worst thing that could happen to me!" Hazel cut in sharply. "I've tumbled off a horse a million times. All I want is to be showed the somerset trick."

"Then you'll have to get somebody else to show you," I told her. "I never will until I'm pretty sure you can do it without getting hurt."

Hazel's voice wasn't sharp any more, and she said, "I'm sorry, Ralph. Go on and tell me."

"Well," I said, "the only thing that makes the trick work is being thrown out of the saddle so hard you'll stay in the air long enough to somersault all the way over. Everybody thinks the hardest part is spinning over and landing on your feet, but it isn't. The hardest part is learning to stay loose in the saddle right through the stop."

"Hmfff! If that's all there is to it, I betcha my life I can do it after two tries!" Hazel told me. "But it'll prob'ly take me a whole week to learn Pinto his part. Reckon I can be doin' the somerset by the time Batch gets back from the trip he's on?"

"No, not for at least two months," I told her. "I practiced a whole summer before I ever landed square on my feet."

Hazel pinched her mouth up tight, then she said, "Betcha my life it don't take me no two months, nor one, neither! But if we don't quit fiddlin' around and get to practicin', I'll never get Pinto learnt."

"Well," I said, "we'll have to start off real easy till we find out how hard we'll bump against the pommels when we stop. I'll do the hissing, and the only thing you'll have to remember is to stay loose in the saddle."

Hazel didn't answer, but pulled Pinto around to face the little valley. Her lips were pinched together, and she had a tight hold of the reins.

"You'll never do it tightened up like that!" I told her. "You'll have to slump loose in the saddle!"

"I ain't tightened up! Quit killin' time!" she snapped.

I started the horses away at a slow rocking canter. Then, before they'd gone a dozen lengths, I hissed. Pinch stopped as if he'd run into a wall, and, even at that slow gait, I slammed hard against the pommel of my saddle.

Pinto didn't do quite so well, but Hazel braced her feet in the stirrups and threw her shoulders back. She knew what she'd done, and as she turned him back, she spluttered, "How's anybody goin' to stay loose and haul in an ornery critter like this one?"

"Maybe it's a good thing he didn't stop too quick," I told her, "because I'm not a bit sure my idea is going to work. I bumped pretty hard against the pommel."

"Hmfff!" she sniffed. "You don't look bad hurt to me!"

"I'm not," I said, "but we weren't going half fast enough to do the trick. If we had been, I'd have hit the pommel hard enough to break a girl in two."

"What do you think girls are made of; glass?" she yapped. "Betcha my life I don't get busted up no quicker'n you do!"

"All right," I told her. "I guess you'll have to find out for yourself."

I didn't have a chance to get the horses away easily on the next run. The moment we turned, Hazel yiped and started them off at a gallop. I didn't dare let them pick up any more speed, so I hissed before they'd gone four lengths. Hazel shot forward in her saddle, doubled over the horn, and clutched Pinto's neck. I didn't go quite that far, but banged hard against my saddle pommel.

When Hazel straightened up, she was yawping for breath, but as soon as she caught it, she lit into me like a wildcat. "You cheater! You cheater!" she shrieked. "You hissed when I wasn't ready! And you done it a-purpose! You done it tryin' to make me scairt to learn the trick!"

"No, I didn't either!" I told her. "I did it so you wouldn't hit that pommel any harder."

Hazel pinched her lips up again, and sat looking at me as if she couldn't make up her mind. Then, she said, "Well, anyways, it ain't fair for you to hiss when I don't know you're goin' to."

I knew that Hazel would brace herself a little bit, and hit the pommel easier if she knew when the stops were coming, so I said, "All right, you do the hissing. But, at first, you'd better try it at a slow canter."

We made three or four more runs, with Hazel doing the hissing, but each time she braced herself in the stirrups before she hissed. I knew that if I told her what she was doing she'd get mad, so I watched her near stirrup, and, the instant it tightened, I lifted my reins an inch.

Pinch was trained to stop short on that lifted rein. Before I heard Hazel's hiss, I felt his rump settle down as he set his legs for the quick stop. We were three lengths back of Hazel when she finally hissed and stopped Pinto.

"You dir— you're cheatin' again!" she hollered. "You pulled Pinch up before I hissed."

"Sure, I did," I said. "I knew when you were going to do it as well as you did."

"You did not, neither! You ain't no mind reader! You're just a cheater; that's all!" she jabbered at me.

"All right," I told her; "let's try it again."

The next stop worked just like the one before. I think Hazel was more peeved at herself than at me, but she blazed, "You cheater! You cheater! You ain't tryin' to learn me! You're just tryin' to make me look silly!"

"No, I'm not," I said. "As soon as you think about hissing you brace yourself for the stop. All I have to do is watch for you to kick your foot into the stirrup."

"I didn't do no such thing!" she snapped. Then she sat, tight-lipped, for a minute, and asked, "How many more tries do you reckon we can get done today?"

"As many as you want," I said, "but it's going to be pretty tough on your legs and stomach."

Hazel wouldn't stop practicing until long after I thought we should have quit, but she couldn't help tightening up a little bit every time. After more than a dozen tries, she was so mad at herself that she was nearly crying.

"That's enough!" I told her. "You're so tired and beat-up now that you couldn't stay loose to save your life."

"I am not! I am not!" she shrieked. "If you can do it, I can do it! Even if it kills me, I ain't goin' to stop till I can do it!"

"You don't think I learned it in one day, do you?" I asked. "I've been practicing this trick for more than three years, and I still can't stay loose every time."

"Well, I ain't even stayed loose *one* time—leastways, not if I done the hissin'—and I ain't goin' to stop till I do!"

I remembered what Mr. Bendt had said to me that morning, and told Hazel, "Don't go raring at it as if tomorrow'd be the day of judgment! Your father knows what we're doing, and he might be worried about us."

"Guess you don't know much about Paw!" she said. "If he said you could learn me, he ain't goin' to worry about it afterwards. But I s'pose we'd best get on back, or Maw'll go to frettin'."

We were about half way to the buildings when Hazel pulled Pinto back beside Pinch, and asked, "Is it sneakin' not to tell somebody somethin' so they won't worry?"

"Well," I said, "I guess it would depend on whether you just didn't tell, or told a lie about it. Why?"

"Well . . . if Maw finds out about this trick-ridin' business, that'll be the end of it. I don't want to be sneakin', but I don't want her to find out about it, neither."

I was pretty sure Hazel was right, and I did want to teach her the trick, so I said, "As long as your father knows, I think it would be all right if you just didn't mention it to your mother —or to Kenny." Hazel grinned, nodded, and spurred Pinto on toward the corrals.

I'd banged against the saddle pommel so much that my legs ached, and I knew that Hazel's must, too. But I didn't realize how bad it was until we climbed out of our saddles. Both of us were as stiff as tin soldiers, and when we tried to walk we waddled like ducks.

I was putting the saddles in the harness shop when Hazel went to the house, but I heard Mrs. Bendt call to her, in a real sharp voice, "What in the world have you children been doin' to get yourselves so crippled up?" I listened as hard as I could, but Hazel spoke too low for me to hear.

Mr. Bendt was waiting by the chuckhouse steps when I went to supper, and his face was set hard. "Didn't reckon tomorrow'd be the day o' jedgment, did you?" he asked.

"No, sir," I said, "but I guess we rode a little more than we should have."

"Reckon that's a good guess," he told me. "Better put some liniment on them legs and turn in early tonight. If you're that rarin' to ride, I'll see you get a bellyful of it 'fore the week's out."

15

A Bellyful of Riding

MONDAY morning I felt as if I'd slept with my legs tied around a barrel, and I could almost hear myself squeak in the joints. I rubbed on plenty of liniment, and made up my mind that I'd walk with my knees close together, so nobody could guess how rough I really felt.

That was the first morning Hank was well enough to eat in the chuckhouse. He still looked sort of puny, but being sick hadn't slowed his talking a mite. Over and over again, he kept telling us how sick he'd been and what the doctor had said to him, and all the different dreams he'd had when he was out of his head. "Yes, sir, by dogies!" he shouted. "I seen them pearly gates a-swingin' open and old Peter . . ."

"Speakin' about gates," Mr. Bendt cut in on him, "you reckon you're stout enough to open and close a gate today? There's a heap o' roundin' up and cuttin' to be done 'fore Batch gets back here at the weekend, and short-handed as I am, I could sure use you to man a gate."

Hank tried his best to cough, and said weakly, "By dogies, I don't know if I can make it, Watt. I'm feelin' mighty, mighty poorly. But with you a-bein' short-handed I'll try my best to get out and around."

"Reckon that would be a good idee!" Mr. Bendt told him. "I'll want you at the corrals right after dinner."

There was a tone in Mr. Bendt's voice that I hadn't heard before, and he didn't speak again until we were out at the horse corral. Then he told Ned and me, "Get your saddles on your best horses, boys. We'll start at the north end and sweep everything this way. 'Fore the week's out we're goin' to put every critter on the home place through the corrals. Batch wants everything booked, the young stock put up to the mountains, and a hundred and twenty head o' trade stock cut out and ready by Sunday. We'll round up forenoons and cut after dinner."

The sun was just rising when Mr. Bendt, Ned and I reined onto the north trail at a good sharp canter, and we didn't slack off till we reached the north fence—seven miles from the buildings. And when he'd said we were going to "sweep" the cattle, he'd used just the right word.

On open range, where a steer can be seen for a mile, cattle can be rounded up and driven in big herds. But in brush country they have to be swept out of each canyon, draw or hollow, the way a woman sweeps out the rooms of her house. And you have to sweep around every thicket and clump of scrub oak the way she sweeps around the furniture.

We started with the canyons in the far northwest corner of the home ranch, right up against the front range of the Rockies. Mr. Bendt did the planning and bossing, but he did an awful lot of the riding, too—and he put his sorrel down canyon sides that looked too steep and rocky for a mountain goat. We worked every canyon separately, with Ned on one side, me on the other, and Mr. Bendt all over it. He was always bringing out cattle we'd missed, but he never blamed us and he never shouted. Around the corrals his voice was deep and rumbly, but in the brush he raised it just enough to make it carry. From a quarter of a mile away, it would come as clear as a bell,

"Above you, boy!" "Catch that side pocket!" "Watch it, Ned; they're turning back below you!" or "Leave any cows with calves, but mark 'em down in your head!"

As we swept each canyon clean, we drove the cattle we'd found past the mouth of the next canyon, to graze along and be joined by the next sweeping. Pinch's shadow was so short it was hidden under his belly when Mr. Bendt called, "That's got it, boys! We'll head on in to the corrals!"

Outside of orders, Mr. Bendt hadn't said anything to me all forenoon. But when we had the herd lined out and moving toward the corrals, he slowed his horse as he rode by me, and said, " 'Pears like Hazel done a pretty good job o' learnin' you to find cattle in brush country."

"Yes, sir, she's a good teacher," I said, and he rode on.

It was nearly four o'clock when we brought that first sweeping in to the corrals, but Mr. Bendt must have planned it that way. As soon as the gate was closed, he said, "Better get washed up and to the chuckhouse, boys. Grub's on the table." Then he looked at me and said, "Eat hearty; you still got a big day's work ahead!"

I don't think I looked up from my plate once during dinner. I was too busy eating and thinking about the day's work that was ahead of me. I knew what it would be, and had trouble to keep from being afraid of it. There was every kind of cattle in the sweeping we'd brought in, and the only cutting horse on the place was in my string. I ate enough, but I didn't stuff. A stomach-ache, to go along with my lame legs and Clay, was something I couldn't take a chance on.

Hank hadn't come to the table, and I hadn't seen Hazel since the night before, but when Jenny brought in the pie, Mr. Bendt said, "Tell Hazel to fetch the herd book and a pencil out to the corral, and tell Hank I'm ready for some gate tendin'! Gettin' his legs under him won't do him no hurt, and might work a little of the wind out of him, so's we can eat a meal o' vittles in peace." Then he looked at me and said, "Throw your saddle on Clay; I'll be at the cuttin' corral!"

I ate my pie in about six bites, then hurried to the bunkhouse and rubbed plenty of liniment on my legs. When I'd saddled Clay and ridden to the cutting corral, everybody else was
there and ready to work. Hazel was sitting on a little platform
by the cattle pens with a book open on her lap, Hank was leaning against one of the gates, and Mr. Bendt and Ned were
mounted—ready to take away the cattle as they were cut from
the herd. Mr. Bendt opened the gate for me to ride in, and told
me, "With only one man on the gates, we'll have to take 'em by
kinds. Take the young stock first; pick 'em off the outside of the
herd as long as you can!" Then he turned back and stood his
horse beside Ned's.

There were about sixty cattle in the corral, and they were
jammed into a far corner. I've heard that a drowning man thinks
of a million things in less than a minute. If it's so, I was pretty
close to drowning as Clay walked slowly toward that herd.
From the way Mr. Bendt had spoken and acted, I knew I'd
have to sink or swim without any help. And in the minute it
took Clay to reach the herd, I'd thought of every thing Mr.
Batchlett, Mr. Bendt, Hazel, or my father had ever taught me
—and I think I prayed a little—but over it all, I kept telling
myself, "Stay loose! Stay loose! Stay loose!"

I don't know what helped the most, but I must have had help
from somewhere. One after another, Clay took the animals I
wanted out of the herd, and when he dodged and side-slipped
I didn't feel as if I'd be spilled at every turn. I knew the job I
was doing was far from perfect, and I tightened up a good
many times when I shouldn't have, but, for the first time since
I'd tried to use him, Clay didn't act as if he thought I was a
stupid fool.

As I cut each animal from the herd, Mr. Bendt rode his horse
in behind Clay and took it away. As he and Ned drove it toward the gate, he'd call to Hazel, "Yearling heifer—roan—
Shorthorn! Durham steer—short yearling—good grade!" or
"Bull—White Face—herd grade—long yearling!"

I knew that marking down the cattle wasn't all Hazel was

doing—that she was watching every move Clay and I made. And I could almost see her keeping score of my mistakes. Each time I tightened up or made a mistake, I wanted to peek up to see if she'd noticed it, but I didn't let myself do it until I had the last yearling cut out and turned over to her father. Then, when I did look up, she didn't say a word. She just let her shoulders slump loose, grinned, and nodded her head. I don't know why, but it made a lump come into my throat. If she'd shouted that I was staying loose and doing a pretty fair job, she couldn't have told me any plainer.

My nerves were zinging when Mr. Bendt turned back from the last yearling and rode toward me. "All right," he said: "now we'll cut out the trade stock! I'll call 'em to you as I want 'em! Fetch that two-year-old White Face bull that's tryin' to pick a fight! Watch ou . . ." Then, without finishing, he reined his horse away and stood it beside Ned's. If he'd gone on and said, "Watch out for his horns," it wouldn't have hurt my feelings. But his *not* saying it made me pretty happy—just having him show that he didn't think I needed to be told.

It's easy to stay relaxed when you're fishing or just watching a herd of cattle graze, but it's hard to do when your nerves are humming like a telegraph wire on a cold night. I'd been keeping an eye on that White Face bull ever since Ned flushed him out of a canyon, and there was no question about his being ugly and looking for a fight. I wasn't exactly afraid of him, but he outweighed Clay by five hundred pounds, and had wide, forward-curved horns. If that kind of a bull charges and gets his head under a horse, he can throw it as if it were a sack of meal—and the rider has about as much chance as a fat pig at a barbecue.

I was telling myself, "Keep loose! Keep loose!" as I turned Clay to face the herd. The White Face bull watched us with his head low, grumbling deep in his throat, and pawing dirt high over his back. I let Clay take a couple of steps straight at him, so he'd know which animal we were after, then drew him off a trifle to get behind and push the bull out. We didn't need to get behind; when we were within two lengths of him, the bull charged.

Quicker than the shot of a pistol, Clay sidestepped the rush and was between the bull and the herd. I let the reins go loose, grabbed the horn, and from then on things happened too fast for me to remember. I do know that the bull charged us at least a dozen times, and that Clay used his own body to twist him and turn him—the way a matador uses his cape in bull fighting. And I know one other thing: that was the first time I ever really got that feeling Mr. Bendt had told me about—the one about dancing with your best girl.

I never knew a horse could whirl, weave, twist, and bounce away as fast as Clay did with that charging bull. But my muscles stayed loose, and the saddle stayed under my bottom all the way. I was getting just a little bit dizzy when Clay yanked the bull around in a turn that was shorter than its own body. It must have made the bull even dizzier than I, because all the fight went out of him. He stood with his head and tail down as Mr. Bendt rode in to take him away. I don't think Mr. Bendt had noticed me once during the whole fight. When he rode past, he was slipping a six-shooter back into its holster, and all he said was, "Lot o' horse, ain't he, boy?"

I was proud to have my voice steady when I said back, "Yes, sir, an awful lot! What animal do you want now?"

I don't know whether Mr. Bendt picked that bull on his first call just to get him out of the herd, or if he did it to let me find out that I'd finally got the hang of Clay—and maybe of myself a little bit. Whichever way he intended it, it worked the second way. From then on I never had to tell myself to stay loose in the saddle, and I was never afraid again. It was in that fight with the bull that the first real understanding began between Clay and me.

One after another, Mr. Bendt called for the cattle he wanted, and as we brought them out he called the description to Hazel. I didn't look up at her until the last of the trading cattle had been cut out of the herd, and then she just grinned and nodded.

The sun was nearly two hours from setting when we began cutting out the brood cows that would be turned back to pasture after the sweep was finished. Most of them were beginning to be heavy with calf, and the job of cutting them away from the herd was easy—now that Clay and I understood each other better. We were about half through the cutting when Kenny came riding to the corral gate on his donkey. He called something, and I heard Mr. Bendt call back, "Tell her to get the grub on the fire! We'll be through a lot earlier than I reckoned on."

I glanced up at Hazel while they were talking, and she pointed back and forth between herself and me, then at her father. I guessed that she wanted me to ask him if we could go and practice when we'd finished with the cattle. After his having told me he'd give me a bellyful of riding, I didn't like to ask, but Hazel kept motioning. So, when I brought the last cow out of the corner, I asked, "Would it be all right for Hazel and me to practice the horses a little while after supper?"

Mr. Bendt's face had been serious all day, but when I asked him it brightened up, and he said, "Betcha my life! Betcha my life, boy!"

He started to ride away, then turned back and said quietly, "Reckon you'd best to do it 'fore we eat. Hazel's maw might not cotton to her goin' out after supper. If I was you, I don't reckon I'd say much about this trick-ridin' business 'round the house. How's the gal doin'?"

"Fine," I said. "I'm sorry she got bruised up so much, but it won't be safe for her to try the diving trick till she can stay loose in the saddle on quick stops."

For a few seconds Mr. Bendt sat as if he were trying to make sense out of what I'd told him. Then he just said, "Betcha my life! Make her learn it good!" and rode away.

All the way to the practice meadow, Hazel was as bubbly as soapsuds. We'd hardly hit the north trail when she called back, "I got it all learnt! I learnt it this afternoon when you was riding Clay—and you done . . . did fine!"

"Maybe I'm getting the hang of him a little bit," I called back. "But what was it you learned?"

"How to keep loose; what else is there to learn?"

"Not much," I told her, "but I still don't know what you're talking about."

"Well, I do! All I got to do is to not let myself know I'm goin' to say, 'Tsssst!' till I hear it. That way I won't get scairt and tighten up."

"It would work if you could do it," I told her, "but I don't see how that has anything to do with my riding Clay."

"That's what you was doin'—right clean up to the time you had the fight with the White Face bull—not lettin' yourself know you was scairt. I seen it plain as daylight."

"Well, I don't know how you could see what I was thinking," I called back, "but I guess you're pretty near right."

"I knew it!" she squealed, as if she'd just found an ostrich egg. "I knew it, and I know something else you don't: Paw was holding a gun on that bull all the time you was fighting him. And he'd have pulled the trigger, too—with all he thinks of them . . . those purebreds."

There wasn't any need for Pinch and me to practice the running and stopping. With the lines draped over the horn, he'd always set his feet at the first sound of the hiss, and all I got out of it was a pounding against the pommel. But I couldn't just sit back and let Hazel practice alone, so when we reached the meadow, I said, "Why don't we trade horses for tonight? Then you won't have to think about stopping Pinto, but only about staying loose in the saddle."

"No, sir! No such of a thing!" she snapped. "When I do the trick for Paw and Batch to see, I'll be doin' it off Pinto, and I ain't going to take no easy horse now! And besides, I'll do all the hissing from now on, 'cause I'll have to be doing it for myself when I really do the whole trick."

I don't think Hazel had learned a thing from watching me ride Clay, but that she'd thought so much about staying loose that she'd taught it to her muscles. However it worked, we made a dozen runs without her tightening up but once, and Pinto behaved a lot better than he ever had before. That was as much as I'd let her do, because I didn't want her to get bruised any more than she had to—and I didn't want her father to tell me again that he'd give me a bellyful of riding.

16

Now, Mr. Man!

EVERY day that week we swept in a corralful of cattle in the forenoon, and cut them out after dinner. Each day I learned the work a little better with Clay—and each evening Hazel and Pinto went through a dozen practice runs without a bobble. But the best part of my days came after everyone else had gone to bed.

When I was unsaddling Pinch after Monday's practice, Lady came to the corral gate and nickered softly to me. It made me ashamed of myself. I'd been so busy with Pinch and Clay that I hadn't paid any attention to her since I'd abused and lamed her. I was still thinking about her when we were finishing supper, and put two biscuits in my pocket, because she always liked them.

After Ned and Hank had gone to the bunkhouse, I went back to the corral gate and whistled to Lady. By that time it was full dark and the moon hadn't come up, so I couldn't see her, but she nickered and came to me. I broke one of the biscuits into small pieces and stood for quite a little while, scratching her forehead as I fed them to her, and telling her I was sorry I'd been so rough with her.

154

As my eyes grew more used to the darkness, I could see that several other horses had come over, and that Clay was among them. I would never have thought of taking him a biscuit or that he would like to be petted. But I was feeling happy about the way we'd worked together that afternoon, so I opened the gate, went in, and walked slowly toward him. He moved away just as slowly, so I stood still—just holding out a piece of biscuit and speaking quietly. Clay stopped when I did, stood for a couple of minutes, then inched toward me. He let me scratch his head and shoulders as he took pieces of biscuit from my hand.

While I was petting Clay, there was a snort from behind me, and when I looked around I could make out the shape of Pinch's jug head. He didn't back away when I went toward him with a piece of biscuit held out, but kept his ears back, and snatched the pieces out of my hand as if he were letting me know that he didn't want any petting.

I was probably with the horses for half an hour, then, when I was going to the bunkhouse I began to feel ashamed of myself again. Blueboy was my horse just as much as any of the others—except Lady—but I hadn't even bothered to look for him. Instead of going to the bunkhouse I went back to the chuckhouse, and rapped on the kitchen door. After a minute, Mrs. Bendt opened it and said, not too pleasantly, "Yes. What is it you want?"

I hadn't expected her to be cross, and sort of stammered, "Nothing. I was . . . I was just wondering if there was an extra biscuit left over from supper."

Mrs. Bendt stopped scowling, and said, "Why, you poor little boy! Didn't you get enough supper? You come right in the kitchen here while I get you a piece of pie and some milk! No wonder you're starved after the way Watt's worked the daylights out of you today!"

For a minute I didn't know what to say or do. I couldn't tell her I wanted the biscuit for Blueboy, and I couldn't think of anything else to say that wouldn't sound silly. Finally I stam-

mered, "Well, it . . . it isn't for me, and I'm not hungry, and
I didn't work very hard today. I just like to keep a biscuit on
hand for . . . sometimes I used to give one to Lady—that's my
horse—when we were at home."

"Well, for pity's sake!" she said, as if she thought I must be
half crazy. "Who ever heard of feeding biscuits to horses? But
you wait a minute; I think there was four or five of 'em left
over from supper—if Jenny didn't throw 'em in the hogs'
bucket."

When Mrs. Bendt had brought me the biscuits, and I'd
thanked her, I took them out and hid all but one of them in the
harness shop. That one I put in my pocket, and went back to
the horse corral.

Lady, Pinch, Clay, and several other horses crowded around,
but my eyes were still partly blinded from the kitchen light,

and I couldn't see anything of Blueboy. I must have made ten trips around the corral before I finally found him—and then it wasn't from seeing, but from hearing him snort as he raced out of a corner.

From the pound of Blueboy's hoofs I could tell what corner he'd run to, and once I knew where it was, it wasn't hard to work my way slowly toward him. There was only one big danger: if I got him too frightened or excited he might stampede and run right over me. I was a little bit worried about it, but I'd learned from Father and Hi Beckman that steady, gentle talking would calm a horse better than anything else. So I inched slowly toward the corner, holding out the biscuit and saying anything that came into my head.

When the moon rose I'd spent more than an hour trying to get near Blueboy, and he'd dashed out of a corner past me six or seven times. I don't know whether it was his getting used to me, my talking, or that he could see me better, but when the top of the moon showed above the hill, he stood long enough to let me get within a few feet of him. I had to remind myself of what Mr. Bendt had said about my having plenty of time ahead of me, but I didn't hurry, and I kept talking as I inched forward with the biscuit held out.

Blueboy stood with his feet braced, his ears pricked forward, and white showing around his eyes in the moonlight. I couldn't tell whether it was from hate or fear, and I knew that at any second he might lunge and strike with either his teeth or his hoofs. Hi used to tell me that a horse could smell fright on a person, and I think it's true, because you can never do much with one when you're afraid. That's why I couldn't even let myself think that Blueboy might strike—and one of the reasons I had to keep on talking.

My head was within less than three feet of Blueboy's—and my heart was pounding as if it would jump out of my chest—when he snatched the biscuit from my hand and bolted away. When I went back to the bunkhouse my nerves were still zinging, and it was a couple of hours before I could go to sleep.

Tuesday night I waited for moonrise before I went to the horse corral, and when I whistled for Lady, Pinch came with her. Clay seemed glad enough to have a piece of biscuit and some petting, but he stood back and made me come to him. Blueboy stayed way at the back of the corral, snorting and stamping a hoof. But that night it only took me about ten minutes to work my way up to him, and he didn't bolt after he'd snatched the piece of biscuit. Still, he wouldn't let me get close enough to put a hand on him.

It wasn't until Thursday that Blueboy would let me touch him, and then it was only because I wouldn't let him have any biscuit until he did. And he moved off to the other side of the corral just as soon as he got it. Friday he was a little better, and let me walk up to him slowly without his backing off. Even then, he didn't want my hand on him, and only let me stroke his muzzle a second before he jerked it away.

Saturday we made the last roundup sweep of the home ranch. It was the one nearest the buildings, and not a very large one, so we had all the cattle in the corral by noon. When I was going in to dinner Hazel met me outside the chuckhouse door, and seemed as excited as if it were already the Fourth of July. "We're having roast pork and applesauce and peach pie," she whispered, "and you eat every single bit you can hold."

"Why?" I asked. "I'm not very hungry this noon."

"That don't make no never-minds!" she whispered again. "You eat every mouthful you can stuff down! I got a special reason; I'll tell you after dinner. And don't you go back to the corrals till I get the dishes done! You wait for me right here!" Then she ran away to the kitchen.

The dairyhands had just butchered a young pig, and the roast pork was real good, but I couldn't hold more than two helpings. And all the time I was eating I could hear dishes rattling and clicking in the kitchen. Hazel must have been washing them just as fast as Jenny could take them in from the chuckhouse, because I only had to wait three or four minutes for her. Then she stuck her head out of the kitchen doorway, and called, "Go get your chaps and spurs on! I'll meet you up to the milk house at the dairy barn." Before I could ask her what in the world it was all about she'd ducked back inside.

I couldn't imagine why Hazel wanted me at the milk house, and particularly with my spurs and chaps on, but I went back to the bunkhouse, put them on and went up to the dairy barn. When I got there she was standing by a pair of scales, and she had both hands on her hips. "Now, Mr. Man," she said, "we'll see if you gained your weight back yet! I a'ready got the scales set for seventy-two pounds."

I knew it would be cheating a little to weigh with my chaps and spurs on, because I'd weighed seventy-two pounds without them and barefooted when I left home. But I knew how much Hazel wanted me to show her the somersault trick before Mr. Batchlett came back, so I kept my mouth shut and stepped on the scales. The bar went up with a good hard bump, and Hazel squealed, "You done it! You done it! Now there ain't no reason you can't show me how to do the somerset trick."

With the amount of riding I'd done that week—and with staying up kind of late every evening—I hadn't been a bit sure I'd gained all my weight back. But from the way that scale arm bumped I knew I had, and I wanted to tease Hazel a little, so I said, "Don't you think it's cheating to weigh with my stomach nearly popping and with my chaps and spurs on?"

Hazel thought about it for a few seconds, then put a finger out to try the scale beam, and said, "Well . . . the chaps might be a little bit cheatish, but what you've et is a part of you now, so it's fair."

"And how about the spurs?" I asked.

"They don't weigh next to nothin'! Just take your chaps off!"

"All right," I told her, "but you'll have to set the scales up a pound."

Hazel looked at my spurs and seemed to be weighing them with her eyes. "Take 'em off, then!" she snapped. "They don't weigh over half a pound, and I ain't going to be cheated by no half a pound!"

When the weighing was over, I was even happier than Hazel. Besides gaining back all the weight I'd lost in the mountains, I gained another couple of pounds. For two years I hadn't been able to gain an ounce, but at last it looked as if I might be growing up a little. "All right," I told Hazel, "as soon as we finish cutting the cattle this afternoon I'll ask your father if I can show you how to do the trick. But you'll have to watch me do it at least a dozen times before you can try it yourself."

"That's just more excuses!" Hazel shouted. "That's just more excuses so's I won't be able to do it by the time Batch gets home—and then you'll go out on the next trip with him—and then I won't never get to learn to do it!"

"Maybe you can try it tomorrow if your father thinks you're ready, but unless you'll promise not to try it today I won't show you how it's done."

"You're a cheater! You're a cheater!" she flared at me. "You're just tryin' to save the trick all for your own self!"

I knew Hazel didn't mean what she was saying, and was only blowing off steam, so I grinned and said, "Promise?"

"Well . . . I s'pose I got to, but it ain't . . . isn't fair," she said slowly.

"Cross your heart?"

Hazel made a quick X with one finger across the front of her blouse, and said, "Now don't go to fiddle-diddlin' around all afternoon with cutting that little dab o' cattle, so's to let it get supper time on us! Get your saddle on Clay while I run for the herd book!"

Clay worked the best he ever had for me that afternoon, and by half past three the last animal on the home ranch had been rounded up, cut out, and written down in the herd book. "That done it!" Mr. Bendt sang out, as Hank opened the gate for the last cow. "By the old Harry, I'd swore we couldn't'a done it— short-handed as we was! You boys done fine—you too, Hank! Let's knock off and call it a day."

Hazel was trying to write down the last cow with one hand and talk sign language to me with the other, so I rode over to Mr. Bendt, and said, "I've gained back more weight than I lost, and I promised Hazel that when that time came I'd show her how I do one of the trick-riding stunts. She's promised not to try it herself today, but is it all right if I show her how it's done?"

Hazel had jumped down from her little platform and was running toward us. When her father saw her coming, he asked real quietly, "Think she's ready? How risky is it?"

I nodded, and said, "Well, you could watch me do it a few times and see for yourself. Of course, she could take kind of a bad spill if she got scared and tightened up at the last second."

By that time Hazel was hopping up and down at the side of her father's horse. "I ain't scairt the least tiny little bit!" she squealed, "And I ain't tightened up once at practicin' all week! And anyways, I ain't going to do it myself today. Can't he show me? Can't he show me, Paw?"

"Can't see no hurt in him showin' you, gal," he told her, "but I ain't about to let you break your neck in somethin' you couldn't prob'ly make out at. You kids go get your horses saddled! Where at do you reckon on doin' this stunt?"

"Well, you said we'd have to do it here at the corrals," I told him, "but I think the horses would do better for the first time or two if we did it where we've been practicing. I'm not much worried about Pinch, but I'm going to use Pinto mostly—he'll probably spook the first couple of times; most horses do."

Mr. Bendt rose in the saddle, so that his head was higher than the corral poles, and looked toward the house. "Hmmm," he said, "where's this practicin' place at?"

"A little valley about three miles up the north trail," I told him; "the one where you swept out the big White Face bull and three heifers."

"Hmmm," he said again. "Reckoned that was it by the way the turf was chawed up. Might not be a bad idee."

17

I Done It! I Done It!

WHEN Mr. Bendt said I could show Hazel how to do the somersault trick, I saddled Pinch and Pinto as fast as I could. Then he rode out to the little practice meadow with us, at a slow jogging pace.

I'd never done the trick without being just a little bit scared, but when we got to the meadow I told Mr. Bendt, "There's nothing about this trick to be scared of if the horses are trained right, and I think these are. Pinch hasn't made a bobble all week, and Pinto's only made a couple of little ones. If you and Hazel will stand your horses right over there, I'll try to do the trick so you can see every part of it. And I'll do it first off Pinch, because he didn't spook the time I did it by accident."

I rode Pinch back to the starting line, took off my spurs, then put him into a hard run. At the moment he was passing Mr. Bendt and Hazel, I hissed and ducked my head and shoulders. The quick, hot taste I always got came into my mouth, I spun in the air, and the next instant Pinch and I were standing with our two heads side by side.

"Good job!" Mr. Bendt called out.

"You done it too fast!" Hazel shouted. "Why didn't you do it slower so's I could see how you done it?"

"I have to do it fast," I said, "or I'd only go part way over. Let's change saddles now and I'll try it off Pinto. The thing to watch is the way I duck my head as I leave the saddle—as if I were trying to poke it between my legs."

Pinto was fidgety with me on him, so I didn't take him all the way back, but turned him into a quick start. As soon as he'd picked up enough speed, I hissed and ducked my head. Pinto set his feet in good shape, but when he felt me leaving the saddle, he spooked and whirled away to the right. He did it so fast that the saddle horn bumped my leg as my foot came up out of the stirrup. It wasn't a hard bump, but enough to throw me a bit sideways and off balance.

I'd practiced the trick so much that my muscles would remember what to do quicker than my head could. My arms didn't go out to balance me, or my legs to reach for the ground, but I stayed curled up like a sleeping cat. I landed sort of cornerwise, on the back of my shoulder, somersaulted on the ground a couple of times, and came to a stop on my hands and knees—right in front of Mr. Bendt's horse. I'd hardly come to a stop before he picked me up and asked, "Are you hurt, boy?"

"No, sir," I told him, "not a bit. I'm all right."

"Betcha my life!" he said, and I heard Hazel gasp. When I looked up, her face was so white that the freckles looked like mud spatters.

"Jiminy!" she panted, as if she were all out of breath. "I thought you was going to get killed."

"That's why I've been making you practice to stay loose," I told her. "You don't get hurt if you stay loose and doubled up; it's only when you get scared and stick out your arms and legs."

"Wasn't you scairt?" she asked. "I was! Green!"

"No," I said, "I didn't have time to be. Where's Pinto? I want to try it a few more times with him; he won't spook after another time or two."

Pinto hadn't run when he'd whirled away, but was standing stiff-legged, with his nostrils wide, watching me as if he thought I'd gone crazy.

"Don't you reckon you've had enough for one day?" Mr. Bendt asked. "Don't you reckon you'd best to leave him a day to settle down 'fore you try him again?"

"I think it would be better if I tried it right now," I told him. "Every horse I ever tried it from—except Pinch—spooked the first time, but after they get used to it they never spook again. If I'd leave him now, don't you think he might be worse next time?"

"Like as not you're right," Mr. Bendt said after a minute. "Like as not! Go on ahead, but watch out there's no loose gear to get tangled up in!"

I took a couple of practice runs on Pinto, but didn't leave the saddle. Then, on the third run, I ducked my head and somersaulted. He spooked again, but not quick enough for the saddle to bump me, and he whirled only half way. So long as the saddle didn't touch me, his spooking didn't bother the trick, but my muscles were still afraid. They kept me curled up in a bunch right through the split second when I should have been throwing my arms out for balance and setting my feet to land.

I hit the ground on my feet, but I was scrooched way down—with my bottom right behind my heels—and my arms wrapped around my stomach. That didn't leave me any way of putting on the brakes, so I bounced like a thrown ball. About that time my head caught up with my muscles in thinking, and I threw my arms out wide to slow me down, but it worked just wrong. For a tenth of a second I must have looked like a wild goose coming in for a landing, then my feet touched the ground again and I flopped forward on my face. The first landing didn't hurt at all, but the flop forward knocked the wind out of me. When Mr. Bendt picked me up, I was yawping for breath like a fish on a hook.

Mr. Bendt saw what the trouble was, and gave me a slap on the back. He wasn't a bit afraid or excited, but his mouth was set hard, and he said, "This ain't no game for girls—boys, neither! How come Beckman learnt it to you in the first place? How come your paw let him do it?"

"They didn't," I told him. "I saw Hi do it once, and then I practiced it by myself—when I was out alone herding cattle —in a good soft sandy place. It isn't nearly as dangerous as it looks. I've taken a thousand spills with nothing worse than getting the wind knocked out of me."

"Well, this ain't no soft sandy place!" Mr. Bendt told me. "Reckon you'd best to call it a day!"

Hazel hadn't made a sound, but when I looked up, two big tears were rolling down her cheeks. I didn't know if it was because she was afraid I'd been hurt, or because she was sure her father wouldn't let her learn the trick. But I did know that he'd never let her learn it unless he saw me do it over and over without a bobble, so I said, "Can I have just one more try? If I don't do it right this time, I won't try it again while I'm here."

Mr. Bendt rubbed his chin with the palm of his hand, as if he were thinking hard, then said, "Reckon every man's due the right to draw one card, but I'm tellin' you—you'll have to come up with a full house or better!"

I'd never played poker, but I'd watched the men at the Y-B ranch enough to know that a full house was a hard hand to beat. And I knew that Mr. Bendt was telling me that, unless everything went exactly right, my trick-riding was over for the summer.

I decided that, with only one card to draw, I'd better not take any chances, so I told Hazel, "We'll have to trade saddles again; I'm going to use Pinch this time."

Mr. Bendt helped me change saddles, and his face stayed hard and set, but Hazel's was nervous. As I kneed the air out of Pinch, she crowded up close beside me, and whispered, "Don't take no chances, Ralph . . . but . . . but . . . make it work."

I didn't say anything back, but nodded, pulled the cinch tight, and hopped to get a foot in the stirrup.

Among all of us, I think Pinch was the only one who wasn't nervous. Hazel was so jumpy that she excited Pinto into dancing, and Mr. Bendt's face was set as hard as rock. As I turned

Pinch toward the starting line, my knees played a tattoo against the saddle, and pins-and-needles ran up and down my backbone. I walked him real slowly, and waited a full minute at the line, telling myself to stay loose and to make the trick work. Then, when my knees stopped trembling, I kicked my heels against Pinch's belly. I don't remember anything about that try, right from the take-off to the moment I found myself standing on my feet with Pinch's head at my shoulder.

I think it was Hazel and Mr. Bendt who sort of woke me up. She was squealing and clapping her hands as if she'd been into the loco weed, and her father called out, "Pick up the chips, boy! It's your next deal!"

"Can I draw more than one card this time?" I called back. "I'd like to try it off Pinto, so he'll get used to it, but I can't be sure it'll work just right the first try."

"Dealer's choice! You've got the deck!" he said, so I shifted my saddle back onto Pinto.

All the time I was changing saddles, Hazel fussed around with Pinto like an old hen with one chicken. She kept patting him, and scratching his muzzle, and telling him not to get fidgety, and to behave himself. Then, when I climbed into the saddle, she looked up and whispered, "Don't kick him hard in the belly. He's as scairt as I am of what might happen, and you'll only make him worse."

"You're the one that's making him nervous," I told her. "If you don't stop fiddling around you'll make me tighten up too, and spoil everything."

Hazel let her arms drop loose, but her face was still excited when I turned Pinto away. His take-off was good, and when I hissed and flipped he threw his head up, but he didn't spook. And when he saw me standing beside him at the finish, he looked at me as much as to ask how I got there.

Hazel didn't pay any more attention to me than if I'd been a post standing there. She ran to Pinto, patted him on the shoulder, rubbed his neck, and told him she'd known he could do it all the time.

I took half a dozen more somersaults off Pinto. They weren't all perfect, but there were no really bad ones, and he behaved in good shape. My worst trouble was with Hazel. She kept yapping at me for doing the trick too fast for her to see, and saying she'd never be able to learn it. At last Mr. Bendt said, "Why don't you ride alongside of him, gal, so's to watch it from close in? But stay off far enough to give him room! Your horse could tromp him if you get in too close."

With Hazel on Pinch, I knew there was no danger of my being trampled. He always stopped quicker than Pinto, and I'd land well in front of him. But I didn't think Hazel could learn much from riding along beside me. At the very moment she ought to be watching what I did, she'd be flung against the saddle pommel, and wouldn't be able to see a thing. At the take-off line, I stopped and told her, "If you're going to learn anything this way, you've got to almost think you're doing the stunt yourself. Try ducking your head a little when you hear me hiss, but look out you don't get it low enough to bump the saddle horn."

I didn't have any time to watch Hazel at the last moment, but, just as I landed, I heard her father call, "Careful, gal! You'll bust your head on that horn!"

On our second run together, he called to her again, "Watch out for that horn, gal!"

Before we left the starting line for our third run, I told her, "Lean a bit to one side, then you'll miss the horn when the pommel stops you and your head jerks down."

That could have been a bad thing for me to tell Hazel. It could have thrown her off balance and made her take a nasty spill, but it didn't work that way. Both horses were going like sixty when I hissed and ducked my head, and as I went spinning through the air I caught a glimpse of something flying right along with me. I didn't realize what it was until I'd landed on my feet and saw Hazel take two or three running steps, then fall forward on her face. For a split fraction of a second my heart stopped beating, and I had that taste like hot blood in my mouth. Then Mr. Bendt shouted, "Hazel!" and leaped out of his saddle.

Hazel fell less than three yards in front of me, but before I could collect my wits and get to her, she'd scrambled to her feet. She was hardly on them before she started bouncing and jumping around like a cat on a hot stove. "I done it! I done it!" she shouted, and her braids flapped like latigo strings on the saddle of a bucking horse. "I ain't hurt one tiny little bit, and I done it!"

I knew she'd done the trick by mistake, just the way I had when the pheasant flew up in front of Pinch. She'd watched me enough that her muscles knew what to do without her head telling them, and she'd been just enough off center in the saddle to be thrown clear when Pinch stopped. I think her father knew it too. His face looked as proud as my father's did when he first saw me do the stunt at the Littleton roundup, but all he said was, "Is that all the worth there is to your word, gal? Thought you promised you wasn't goin' to try that stunt today!"

Hazel stopped hopping, and her face went sober. Then she peeked up at him under her eyebrows and said, "I didn't do it a-purpose, Paw. Honest, I didn't! It just kind of happened all by itself."

That time he smiled, and said, "I reckoned right from the start-off that's the way it had to work. Maybe you'd best to let Little Bri . . . to let Ralph here show you how to keep from fallin' over after you land."

"Well, I think I can tell it to her better than I can show her," I said. "I learned it from watching a pigeon light on our barn. Did you ever notice how they use their wings for brakes, and how they reach out to feel for a landing with their feet? That's the way I do it, but it's too fast to watch in the middle of a somersault, and that's when I begin to push my arms and legs out."

"Betcha my life! Betcha my life!" Mr. Bendt said. "Reckon you can get the hang of it, gal?"

Hazel began hopping again, and squealing, "Sure I can! Sure I can! Let's do it again!"

I knew Hazel would make plenty of bobbles until she'd

practiced the trick over and over, and I didn't want her father
to stop her if she took a few spills, so I said, "You know, she
can only learn it by practicing, and she'll be sure to take some
more spills. But if she doesn't get scared and tighten up, she
can't break anything."

"Hmmm! Nothin' but her neck!" he said. Then he laughed
and told Hazel, "Reckon I'm loco as a range maverick to let
you try it, gal. Your maw would peel the hide off me if she
knowed of it. But now you done it once you'd best to go on
and learn it the safest way there is." His face set hard, and
he went on, "Look here, gal! The boy'll be away with Batch
most of the time. I want your word that you won't try this
stunt alone! Is it a go?"

Hazel swiped a quick X on the front of her blouse, and
said, "Cross my heart! But it's all right if we practice when
Ralph's on the home ranch, ain't it, Paw?"

Mr. Bendt nodded slowly, and I did the trick a few more
times to show Hazel how I kept from falling forward. When
it came time for her to try the trick alone, I could see she
was nervous, so I rode to the starting line with her. We'd
turned the horses, and while I was telling her to stay loose
and not to be afraid, her lip began to quiver. "Ride with me,
Ralph," she almost begged; "I'm scairt."

I knew that the longer we waited the more afraid she'd
get, so I yipped, "Let's GO!" and kicked my heels against
Pinch.

Both horses jumped at the word, and we were racing neck
and neck by the time we'd gone fifty yards—then I hissed.
I had to—so Hazel would somersault again without thinking
about it or having time to tighten up. It worked fine. She
went all the way over, lit on her feet, staggered a couple of
steps, then stopped without falling down. She didn't remember
to put her arms out till she was already on her feet, but I
knew she had the trick learned—and so did her father.

He didn't even bother to come over to us, but called, "Two
more times and we're goin' in! Your maw'll be wonderin' where
we're at."

18

A Glow of Light

THAT Saturday was a good day for me in lots of ways. I'd found that I was growing again, Mr. Bendt had said I'd done a good job cutting cattle, and I'd taught Hazel to do a hard trick-riding stunt without getting hurt. But the two things that made me the happiest came after that.

We'd eaten supper and I was sitting on the bunkhouse steps with Hank and Ned when I heard a cow bellow from far to the east. I listened, and heard another bellow with a different tone. Mr. Bendt was at the harness shop, and I called to him, "I think one of the trail herds is coming in! I heard cows bellowing way off to the east!"

Mr. Bendt came out and listened for a minute, then called back, "Betcha my life it's Batch! You boys want to saddle up and come along to meet him?"

Ned and I started to get our saddles from the harness shop, but Hank beat us there. He hadn't been on a horse since he'd been sick, and had been acting as if he were too weak to open the gates, but he yanked his saddle down and hurried off to catch up a horse.

I hadn't used Lady all week, so I whistled for her when I

reached the corral. It didn't surprise me much that Pinch and Clay came to the gate with her, but I could hardly believe it when I looked up and saw Blueboy follow them half way across the corral. He stuck out his muzzle and sniffed while I was saddling, then stamped a fore hoof and turned back.

Both trail herds had met in the early afternoon, and Mr. Batchlett had thrown them together. When we were still half a mile away, I could hear Sid and Tom yipping and driving. We met them about two miles east of the corrals when twilight was just beginning to settle. There were over a hundred cattle in the combined herd—all cows that were going to have calves before long—and they were so trail-weary they were hard to keep from scattering.

We spread out wide, so we wouldn't turn the herd, and I went to the side where I'd heard Sid's voice. "Hi, there, Little Britches!" he called, when he saw me coming through the brush. "How you doin'? How's that little Jenny Wren?"

"Fine!" I told him. "Everybody's fine, even Hank. He rode out with us. Did you have a good trip?"

Instead of answering me, Sid started to say something about Hank being a lucky old buzzard to get sick and have Jenny take care of him. But some cows pushed out of his side of the herd and he had to ride after them. I rode a little farther on and began pushing back stragglers. In a few minutes I heard Hank doing the same thing still farther toward the back of the herd. From the way he was shouting, anyone might have thought he was trying to handle the whole herd alone.

As twilight deepened the tired cows tried to leave the herd and find places to bed down. If I'd used my head I'd have known how they'd act, and would have ridden Pinch. But I didn't think about it when I'd saddled, and Lady wasn't much good in scrub oak. A dozen cows had slipped past us— and things were about as bad as they could be—when I heard Mr. Batchlett's voice from back where Hank was, "Take it easy, Hank! They'll scatter if you rough 'em!"

I hadn't seen Hank since we met the herd, and in that tall scrub oak he couldn't have seen me, but he shouted back to Mr. Batchlett, "Don't you fret none about me, Batch! I got 'em fenced in tighter'n hog wire, but that there kid's in plenty trouble up yonder."

In a minute or two Mr. Batchlett rode into sight and began rounding up my stragglers. I helped as much as I could, but it was a poor job, and he had to double back for cows that I'd let slip past me. He didn't say a word when he rode up, and all he said when he left was, "Keep 'em in close as you can!" Then he rode on toward where Sid was working.

I didn't see anybody else till we had the cows out of the brush and headed across the valley to the corrals, and I didn't want to. All week I'd been proud of the job I was doing, and had been anxious for Mr. Batchlett to get back, so he could see how much I'd learned. Then, when he'd come, he'd found me doing a terrible job, and Hank had made it sound as if

I never did any better. After that, I was sure Mr. Batchlett wouldn't take me on a trading trip with him, and I thought he might pay me off and send me home.

All the others stood around after the herd was in the corrals, but I unsaddled and went right to the bunkhouse. I didn't light the lamp, but undressed and crawled into my bunk. It wasn't that I was tired; I wasn't. I just didn't want to see anybody, and particularly Mr. Batchlett.

I must have lain there fifteen or twenty minutes when I heard Mr. Bendt's and Mr. Batchlett's voices coming toward the bunkhouse. I was sure Mr. Batchlett was going to turn in early, and I didn't want him to see me awake when he lit the lamp—and to have him tell me I was no good and that he was going to pay me off. So I turned over to face the wall and tried to snore quietly, as if I were sound asleep.

We always left the bunkhouse door open on summer evenings, and I heard the voices come nearer and nearer till they stopped there, outside the doorway. Mr. Batchlett was telling Mr. Bendt something about his trip, but I didn't pay any attention until I heard him ask, "Where'd Little Britches go to? Ain't seen him since we come in."

"Betcha my life him and Hazel's up to somethin'," Mr. Bendt sort of chuckled. "Them kids is as full o' beans as poorhouse chili."

Mr. Batchlett's voice hadn't sounded as if he were peeved at me, so I turned back from the wall. Just then there was a glow of light from the doorway, and against it I saw the dark shadows of two pairs of wide shoulders and two hats nearly as wide. The men were sitting on the bunkhouse steps, and Mr. Batchlett was lighting a cigarette. When he'd snapped out the match, he asked, "How's the kid doing? Still raring into things like he was killin' snakes?"

"Never seen the beat! Must'a been that stay abed, or Hazel, or . . ."

"What's he been up to now?" Mr. Batchlett asked, with a little edge to his voice.

"Ever see him do that trick where he dives off a horse and lands on his feet?"

"Yep, half a dozen times," Mr. Batchlett said. "Quite a stunt, ain't it?"

"Betcha my life! He's been learnin' it to Hazel."

"Break their necks, the both of 'em!" Mr. Batchlett said. "Ought to had better sense than to fetch him out here. Been gettin' too much attention around town—ruins a kid that age. Had some hopes for him when I left here, but . . ."

A big lump came into my throat, and I was turning back toward the wall again when Mr. Bendt said, "Trade you Tom for him."

"What's that?" Mr. Batchlett snapped.

"Trade you Tom for him," Mr. Bendt said again. "Him and Hazel's the best team of calf hunters ever I seen, and you'd ought to lay eyes on him and that old Clay horse cuttin' cattle —smoother'n cat hair. Old horse gets around mighty spry with a light kid on him—cut and handled every critter on the place in less'n six half days."

"Well, I'll be go to . . . ! Reckon maybe the kid was right. Reckon maybe that losin' up in the mountains didn't do him no hurt," Mr. Batchlett said, and I knew he was remembering what I'd said to him when he'd left for his trading trip. Then he asked, "Usin' his head, you say?"

"Ought to seen him learnin' Hazel that trick stunt; learnt it to her like a schoolma'am—wouldn't let her make no move till she'd learnt the one before it dead right. Fetched her through without a scratch. 'Course she ain't no ways good as him at it yet, but she's honin' to show it off to you." Then he chuckled, and said, "Won a poker hand off'n me, the kid did! Come up with a full house on a one-card draw."

"Don't reckon his maw would . . ."

"Oh, 'twasn't no card game, Batch! It was on learnin' Hazel that stunt. I reckoned 'twas too dangerous for her, and was about to freeze him out o' the game, but he called my hand. Wasn't ornery. Just called for a one-card draw and laid his hand down."

I didn't feel right about lying there and listening when they were talking about me, and I couldn't get out of the bunk-house, so I coughed.

"Reckon Hank turned in early," Mr. Blatchett said quietly. Then he asked, "The kid gained any of his weight back?"

From then on they kept their voices low, but it was so still that I couldn't help hearing, and I couldn't just sit up and say, "I'm not Hank, and I can't help hearing you."

"All back, and a couple to spare," Mr. Bendt said. "Says he reckons he's started to grow again—first weight he's gained since his paw passed on."

"Reckon I'll be takin' him along next week," Mr. Batchlett said. "Told him I would if he gained back and done a good job while I was away. Dang shame he ain't got a better string of horses for trail work! Couldn't keep his hands off that blue devil, and his own mare ain't worth a dime in the brush. Pinch is too old for hard trail work, and Clay's needed here. What you reckon ailed the kid to pick that kind of a string?"

"He didn't pick none but Blueboy—and you're the man ought to know why he done that," Mr. Bendt said slowly. "Hazel picked him the rest of 'em." Then he chuckled again. "And I'm getting a sneakin' idee why she done it."

I wanted to know what Mr. Bendt's idea was, but Mr. Batchlett didn't ask him. Instead, he asked quickly, "That little devil been on Blueboy? I told him to stay off."

"Nope! Nope! Ain't had a strap, a rope, or a leg on him since you been gone. But he's workin' on him. Been out there in the horse corral till late in the nights—soft-talkin' him and feeding him biscuits that he tells Helen he wants for his mare. And dag-goned if the ornery maverick ain't cottonin' up to it like a spring foal. What routes you figure on workin' this next trip out?"

I couldn't guess how Mr. Bendt knew about my working with Blueboy, and I couldn't ask. I didn't cough again, but lay with my eyes and ears wide open.

Mr. Batchlett lit another cigarette, and didn't answer for two or three minutes. Then he said, "Figured I was licked on putting out more than two teams this next trip, but with the kid . . . and this little Sid turned out to be a right smart trader—joshes a man into a pretty good deal and makes him like it. Might send him back into the South Park country. Lots of good milkers over there that's due for fall calves, and the ranchers don't want to winter 'em through. They'll trade even-up for a dry cow that'll drop a spring calf."

"Who you aim to send along for driver?" Mr. Bendt asked.

Mr. Batchlett dropped his voice even lower than it had been, and asked, "You reckon old Hank's in shape to go?"

"Betcha my life!" Mr. Bendt whispered back. "Old bluff's been belly-achin' 'round here all week account of I put him to swingin' a gate, but he sure perked up when he heard you was comin'. Do him good to wear out a little saddle leather." Then his voice boomed up again, and he asked, "Who you figure to send out with Zeb? You ain't countin' on taking the kid and Tom both away from the home ranch, are you, Batch? I got to have . . ."

"Wasn't counting on it," Mr. Batchlett told him. "Wasn't counting on having three teams out when I sat down here. Reckon I'll ride on over to The Springs tomorrow; see what I can pick up to go along with Zeb. He can get along with most anybody, but I wouldn't dast send a new man with Sid or Hank. Little Sid ain't got that red hair for nothing, and Hank would like as not get a new man lost."

"Sendin' Zeb back down Pueblo way?"

"Aim to," Mr. Batchlett said. "That'll leave him where he can keep an eye on the peak, and he says there's still some good cows to be had down that way."

"And you?"

"Well . . . I been studyin' on it here for a bit," Mr. Batchlett said slowly. "Been wanting to get down the Arkansas Valley for the past three, four years. Like to take a look at that country as far down as the Purgatory. Hear there's some right good ranches down there; ought to be some good trades to be made."

"Mighty long swing for two weeks, ain't it, Batch?"

"Longish, but I aim to take all young stock, push straight across country to the Purgatory, then trade back along the Arkansas. If I'm lucky enough to trade for late fall calvers they'll travel good, and I ought to make out all right. Wish, by dang, that kid had picked a better string of trail horses!"

"Wish, by dang, you. was takin' Tom," Mr. Bendt told him. "With three teams out there'll be a heap of cuttin' work to do around here, and havin' the kid to handle Clay would leave me loose for other jobs I ought to get done."

"Nope!" Mr. Batchlett said, and I saw his shadow against the sky as he stood up. "I promised the kid I'd take him if he done a good job, and I ain't going back on it. Reckon I'll turn in; it's been a long day. Tell Hazel I'll be rarin' to see her do that trick of hers in the mornin'."

I'd turned back to face the wall before Mr. Batchlett came into the bunkhouse, and was breathing slow and steady when he lit the lamp. I'm sure that when he saw me he thought I was asleep, because he half mumbled, as if he were talking to himself, "Little devil! I'd sure have bet against you 'fore you got lost, but I reckon you're goin' to make it."

I wanted to sit up and thank him, but, of course, I couldn't.

Mr. Batchlett moved around the bunkhouse quietly for a couple of minutes, then blew out the lamp, and I heard the tight horsehide squeak as he got into his bunk. In a few minutes he was breathing long and steadily, but I didn't want to go to sleep then. It was too nice just to lie there and remember back over the things I'd heard him and Mr. Bendt say while they were sitting on the steps.

The moon had risen when I heard the other men coming toward the bunkhouse. I could hear Tom's and Sid's voices, but Hank was drowning them out. "By dogies," he shouted, "I'm

a-tellin' you, it's a-goin' to rain cats and dogs 'fore noontime
tomorra! Can't nobody fool us oldtime cowhands on the
weather! Take note how that there moon's a-canted over to
spill the water! Why, I recollect when . . ."

Boots scuffed as someone came up the steps, there was a
glow from a struck match, and Tom's voice came—low but
sharp—"Shut up, Hank! The boss is sleepin'."

The glow brightened as Tom lit the lamp, then there was
the gentle scuff of boots on the steps and floor, and Sid whispered, "Well, I'll be dogged if old Little Britches ain't turned
in, too! Reckoned he'd went off to the house to visit with Jenny
Wren and the girls. Can't make out why he turned in so danged
fast! Still kind o' puny, I reckon."

Ned's slow twang came from somewhere across the bunkhouse, "Beat out, I reckon! Watt's been poppin' the whip all
week long. Rounded up, cut and booked the whole shebang.
Britches, he done all the cuttin'."

There was no more whispering, and one by one I heard the
horsehides squeak as the men turned in. As I lay listening I
heard the breathing grow longer, and the sound of gentle snoring came from here and there around the bunkhouse, but the
lamp was still burning. I thought the last man to turn in had
forgotten to blow it out, and was just going to get up and do
it myself, when I heard a low drone, "*She wore a yella ribbon
around her neck.*"

I didn't roll over, but turned my head slowly till I could see
out into the room. Zeb was sitting, slouched on the small of his
back, and with his bare feet crossed on the table by the lamp.
A pair of steel-rimmed glasses were perched on the end of his
long nose, and he was darning a hole in the heel of a sock. With
each dip of his needle, he was mumbling one syllable of, "*She
Wore a Yella Ribbon.*"

There haven't been many times when I've been happier—just
lying there in my bunk and listening to Zeb drone, and thinking how glad I was that Hank had got us lost in the mountains.
If he hadn't, I might not have waked up to a lot of my own

mistakes, and Mr. Batchlett would have sent me home.

Zeb must have darned socks for nearly an hour, then I heard his chair squeak, and the padding of his feet on the floor boards. I tried not to change the rhythm of my breathing as the sound stopped, almost beside my bunk. And I didn't let a muscle quiver when I felt a hand touch my back. But when it lifted the blanket carefully and drew it up over my shoulders a lump began to swell in my throat.

I couldn't go to sleep, and there was no sense in lying there awake. So, as soon as Zeb began to snore, I slipped out of my bunk, felt for my clothes, and tiptoed outside. After I'd pulled on my overalls, shirt and boots, I went to the harness shop for a biscuit, and wandered over to the horse corral. The moon looked like a tilted golden saucer, and there was just enough light that I could see the horses standing in groups at the far side of the corral.

I stood outside the gate and watched them for a minute or two, then gave a soft bob-white whistle—the call I'd always used for Lady. There wasn't a stir among most of the horses, but a few heads lifted and turned toward me. When I whistled again, four dark shapes separated from the groups and came toward me. One of them was Blueboy, and he didn't stop half way, but came right up to the gate with Lady, Clay, and old Pinch—nickering a whisper deep in his throat for a piece of biscuit. He let me scratch his forehead, the way the rest of them did, and stood quietly while I soft-talked—telling them about the trip we were going on to the Arkansas, and that they were the best string of horses in the world.

19

No Profit A-fightin'

WHEN I went to the chuckhouse the next morning everybody seemed as excited as they had been the Sunday we picked our horse strings. Sid kept calling Jenny, "Jenny Wren," and trying to make jokes she'd laugh at—but she wouldn't. And Hank was wound up like a new dollar watch. He'd heard that he and Sid were going out as a team, and was hardly down at the table before he shouted, "By dogies, Batch, you sure ain't made no mistake! With this here little redhead to give me a hand, I'll show you a job o' tradin' like you ain't saw in many a year! No, sirree, by dogies, they don't make tradin' men no more! Why I recollect when we was a-fetchin' trail herds up from Texas, I and old Tom . . ."

"Pass the flapjacks!" Mr. Batchlett cut in. Then he began talking to Mr. Bendt about cutting out seventy head of young stock for our trip down the Arkansas.

Hazel came into the chuckhouse three or four times, to bring coffee or help Jenny carry out dishes. Every time she tried to whisper something to me, but she did it so low and fast that I couldn't understand what she was saying. When we were nearly through eating I noticed her just inside the kitchen door-

way, ducking her head and making the motions of throwing a
saddle onto a horse. Of course I knew then that she was telling
me to get saddled up so she could show Mr. Batchlett the
somersault trick. I nodded to let her know I understood, and
within two minutes I heard dishes clicking and clattering in
the kitchen faster than Hank's false teeth did when we were
lost in the mountains.

While the trading teams had been away I hadn't noticed that
Jenny paid the least bit of attention to Ned. But at breakfast
that morning she kept asking him if he'd like more coffee, telling him she liked his Sunday shirt, and things like that. Then,
when Sid was telling a joke, she looked out the window, and
said to Ned, "I thought I heard a little redheaded woodpecker,
but I must have been mistaken."

Everybody but Sid laughed—and he tried to—but his face
and neck got as red as his hair. I thought he might blow off, but
Mr. Batchlett cut in again. "How about it, boys?" he asked;
"Want to pitch in and get the trail herds made up this morning?
I'm aimin' to ride over to The Springs this afternoon; any that
wants can ride along. We'll have to work right through the
Fourth, and this is the only chance you'll get for a celebration."

The men all nodded, and the last thing I saw when I was
leaving the chuckhouse was Hazel in the doorway. She had a
plate in one hand and a dishtowel in the other, and was making
diving motions with her head.

I didn't know just what Mr. Bendt might want me to do
about helping to make up the trail herds, so I walked up beside
him on the way to the horse corral, and asked, "Which horse
should I put my saddle on this morning?"

He looked down at me, closed one eye, and said in a low
voice, "If you don't want to get et up alive, you'll put it on
Pinch while I'm puttin' Hazel's on Pinto. If she don't get to
show off that trick stunt to Batch 'fore Sunday School time,
she'll bust a hame string."

Mr. Batchlett and all the men—even the dairyhands—must
have known Hazel was going to do the somersault trick before

we worked the cattle. When Mr. Bendt and I brought the saddles, they were standing around behind the horse corral, and Hank was telling in a loud voice about riding tricks he used to do when he was a boy.

We hardly had the saddles on when Hazel came running from the house. She was holding the herd book in one hand—sort of waving it around so it would show from behind—but with the other hand she was hugging a new ten-gallon hat against her chest. As she ran up to the corral gate, her father called, "Hazel, what you doin' with that new Stetson I bought you for the roundup?"

"Well . . ." she panted. "Well . . . the Fourth o' July is only two days off, and I'll need . . . I'll need . . ."

In less than a second I knew what she'd need, and Mr. Bendt did too. Before she could go on, he said quietly, "Betcha my life! Betcha my life, gal! Now don't go to gettin' all het up or you won't do too good. The boys is waitin'."

Until then, I'd thought, of course, that we'd be going to the little meadow for Hazel to do the trick, so I said, "If she's going to do the trick here at the corrals, I won't have any need for Pinch."

"Yes, you will too!" Hazel snapped at me. "If you don't ride with me and do the hissin' I'll get scairt, and then I'll tighten up, and then I'll make a mess of it."

I still thought it would be better if Hazel did the trick alone. If I lit on my feet and she bobbled it, she might be ashamed. So I said, "I'll make a few practice runs with you here in the corral—the kind where we don't leave the saddle—then, if you're loose enough, you can do better alone."

"Nope!" Mr. Bendt told me. "You go on and take your practice runs, but it's your trick, you learnt it to her, and you'll do it together—she'll feel more to home." Then he tossed Hazel up onto her saddle and left the corral.

The practice worked fine, and Hazel stayed as loose as a rag doll in the saddle. After Mr. Bendt opened the gate and we rode out, I didn't say a word about the trick, but kept soft-

talking about anything else—the way I'd have talked to a nervous horse. When we were fifty yards beyond the men I turned
the horses. Then, before Hazel had time to get scared, I
snapped, "Let's GO!"

I kept Pinch well clear of Pinto, and the little crowd of men
seemed to rush toward us as we raced. When we were almost
on them I hissed and ducked my head. The next moment we
were standing in a row, with Pinto's head between Hazel and
me, and Pinch's at my right. As I looked along the line, Hazel
swept off her new Stetson and bowed—the way I'd told her
I did it at the Littleton roundup.

The men whistled and shouted for us to do the trick again,
but I told Hazel I didn't think we'd better. With the little bit
of practice she'd had, there wasn't one chance in fifty of our
doing it that well again—and there wasn't one chance in fifty
million that any other girl could have done it that once.

I never saw another cutting horse work with the sureness and
speed Clay showed that Sunday. Long before noon we had
three trading herds cut out and ready to take the trail Monday
morning. Mr. Batchlett bossed the making up of the herds and
told me which animal to bring out each time, and when we'd
finished, he nodded, and said, "Good job, Little Britches!"

Before I could tell him that it was Clay who had done the
good job, he wheeled his horse away and called to the men,
"I aim to ride in to The Springs in half an hour. Get your glad
rags on if you want to come along—we'll eat in town." Then
he rode away toward the house with Mr. Bendt.

I didn't want to go to Colorado Springs, but I did want to
talk to Mr. Batchlett before he went. With Clay having to stay
on the home ranch, and with me going on a long trip, I'd need
Blueboy in shape to use. From the day I'd picked him I hadn't
ridden him an hour, and he'd fought me every minute. I hoped
that during the past week he'd settled down enough that I
could handle him—but I thought I should ask Mr. Batchlett
before I tried it.

As soon as I'd unsaddled Clay I went to the bunkhouse, but Mr. Batchlett wasn't there. Tom and Ned were trying to shave in front of a little mirror a foot square, and Hank was hollering for his turn. Sid was nowhere in sight, but Zeb was sitting on the steps, patching a pair of overalls, so I sat down beside him.

I knew a half hour must be up before Mr. Batchlett and Mr. Bendt came from the house. They'd both shaved, and kept right on talking while Mr. Batchlett changed his shirt and boots. I got up and stood around, waiting for a hole in their talking. Then I asked, "Would it be all right for me to ride Blueboy this afternoon? I'll need to get him . . ."

"Dasn't risk it," Mr. Batchlett told me. "He's too dangerous for you to be messing around with by yourself."

Zeb looked up from his patching, and said, "Me and Sid'll be hereabouts. We could lend a hand if needs be."

Mr. Batchlett stopped for half a minute and stood looking at the steps. "Bad streak in that outlaw," he said, as if he were talking to himself; "can't tell when it'll bust loose." Then he looked at me, and asked, "Why'd you pick him?"

"Because I . . . because . . ." I was going to say, "had to have him," but I knew it would sound silly, so I stopped.

Mr. Batchlett must have read what was in my mind. He gave me a quick slap on the shoulder, and said, "All right, Little Britches, I ought to know without asking, and I do. Go ahead, but be danged careful!" He started on, then turned back, and said, "Don't saddle him without two men around, and don't get on him without a man mounted and alongside!"

I stood in the bunkhouse doorway and watched the riders out of sight. Then I went inside to write a letter to Mother, but I couldn't think of much to say, so I just wrote:

"I am going on a trip to Pergatory with Mr. Batchlett. I have a blue horse in my string that is the most butiful horse I ever saw. I think he is begining to like me. I have gained 2 pounds. Your loving son Ralph."

When I'd finished my letter, I thought I'd better rig a double cinch on my saddle before I tried Blueboy, so I went to the

harness shop to do it. Sid was there, and working over something at the bench. When I went in, he sang, "Hi-ya, Little
Britches! Come look what I done made for that little old Jenny
Wren! Been workin' on it odd minutes o' night herdin'. Pounded
out the dee-zign on the saddle horn with a boot heel. Batch, he
let me ride on into Pu-ay-blo to get the buckle off'n a harness
store."

Sid held up as pretty a horsehide belt as I'd ever seen. It was
seal-brown, almost as soft as velvet, and polished till it glowed
—with a vine pattern hammered into it. The buckle was dull
silver, with a bright gold horsehead set in the middle. I never
would have put all that work into anything for a girl who
treated me the way Jenny treated Sid, but, of course I couldn't
say so. He was still polishing the little belt and talking about
Jenny when she and the girls drove into the yard from church.

While I was waiting for the dinner bell to ring, I finished rig-
ging my saddle, then went to the bunkhouse to put on a clean
shirt. Zeb had finished his patching, and was washing the
overalls in a bucket of water beside the steps. He didn't say
anything as I went in, and he didn't look up when I came out,
but said, "Better fetch me that shirt, son. Ain't no sense in the
both of us gettin' into the suds, and might happen you'll need a
change whilst you're on the trail."

It wasn't until I took the dirty shirt back to Zeb that I noticed
my spare pair of overalls, all washed and hanging on the fence.
When I tried to thank him, he only shook his head and went
right on washing—and crooning, "Yella Ribbon."

All the dairyhands had driven into town as soon as the milking was done, so there were only the three of us at the table
that Sunday noon. Zeb didn't look up from his plate till he was
finished, then cut himself a big chew of tobacco and went outside. I couldn't saddle Blueboy till Sid was with me, but he
dawdled over his pie so long that I went out and left him at
the table.

Zeb was waiting for me when I came out. He rifled a thin
squirt of tobacco juice, got up from the steps, and walked along

with me toward the horse corral. "Been studyin' 'bout that blue hoss," he said when we were halfway to the corral. "Awful full o' fight, ain't he?"

"Yes, he is," I said, "but he's been letting me feed him some pieces of biscuit this past week."

"No profit a-fightin' a man as ain't lookin' for a fight," Zeb said, then he spit again and we went on.

I was pretty sure Zeb was telling me that when I'd tried to ride Blueboy before I'd let him know I was looking for a fight, and that he'd keep right on fighting me as long as I gave him anything to fight against.

We carried our saddles to the horse corral, and I took along a biscuit, but we had to wait fifteen or twenty minutes for Sid. While we were waiting Zeb stood outside the gate and mumbled, "*Yella Ribbon*," and I went in and fed pieces of biscuit to all four of the horses in my string. Blueboy even stood while I reached back for the hackamore Zeb passed me through the gate, and he didn't try very hard to pull away when I slipped it over his head.

Sid was whistling like a meadow lark when he brought his saddle, and as he came up to the gate he let out two or three coyote yelps. Even after Zeb had whispered, "Watch out afore you spook the hoss!" he kept whistling, and he wasn't much help in saddling Blueboy.

I didn't stop soft-talking to Blueboy until all three of us were in the saddle and Zeb had opened the gate. For the next few minutes I couldn't have soft-talked to save my life. The second he saw the gate open, Blueboy went up like Old Faithful Geyser. And when his fore hoofs hit the ground he was running —running with his head and neck stretched out and his hoofs beating like sticks on a snare drum.

When Blueboy went up I had to double over, with the saddle horn in the pit of my stomach, and when he came down I bounced high. The natural thing to do was to haul hard on the hackamore rope, to hold me tight down in the saddle, but I wouldn't let myself do it.

Blueboy streaked along the wagon road across the valley, just as he had done when he ran away with me before. Sid raced behind, and yelled for me to jerk the hackamore, but I left it loose, and tried to keep my heels from kicking Blueboy in the belly. The other time, he'd left the road at the end of the straightaway, and raced up the hill through the scrub oaks, trying to rake me off on each one. This time he followed the winding of the road, and hardly slowed his driving pace all the way up the long hill.

He raced across the top of the rise and onto a rock-strewn piece of road that corkscrewed through the deep gulch beyond. It seemed crazy to let a horse race down that road without at least holding his head up tight. With it down, a stumble would have somersaulted us, but I decided I'd rather risk my neck and his than to let him think I was fighting him, so I left the hackamore loose and rode it out.

Blueboy went through the gulch and up the rise beyond without a break in his pace, then I felt his stride lengthen, and the sound of his breathing came back above the clatter of his hoofs. There'd been times on some of those hairpin turns when I hadn't been sure I'd be able to stay in the saddle, but that feeling was all gone now. I eased a hand up along Blueboy's neck and began soft-talking again.

For at least three miles Blueboy held that racing, killing pace, and I was sure he was going to run himself to death. Then his head began to rise, his ears lifted, and I knew he was watching me from the corner of his eye.

I didn't let myself change the tone or timing of my soft-talk, I didn't try to drive or slow him, and I kept one hand rubbing along his neck. In another half mile Blueboy had dropped his gallop to a swinging canter, and wasn't blowing any more. His breathing whispered through his nostrils with as little effort as his white-stockinged legs reached forward for the road. I looked back for Sid, but he and his piebald horse were nowhere in sight.

I think I could have turned Blueboy easily then, but I wanted him to be sure I wasn't fighting him, so I let him go on for another mile. I'd never felt small on a horse before, but there was something about Blueboy that made me feel even smaller than I was. It couldn't have been his size—he wasn't much bigger than Pinch—but I think it was his drive and power. When I turned him back, it was only because I thought Zeb and Sid might be worried, and I brought him around in a wide circle—with only the slightest draw of the hackamore rope against his neck.

Blueboy didn't break his canter when I turned him, and I didn't want him to. He'd held the pace steadily for a couple of miles when we topped a rise and I saw Sid coming up from the gully below. His horse was making hard work of the hill, and was blowing badly. Sid let him down to a walk, and called up to me, "Way you took off, I reckoned you'd be in Kansas 'fore now. Why didn't you jerk that hackamore and haul him in? Sure you ain't broke his wind?"

I didn't want to make Blueboy nervous by shouting back, so I waited till I'd ridden down to Sid, and told him, "I didn't need to haul him in, because, after the first mile, he wasn't running away. And it looks to me as if Pie is the one that might be wind-broken."

Sid turned his horse, and we jogged side by side, with Blueboy breathing easily and the piebald fighting for each lungful of air. "By jiggers, it's a wonder if I ain't went and broke his wind!" Sid spluttered. "If that danged maverick wasn't runnin' away with you, why didn't you turn him back 'fore you scairt the livin' bejeebers out'a me? What you messing with him for? He won't never be no more use to you than a wooden leg! Ain't it best if we take him up to the mountain pasture and turn him loose? One day that dag-goned outlaw's goin' to kill you if you don't get shut of him."

I couldn't be sure Sid wasn't right, but from the way I felt right then, I was willing to take my chances of being killed. I knew without Sid's telling me that Blueboy would probably never be any good for a cowhorse, but something made me feel as if I needed him and had to have him. I couldn't say those things to Sid without sounding foolish, so I just said, "I couldn't turn him back now, Sid—not unless Mr. Batchlett told me I had to."

Sid had started all over again about Blueboy's being a worthless outlaw when we heard the pound of a running horse's hoofs. I guessed who it would be, and leaned a bit in the saddle. Blueboy leaped forward as if I'd spurred him, and raced up out of the gully. As we topped the hill I saw Pinto running toward us. Hazel was clinging to his bare back, and whipping him with the line ends at every stride. I forgot all about making Blueboy nervous, and shouted, "What's the matter, Hazel? What's happened?"

For a moment I thought she was going to fall. She jerked up straight for an instant, then slumped in a heap on Pinto's back. When I got to her she was laughing and crying at the same time, and her words came in gasps. "I . . . I reckoned he'd . . . he'd killed you," she sort of burbled. "I seen how he was runnin' . . . crazy mad, with his head down . . . like a killer stallion."

Blueboy didn't like to be stopped. He sidestepped and bobbed his head, but didn't act mean or try to break away, so I said, "Look at him now! He doesn't look crazy or mad, does he? Zeb told me how to handle him, and it worked all right. Blueboy wasn't mad, he was just trying to find out if I was looking for a fight." Then I realized that Zeb should have been close behind Sid if he'd come with us, so I asked, "Where is Zeb?"

"That crazy old coot!" Hazel blurted. "When I run to get Pinto he was settin' by the horse corral gate—just settin' and spittin' at a rock."

Zeb never told me I did a good job in handling Blueboy, or that he thought I was a good rider, but, after that, he didn't need to—and I loved him for it.

I was sorry Hazel got so scared when she didn't need to be, but it made me a little bit happy that she worried about me. Maybe that's what made me remember that I wouldn't see her for a couple of weeks, and why I thought it might be nice to ride out to the secret spring and back. Hazel thought so, too, and her mother said it would be all right, so I saddled Lady and Pinto and we went.

It was still fairly early in the afternoon, so we spent about an hour watching some rabbits play by the basin below the spring. And I made a slingshot out of a latigo string and a willow crotch—to scare away the weasel if it came again. Then Hazel thought it would be fun to go around to the beaver dam in the valley west of the buildings. She said that if we crept up to it real quietly we might see a beaver swimming.

We left Lady and Pinto nearly a quarter of a mile below the beaver dam, and went up the little valley by the cattle path through the willows. We went as quietly as we could, but when we got to the dam we didn't see any beaver. There was an outcropping of rock on the shady side of the pond, and Jenny and Sid were sitting on it. She was holding the belt he'd made for her, looking down at it and rubbing her fingers over the buckle. Sid was looking down too, picking petals off a flower and dropping each one into the water. Jenny was saying something, though her voice was too low to be heard across the pond, but it didn't sound as if she were making fun of Sid the way she usually did.

The minute we saw them, Hazel put a finger to her lips and motioned for me to go back the way we'd come. I didn't make a sound until we were halfway back to the horses, then I said, "That's the funniest thing I ever saw! From the way Jenny's been treating Sid I thought she hated him."

"Hmmmff! That's all you know about women!" Hazel told me, as if she thought I was just plain stupid.

I couldn't help remembering her calling me a dirty squealing pig, and making fun of me when I slipped off Kenny's

donkey, then her crying when she thought Blueboy had hurt me, so I said, "I guess I don't know much about women, but they're an awful lot harder to figure out than horses."

Hazel didn't even bother to answer, but sniffed again, and walked on down the path through the willows.

20

Trinidad

SID AND Jenny must have left the beaver pond right after Hazel and I did. We rode straight back to the corrals, and they came into the dooryard while I was unsaddling. Jenny had her arm hooked inside of Sid's, and they were walking slowly, still talking. By the time I'd spread the sweat blankets to dry and gone to the bunkhouse, Sid was already there. He was whistling like a meadow lark, and getting a big piece of seal-brown leather out of his war sack.

With Sid busy and Zeb taking a nap, there wasn't much for me to do, and I began to worry about the trip I was going on with Mr. Batchlett. I'd be his driver, and it was the driver's job to do the packing, cooking, and camp making, but I didn't know any more about it than a jack rabbit.

At the Y-B ranch we'd always had a chuckwagon when we were out on the range, and I was supposed to have been the cook's helper, but the most he'd ever let me do was to haul wood and water and peel potatoes. I couldn't even make flapjacks, and didn't have any idea how to make a trail pack or what to put in one. Besides that, we were going to start away from the home ranch at the crack of dawn, and I'd look pretty silly if I didn't have our packs made up and ready.

I could think of only one way to begin. I got a piece of paper and began writing down everything I could remember that we'd had in the Y-B chuckwagon. I was still trying to remember things when Zeb yawned, stretched, and sat up on the side of his bunk. "Tobacca's better chawin' than pencils," he said. "What's got you throwed?"

"Well," I said, "I'm trying to write down the things Mr. Batchlett and I will need for our trip, but I've already got enough to load nine horses, and know there must be something I've forgotten."

"Always is," Zeb yawned. "Ever make up a trail pack?"

"No, I haven't," I said, "but I think I've remembered almost everything we had on the Y-B chuckwagon."

"Wouldn't doubt me none," Zeb yawned again. "I seen packs the likes o' that. Want I should lend a hand?"

Zeb did more than lend a hand: he did nearly the whole job of making up the packs for both his trail trip and ours. As I brought flour, sugar, canned goods and frying pans from the kitchen, he explained why everything had to go just where it did, and how to balance a pack to make it ride square on a horse's back.

We'd finished our packing, and were sitting on the bunkhouse steps in the deep twilight, when I heard a faint shout from far away toward the east. As the breeze shifted a bit, the sound of shouting came clearer. Zeb turned on one elbow, looked into the bunkhouse where Sid was busy with his leather, and drawled, "Reckon you might as leave go to makin' pack, Sid. Hank, he's had him a Fourth o' July celebration."

It was full dark before the men reached the home ranch, and we went out to the horse corral to meet them. As they rode toward us across the little valley we could hear them laughing and talking, but Hank was the only loud one. He'd never stopped shouting from the time we'd first heard him. When he rode up to the corral gate he was hanging half out of his saddle, and yelling, *"I'm a wild coyote (hic)—a-huntin' for a high place to howl!"*

In the darkness I didn't notice the new man until Zeb had lifted Hank out of his saddle and started for the bunkhouse with him. The man was as big as Mr. Bendt, dressed in fancy cowboy clothes, and riding a silver-studded saddle on a palomino that looked like a circus horse. He was leading another palomino with a big trail pack on its back. The new man didn't step down from his saddle when the others did, but said to Mr. Batchlett, "Where's the bunkhouse at? Reckon I'll stow my gear."

Mr. Batchlett was unsaddling, and said, without looking up, "The boy'll show you."

The cutting corral and harness shop stood between the horse corral and the bunkhouse, so I couldn't point it out, but said, "It's over here; I'll show you," and led the way.

The man rode along beside me until we were past the cutting corral, then asked, "The old man your paw?"

"No," I told him, "I just work here."

Then, when we'd rounded the harness shop, I said, "There's the bunkhouse right there," and started to turn back.

"Come here, kid!" the man ordered. "Lug my stuff inside!"

I didn't like having a new man order me around like that, and I knew that if I let him boss me once he'd always do it, so I turned back toward him and said, "Mr. Batchlett gives the orders around here."

"And when he ain't around, I'll do it! See!" As he said, "See!" he popped the quirt on the end of his bridle reins at my shoulder. It would have drawn blood if I hadn't ducked quicker than a prairie dog. When the quirt snapper missed me it cracked like a pistol shot, and before I caught my balance the bunkhouse door opened. Against the yellow light of the lamp behind him, Zeb's black outline towered to within two inches of the top of the doorway, and he drawled, "What's the ruckus?"

I kept quiet, but the man sort of growled, "Any more yap out o' this smart-aleck kid, and I'll . . ."

"Doubt me I would," Zeb drawled into the growling. "If

you're the new hand, light down and fetch your stuff in."

I stood where I was, ready to duck if the man popped the quirt again, but he didn't. He climbed out of his saddle and began untying the lashings on his pack. Zeb didn't move from the doorway, but motioned for me to go back to the corral.

I'd only gone part way when I met the men. Tom was dragging both his saddle and Hank's by the horns, and Ned was staggering a little, with his saddle hugged up against him in both arms. Mr. Batchlett and Mr. Bendt were laughing, and asked Sid why he hadn't gone along for the celebration, but neither of them seemed a bit drunkish.

Mrs. Bendt had waited supper, and Jenny rang the bell while the men were putting their saddles away, but Ned and Tom weren't hungry. As I watched them go toward the bunkhouse I noticed that the new man's horse was all unpacked, and that Zeb was leaning against the door jamb.

The dairyhands went right at the milking when they got home, and none of them came to the chuckhouse for supper. At first there were only four of us at the table: Mr. Batchlett, Mr. Bendt, Sid and I. Jenny brought the meat and potatoes, and we'd filled our plates before Zeb came slouching in. When Mr. Batchlett saw he was alone, he asked, "Where's Trinidad? Didn't you tell him to come in and eat?"

"Unsaddlin'," Zeb drawled, as he sat down. "Don't calc'late he's back'ards. He'll be along."

I'd had my second helping of meat and potatoes, and Jenny was bringing in the pie when the new man came into the chuckhouse. He had his hat on, but when he saw Jenny he swept it off and stood staring at her. Mr. Batchlett looked up, and said, "Miss Warren; Trinidad Bates. He'll be going out as driver for Zeb, Jenny."

When I looked around, Trinidad was holding his hat against his chest, and bowing so low that only his curly black hair showed. "Jenny Warren," he said in a voice that was almost singing, "a beautiful name for a beautiful lady. One day soon I will sing and play for her."

Jenny's face turned as red as a windy sunset, and she bowed her head a little, but Mr. Batchlett cut in, "This day you'd best to sit in and eat your grub; it's gettin' cold." Then he looked at me and said, "Reckon you'd best to find us a lantern after you've had your grub. We got a job of pack makin' to do 'fore we turn in."

"It's all done," I told him. "Zeb did it this afternoon. All we'll have to do in the morning will be to put in our bedrolls and war bags."

"Good!" Mr. Batchlett said, and nodded toward Zeb. Then he looked back at me, and asked, "Ride Blueboy today?"

"Yes, sir," I said, "I rode him half way to The Monument and back, and he didn't buck or fight the hackamore."

"Run away with you?"

"Well . . ." I said, "he kind of acted like it . . . but he wasn't toward the end, and . . ."

"Couldn't hold him, eh?"

Before I could answer, Trinidad asked, "That blue devil with the white socks?"

Mr. Batchlett nodded.

"Too much horse for a kid!" Trinidad said, but looked at Jenny instead of Mr. Batchlett. "Outlaw showed fight when I turned my palominos into the corral. Needs handlin'! I'll take him in my string."

"He's took," Mr. Batchlett said, without looking away from me. Then he asked again, "Couldn't hold him?"

"I didn't try to," I said. "Zeb said he wouldn't fight back if I didn't fight him."

Zeb had pushed his chair back and was leaving the table when I spoke, but he slumped back into it and said, "Naw! Said there wa'n't no profit a-fightin' a man as wa'n't lookin' for a fight." And when he said it he was looking right square into Trinidad's eyes.

I guess everybody knew Zeb was talking to Trinidad instead of me. We were all watching them when Mr. Batchlett said, "Takes two to make a fight. Sit tight a minute, Zeb! I want to lay out your trip with you." Then he nodded to me and said, "Better turn in, Little Britches! We'll be hitting the trail at crack o' dawn."

Sid had finished his pie when I left the table, but was sitting with his fork in his hand, watching Jenny with eyes as big and soft as a sheep's. She was pouring Trinidad's coffee, and he was saying something to her, so low I didn't hear it. Whatever it was, it made her face as red as it had been when he bowed to her.

When I went to the bunkhouse Tom, Ned, and Hank were snoring to beat the band. I didn't want to wake them by lighting the lamp, so felt my way to the bunk. As I reached my hand out, my fingers struck tight wires that twanged sharply. I couldn't have jumped back quicker if I'd found a rattlesnake in my bunk. When my heart stopped pounding I lit the lamp. My bunk was piled high with fancy clothes, boots, and saddle bags. A guitar was propped against the headboard, and lying on top of everything was a silver-studded gun belt and holsters —with two pearl-handled six-shooters, and every loop of the belt filled with .45 cartridges.

All the bunks in our bunkhouse were double ones, and the posts between them ran up to the roof. About a foot and a half above the floor, a tanned horsehide was stretched tight to make the spring for the lower bunk. There were three double bunks on each side of the room, and one across the back wall.

When you went to work on a ranch, nobody ever said, "This will be your bunk." You looked around till you found one without a blanket on it, then pushed your war sack underneath and moved in. No cowhand would take an upper bunk if he could get a lower one, but it was first come, first served. Once you'd moved in, the bunk was yours till you quit or got fired, and it didn't make any difference whether you were top hand or the horse wrangler.

When I'd gone to the bunkhouse the first evening I'd come to the home ranch, there had been blankets on the three lower bunks along the south side of the room, so I crawled into the front one on the other side. Sid had taken the one next to me, then Hank, and Zeb had the one across the back, but all the uppers were empty.

When I found all Trinidad's stuff on my bunk, I looked to see if he'd bothered my war sack. Both it and my blanket were gone. At first I thought he'd thrown them outside, but when I stepped up onto a chair I saw them, slung into the far corner of the upper bunk above Hank.

I had to stand there a few minutes before I could make up my mind what to do—and I was so mad that I bit my lip till it bled. I couldn't run back to the chuckhouse and tattle to Mr. Batchlett. Hank, Ned, and Tom were too drunk to be of any help to me, and it would have been almost like tattling to have waked them anyway.

I thought about yanking Trinidad's stuff off my bunk and slinging it up where he'd slung mine—but I didn't more than think of it. He hadn't been fooling when he'd popped that quirt at me, and he might come back to the bunkhouse before any of the other men did. I decided that it would be best to climb up where my blanket and war sack were and say nothing—but I decided something else, too. As much as I liked my job, and as much as I wanted to keep it, I'd quit if Mr. Batchlett let Trinidad keep my bunk. Then I blew out the lamp and shinnied up into the bunk above Hank.

I'd lain there about half an hour when I heard voices coming toward the bunkhouse. A minute later boots scuffed on the steps, I heard the scratch of a match on rough cloth, then the tinkle of the lamp chimney, and the bunkhouse glowed with light. At about the same moment Mr. Batchlett called, "Little Britches!"

I sat up and said, "Yes, sir."

"What you doin' up there?" he asked. "Did you trade bunks with Trinidad?"

"No, sir," I said, "but this is where I found my blanket and war sack when I came out from supper."

When I first sat up, the light from the lamp blinded me. As I blinked, my eyes cleared, and I was looking down on three tall, big men—each of them standing as still as if he'd been frozen. Trinidad stood in front of the bunk that had been mine, and I couldn't see his face. Zeb was just inside the doorway, crouched to a few inches shorter than his six-feet-four, and with his long arms hanging a little out from his body. From above, he looked like the gorilla in the Denver Zoo, and he was watching Trinidad with the same look that the gorilla had when he watched the people in front of his cage.

Mr. Batchlett was looking at Trinidad, too, but it wasn't the first time I'd seen the look that was on his face. I'd seen it when I'd ridden a matched race against his horse the summer before. His rider had spit tobacco juice in my face when we were in the home stretch, and if the other men hadn't held Mr. Batchlett I think he'd have torn that rider to shreds. He didn't make a sound as he watched Trinidad, but stood there by the bunkhouse table with his hands right in front of his pants pockets—as if they were poised to grab the handles of six-shooters.

There was something about the whole sight that made me hold my breath, and my heart was thumping crazily when Trinidad said in a sort of dry, husky voice, "I got a bad leg; can't make it into them high bunks."

Mr. Batchlett flicked a glance up at me, and said, "Hop down!" Then he rapped out to Trinidad, "Git movin'!"

As I jumped down to the floor, Trinidad stood looking back and forth from Mr. Batchlett to Zeb—as if he couldn't make up his mind whether to move his stuff into the upper bunk or to make a break for the doorway.

My heart jumped into my throat as I noticed one of Trinidad's hands moving slowly back toward the bunk, but I wasn't the only one who noticed it. Zeb crouched lower for a spring, and Mr. Batchlett said, "I wouldn't!" in a voice that was as flat and cold as pond ice. Without the least bit of hurry, he walked toward Trinidad, reached around him, and picked up the gun belt and six-shooters. "I'll take care of the artillery while you're here," he said, "my men don't have no need for it. Now get your dunnage out o' here! This boy needs his sleep."

21

Trail Driver

By FOUR o'clock Monday morning we'd had breakfast, Mr. Batchlett had helped me lash my trail pack onto Lady, and I was saddling Pinch. I didn't want to come right out and ask if I could take Blueboy along, so I said, "Would it be better to put a drag rope on Blueboy and turn him in with the herd, or should I tie him to Lady?"

"He wouldn't be no use to you," Mr. Batchlett said. But my face must have shown how I felt. "Oh, tie him to the pack if you want to," he added; "you're goin' to be mighty short of horseflesh for a long trip."

There were seventy head of cattle in our trail herd, all two-year-old steers and White Face bulls. In the cool of early morning they stepped out at a good pace, and by sunup we had the worst of the brush country behind us. About an hour later, Mr. Batchlett dropped back to where I was pushing up the stragglers, and asked, "How you makin' it?"

"Fine!" I told him. "If it's as easy as this all the way, I won't have a bit of trouble."

"It won't be!" he said. "It'll be rough as soon as these

critters get a little tender-footed, and if water's scarce it
might turn out to be doggone rough." He rode along beside me
for a minute or two without a word, then said, "It ain't too
late if you want to turn back and send Tom along."

I couldn't be sure he wasn't telling me that he was sorry
he'd brought me, and that he'd rather have Tom, so I had to
think a little before I said, "If you'd rather have Tom I'll go
back, but I'm not afraid of a hard trip."

"I'd lay my chips on you," Mr. Batchlett said, as if he were
still thinking it over, "but I don't want to do nothin' to make
your maw sorry she let you come out here."

"If she hadn't thought I was going to do a man's job, she
wouldn't have let me take a man's pay for coming," I told
him. "She'd be sorrier if I didn't go with you than if I did
and had a hard trip."

"Then forget about Tom," he said, "but it's sure goin' to be
a man's job. I aim to hit the head of Black Squirrel Creek
by nightfall; that's close onto thirty-five miles. If there's water
there, we'll be all right; if not, we could be in bad trouble.
Spare your horse when you can! I aim to stop and day-graze
on the divide above the head of Cherry Creek." He didn't
mention Tom again, but touched his spurs to his horse and
rode back to his side of the herd.

We crossed the Denver highroad about twelve miles north
of Colorado Springs, and watered the stock at a ranch that had
two windmills. From there we drove east onto the high divide
that separates the water running into the South Platte and the
Arkansas rivers. It was broken by high rolling hills, and dotted
with clumps of brush or scrub oak. I had never seen that
country before, but Mr. Batchlett seemed to know every foot
of it. We didn't follow a straight line, but wound around the
high hills and deep gulches.

Because of his habit of pinching the laggards, Pinch was
better for working the drag than Mr. Batchlett's chestnut. So,
without any planning, we each took our own position with
the herd. Mr. Batchlett rode near the front, turning the leaders

into the right draws and valleys, and I pushed the laggards
along and held in the stragglers.

As the sun rose higher, its heat bore down from the clear
sky, and bounced up from the dry buffalo grass under foot.
I guessed it to be about ten o'clock when Mr. Batchlett dropped
back for the first time. "Ease off a bit!" he told me. "We're
pushin' 'em a little too hard. If my recollection's good there's
a pretty fair valley beyond them hills yonder. We'll drift 'em
along to it and day-graze 'em three-four hours. They won't
feed good if we dry 'em out too much before we leave 'em
graze." Then he rode back to the point again.

There had been nothing in what Mr. Batchlett said to make
me happy, but it was in the way he'd said it—not as if I were
a boy, but another man. The sun didn't feel nearly so hot
after that, and the dust that rose from the cattle's hoofs didn't
seem to be smothering me. I wouldn't have traded jobs with
the President of the United States.

Mr. Batchlett had been right about the valley. After we'd
drifted the herd along for another hour, we came out into
a valley that was shaped as if a great bowl had been pressed
down among the hills when the earth was made. In the center
there was a little pond, hardly more than a puddle, and a few
stunted cottonwood trees grew around it.

Before the pond came into sight, the cattle and spare horses
smelled the water and quickened their pace. Mr. Batchlett
took the coffee-pot from his trail pack, and cantered ahead of
them to fill it before they muddied the water. By the time I'd
brought in the stragglers, he had a little fire going under the
cottonwoods, and the pot on to boil.

All morning I'd been worried about its being my job to do
the cooking, but Mr. Batchlett didn't seem to expect it of
me, and went about it as if he were the driver instead of
the trader. He didn't give me any orders, but unlashed both
of the packs, lifted them down, and took out the things he'd
need for cooking dinner.

I'd never been on a trail trip before, but I'd been around

cow camps enough that I knew what had to be done, so I
unsaddled Pinch, hobbled him, and turned him loose to drink
and graze. Then I caught a spare horse, hobbled it, and tied
the drag rope up around its neck. After I'd taken care of Mr.
Batchlett's horse string, I picked up a pair of hobbles and
started toward Blueboy with them. I didn't know Mr. Batchlett
was watching me, but he called, "Leave him be! Tie him to a
tree here, and hobble your mare! He's tough; he'll make out
all right without grass! If he's goin' to be any use to you,
it'll be for day-herding."

Deep down inside, I knew that Blueboy wasn't a cowhorse,
and that I'd never be able to make one of him. He was all
run and drive, without any patience or cow savvy, and he'd
always fight me if I tried to rein him hard enough for working
cattle. I didn't like to admit it even to myself, but I knew
that I'd brought him along because I couldn't bear to leave
him behind.

When Mr. Batchlett called to me, a lump came into my
throat. It wasn't because of what he'd said about Blueboy,
but about day-herding. I was his driver, was getting full cowhand's wages, and I wanted to do my job the way any other
cowhand would have done it. When a trail herd stopped for
day-grazing, that was the driver's time to get what sleep he
could. It was his job to do the night herding while the trader
slept. From what Mr. Batchlett had said, it was plain that he
was going to do the night herding himself. I knew he wouldn't
have done it if he'd had Tom with him instead of me, and
wanted to tell him that I'd rather do the night herding like
any other driver. But I couldn't be sure that he'd trust me
alone at night with cattle in a strange country, so I watered
Blueboy, tied him to a tree, and kept my mouth shut tight.

"Fetch your canteen!" Mr. Batchlett called to me while I
was tying Blueboy. When I got to the fire, he went on, "This
puddle water ain't fit for a man to drink without boilin', but
there's no telling when we'll strike any better. It's got the
taste of all the cows this side the Platte in it, but it'll be

better than none. Hold out your bottle!" As I held out my canteen, he filled it with boiling water from the coffee-pot, then threw a big handful of coffee into the pot and set it back on the fire. "A man can make out most any place," he said, "if he's got good stout coffee." Then he lifted the lid and tossed in another handful.

The coffee was so strong and bitter that it made my mouth pucker, but the dinner was a good one. Mr. Batchlett had fried a dozen thick slices of bacon, cooked a can of beans in the hot grease, and baked biscuits in an iron pot. When we'd finished eating, he scrubbed out the frying pan with dry grass, and asked, "Reckon you can get a saddle on Blueboy alone, or want I should lend a hand?"

At the home ranch I'd always saddled Blueboy from the top of the corral fence, and always had someone to help me. But, after Mr. Batchlett's putting me on day-herding, I didn't want any help that any other cowhand wouldn't have had, so I said, "I think I can do it alone, but if I need help I'll call you."

I picked up a biscuit that was left over, took my saddle and blanket, and walked slowly to the place where Blueboy was tied. I didn't make any quick moves, but fed him a little of the biscuit, untied him, and moved him to a place where a couple of trees stood just below a little cut-bank. After I'd scratched his neck a minute, I eased the folded blanket over his back, and climbed up onto the bank with my saddle.

Blueboy spooked away when I lifted the saddle toward him, bumped against one of the trees, and bounced back, so all I had to do was to drop the saddle on him. Once it was on, he stood fairly quiet while I pulled up the cinch and slipped the hackamore over his head. I didn't notice that Mr. Batchlett had mounted and ridden over until, from just above me on the bank, he chuckled and said, "Reckon you'd best to take that set-up along with you. It won't be long now till we'll be gettin' into flat country."

I wasn't too sure of what Blueboy might do when I mounted him, and I don't think Mr. Batchlett was nearly as sure as I.

He shook out a loop in his catch rope, and pulled his horse in tight against Blueboy's off side. I went up as easy as I could, and was careful not to haul on the hackamore rope. Just as he had done the day before, Blueboy reared straight up and came down running hard. But this time he wasn't holding his head so low, his ears weren't pinned back tight, and there wasn't that driving feel under the saddle.

Mr. Batchlett's chestnut was fast, but Blueboy left him rods behind in the first ten seconds. I tried to stay loose in the saddle, brought the hackamore lines up snug but not too tight, and drew one gently against the side of Blueboy's neck. He didn't answer it sharply, but bore off into a sweeping circle. I let it be a good wide one, and began bringing him around toward the place where I could see Mr. Batchlett pulling in his chestnut.

From the moment I began to rein Blueboy I knew he was willing to do what I wanted. Mr. Blatchlett knew it too, and when we pulled up beside him, all he said was, "I'll be turnin' in for a spell. Leave the herd spread out, so long as it don't scatter!" Then he reined his horse back toward the cotton-woods, hobbled it, and turned it loose.

There was nothing for me to do on that day herd. The grass in the valley was good, the cattle and spare horses were well watered, and there was no reason for them to scatter. It gave me about three hours to do the kind of work I'd always wanted to do with Blueboy; to learn how short I could turn him, how hard I could pull him in without making him angry, and to get him used to my feel in the saddle. At first he reared and plunged when I tried to turn him too short. But as we grew more used to each other, he fought the reins less, and his turns and stops began to smooth out a little.

I guessed it to be about half past three when Mr. Batchlett ya-hooed and motioned for me to round up the herd and bring it in. I knew I couldn't do it the way I would have with Pinch or Lady, but I held Blueboy in as much as I could, circled the herd, and began drawing it toward the cottonwoods. The biggest trouble I had was that Blueboy was too much wild horse—that he'd been too used to doing his own herding in the driving, slashing, wild stallion way. If an animal lagged or tried to dodge away, he wanted to rush it and slash hide with his teeth.

Mr. Batchlett stood and watched until I had the herd fairly well drawn in, then he called, "Leave 'em be!" and motioned me to him. "You done pretty good," he told me as I rode up, "but you'll never make a cowhorse out of him if you both live to be a hundred. Too much wild stud in him! I ought to have turned him loose in the mountains when he was a yearlin'. Pull your saddle off; I reckon he'll trail with a drag rope now. Better catch up your mare for the rest of the day."

The afternoon went a good deal like the morning, except that a few of the steers began to get tender-footed, and Lady wasn't nearly as good as Pinch at keeping them afraid of her. With a long drag rope that he'd step on if he tried to run, Blueboy trailed well and caught up on his grazing. By late afternoon the high hills, the brush, and the scrub oaks were behind us, and the prairie stretched out ahead in long rolling swells.

The sun was sinking low in the west when Mr. Batchlett dropped back to me for the first time that afternoon. "How's them tender-footed ones holdin' up?" he asked me.

"Pretty well," I told him. "I think it's more laziness than sore feet with most of them."

"Reckon so," he said, as if he were thinking of something else. Then, "I ain't been over this country in ten years or more. Not much in the way of landmarks to recall, but if I ain't twisted and too far north we'd ought to have raised the head of Black Squirrel Creek. Didn't see nothin' that looked like cottonwoods off to the right, did you?"

"No, sir," I said, "but if any had been there I think I'd have seen them. This is new country to me, and I've been kind of looking it over so I'd remember it."

"Not a bad idea," he said. "Reckon I'll head a little more

to the southeast. We'll be in a bad way if we don't hit water by nightfall. This hot wind's dryin' out the cattle." Then, as he rode away toward the point of the herd, he called back, "Keep a sharp eye out to the southward!"

I'd been so busy during the afternoon that I hadn't noticed the hot wind until he mentioned it. It was coming in from the south, off the New Mexico deserts, and the air hadn't cooled at all with the sinking of the sun. Mr. Batchlett turned the herd well south of east, and rode to the top of every hill, looking off to the south for the cottonwoods that would mark Black Squirrel Creek.

Just before sunset Blueboy spooked at a jack rabbit that jumped out of a clump of Spanish dagger. He raced away up a hill to the north—holding his head far to the side, to keep the drag rope out from under his feet. I had to spur Lady hard to get around him and head him back. As we topped the hill, I glimpsed a thin line of green along the gray-brown of the horizon—but it was far to the northeast.

Mr. Batchlett raced his horse up to me when I shouted and motioned to him. At first he couldn't see the line of green, then his eye caught it, and he said, "You're right! You're right as rain, boy! That's what happens to a man when he mistrusts his judgment and goes to worryin' too soon. If I'd held straight on east, wo'd have fetched the headwaters of the Black Squirrel an hour ago. For its first five-six miles, it runs toward the southeast." Then he raced his horse back to turn the herd.

It was deep twilight before we got the trail-weary herd over the last hills and to the cottonwoods—and when we got them there Black Squirrel Creek was nothing but a bed of powder-dry sand.

Often a prairie creek that seems dry will have water under the sand, but the Black Squirrel was dry as deep as we could dig. Most of the men I'd worked for would have sworn at their bad luck, but all Mr. Batchlett said was, "Well, son, we've got a rough night's work ahead! Ought to have knowed that hot wind would dry up this creek! Ought to have rode day herd and let you catch a wink o' sleep! Catch up my horse string while I rastle some grub together! Your mare's put in a big day, and you got to have a pack horse—no sense tryin' to tote a pack on Blueboy."

By the time I'd caught the horses, Mr. Batchlett had the packs unloaded, a fire going, and beans and bacon on to fry. "Leave me have your canteen!" he said, as I came up to the fire. "Coffee'll hold you together better'n water on a night ride; keeps a man from drowsin' off in the saddle." As he spoke, he emptied both canteens into the pot and put in three big handfuls of coffee. "That ought to do it!" he said, as he flipped the lid down. "Coffee that's too strong for night ridin' won't run out of the pot. Light into them beans! I aim to get lined out for Big Horse Creek before full dark falls. There won't be no moon till close onto mornin'."

The night drive from Black Squirrel to the Big Horse wasn't easy. But I was lucky to have Pinch under me—and good strong coffee in my canteen. The hot wind kept up right through the night, but the stars were bright and the cattle didn't try to scatter. My biggest trouble was with the tender-footed ones. If I didn't watch them every minute, they'd pull off to the side and lie down.

The cattle in the herd bawled more and more as the night went on, but those that tried to fall out never made a sound. In the darkness, I was afraid I might have passed some of them and lost them. It worried me most after I'd run out of coffee. No matter how hard I tried, I couldn't help drowsing off in the saddle. Each time my head jerked and I woke up, it seemed as if I'd only closed my eyes for a second. But once, I woke up to find Pinch standing stock still, asleep on his feet, and the herd out of sight ahead. Another time I woke to find him nipping at a steer that was lying down, but I'd never even seen it leave the herd.

It was only about sixteen miles from the Black Squirrel to the Big Horse at the place where we crossed, but it took

us all night to make the drive. In the first gray of dawn, the spare horses started leaving the herd at a trot, and Mr. Batchlett called out to me, "Water up ahead! The horses smell it!" A few minutes later the dark outline of trees showed against the pale sky to the east.

There was only a trickle of water in the Big Horse Creek, and the stock fought each other for it. As the bulls and larger steers fought the smaller and weaker ones away, Mr. Batchlett called to me, "Spread 'em down the line; I'll spread 'em up—give 'em all a chance!" By clear dawn the cattle were strung out for a quarter mile along the damp snake of sand in the creek bottom—bellowing, pawing into the sand, and sucking up any drop of water they could find.

I was so tired and sleepy I was seeing double, but Mr. Batchlett seemed as fresh as ever. "That was a close one!" he called as we met again at the center of the strung-out herd. "Hated to put you through it, boy! But we'd have lost the weakest if we'd waited to cross in daylight—lost 'em if you hadn't saw them cottonwoods before dark come on!"

"I'm afraid we've lost some anyway," I said. "I drowsed off once or twice after my coffee ran out, and I'm afraid . . ."

"Don't fret you!" he told me. "Old Pinch wouldn't pass up none of 'em. Never seen a better drag horse."

"Well, once when I woke up he was sound asleep on his feet," I told him.

"Poor old devil!" Mr. Batchlett said, and gave Pinch a slap on the rump. "Shouldn't ought to took him on a rough trip like this; he's twice as old as you are. He belongs on the home ranch; he's earned it." Then he grinned at me and said, "Reckon a little coffee and some flapjacks wouldn't do you no hurt. Rastle up some firewood while I make a count and dig up a pot o' water!"

I gathered a little pile of wood, but must have drowsed off when I laid down the last armful. I was dreaming I was at home when Mr. Batchlett called out from right behind me,

"Full count! We'll have coffee boilin' in a few minutes! Got to drift the stock along down-creek right away! With this wind blowin', they've got to have more water."

I unsaddled Pinch while Mr. Batchlett cooked breakfast, but I had trouble in staying awake to eat. Once he slapped me on the face—not hard, but enough to sting. "You need grub," he told me when I jumped and woke up. "Get some coffee and bacon in you, then you can turn in for a bit while I drift the stock on down-creek."

22

Fireworks

I WOKE up lying on a pile of leaves at the foot of a cotton-wood. Lady was saddled and tied to a tree, my boots were off, and the sun was about four hours high. I sat up and looked all around, but there was nothing to see except trees, the prairie, and a dry ribbon of sand. A hot wind was blowing, my mouth was dry, and a crack on my lip was bleeding. It was a minute before I remembered where I was.

I supposed Mr. Batchlett had let the cattle work their way down the creek, grazing, and drinking where they found water. So I pulled on my boots and swung into the saddle, but I'd ridden a good five miles before I caught up to him. He was pushing the herd along the dry creek bed as fast as it would travel. "Weather man's sendin' the fireworks for the Fourth!" he called, as I rode up. "It's sure goin' to be a scorcher! Feelin' better?"

Until Mr. Batchlett mentioned fireworks I hadn't thought of its being the Fourth of July, but the wind did feel as if it were coming off a fire. "I feel fine!" I told him. "I felt all right before, only I couldn't keep awake. Haven't you found any pools of water yet?"

"Nary a drop! Won't be, this high up the creek, and with this wind blowin'." He leaned from his saddle, scooped up a handful of powdery sand, and tossed it high. Watching it whip away, he said, "Bad enough now; hope this wind don't veer to the west—dirt's commencin' to rise a'ready! We got to hightail for water or we'll lose these critters!"

We hightailed five or six miles down the creek bed, but found only one shallow pool of water. The loose horses and stronger stock smelled it before we reached it, and ran ahead. Mr. Batchlett wanted the horses to drink, but to hold back the stronger cattle and let the weaker ones at the water. I double-knotted my throw rope and swung it like a flail, but fighting those water-starved bulls and steers was like fighting so many wild elephants. Mr. Batchlett couldn't do much more with them than I, and before we could get the weaker cattle up to drink, the water was gone.

The sharp gravel in the creek bed cut into the cleft of the cattle's hoofs, so we had to fight the herd out onto the prairie, where there was no protection from the sun and the burning wind. With each hour the dust in the air grew thicker and the herd harder to handle. The weaker and tender-footed wanted to turn tail to the wind and stand, the stronger ones kept trying to break back to the creek in the hope of finding water. Each mile, Mr. Batchlett held the herd alone, while I rode to the creek and searched up and down it for any drop of water.

By early afternoon the wind had turned full into the southwest. The air was so thick with dust that the sun looked like an orange-yellow blot. All my coffee was gone, and Mr. Batchlett used part of his to wet spots on our bandannas. We tied them over our mouths and noses, trying to keep out some of the dust. In two minutes the spots were patches of mud, and in another two they were dry again. The wind hissed through the short, curled buffalo grass with a sound like steam escaping from a boiler. At the creek, it roared through the wildly flailing branches of the cottonwoods. Tears ran from the animals' eyes and ours, turning into streaks of thick mud. To drive half-blinded cattle against that quartering wind was almost impossible.

I'd swung my knotted rope until both arms ached, and Lady was all in when Mr. Batchlett rode up. "Catch up Pinch, and drive 'em hard!" he shouted. "Got to reach shelter and water before nightfall or we'll lose 'em all!"

I caught Pinch, and drove him so hard he staggered, but I could barely keep the tender-footed and laggards moving. The sun was entirely gone, and twilight began falling when I knew it couldn't be more than five o'clock. Half the time I could see only the laggards, but every once in a while Mr. Batchlett rode past me through the dust, and shouted, "How you makin' out?" "You're doin' fine!" "That's the stuff; keep 'em movin'!" or, "Here! Get a swig o' this coffee!"

Twilight had deepened nearly into darkness when he rode up and passed me his canteen. "Get to the creek!" he shouted. "Follow it till you find damp sand, and dig for water! If it's plumb dark before you get back, keep hollerin'! I'll be downwind to hear you."

I tried to shout back, but my throat was so dry that I only made a croaking sound. What I wanted to tell him was that a couple of cattle were down farther back, and that I hadn't been able to get them up. When I found I couldn't shout, I tried to tell him in sign language, but he shook his head and motioned me to ride for water.

In the quarter-light, with the trees whipping and groaning, the creek bed was a scary place. I was afraid, but kept low in the saddle, looking for any damp spot on the sand. I tried to spur Pinch into a canter, but the best he could do was a shuffling trot. By the time we'd covered two or three miles, his head was hanging so low it was just above the sand. I was sure, from the way he was swinging it back and forth, that he'd give out any minute—but that was because I didn't know old Pinch well enough.

At a place that looked just as dry to me as any other, he

stopped, circled, and began to paw into the gravel. When I slid out of the saddle I could see that water was seeping into the hole he'd dug. I found a piece of a broken limb and dug the hole deep, but didn't drink or fill the canteens until Pinch had drunk all he wanted.

Water was still seeping into the hole after I'd filled the canteens and drunk again. We needed every drop of water we could get, but I had nothing to carry it in, and was afraid I couldn't find the place again after dark. I could think of only one way to do it: I walked Pinch back up the creek bed counting each step as he took it.

It was almost full dark, so, when I thought I was nearly back to where I'd started from, I began hollering. Pinch had taken seven hundred steps more before Mr. Batchlett rode out from among the trees. The moment I saw him, I shouted, "It's fifty-one hundred and thirty-six steps!"

"What's that?" he shouted back. "Did you find water?"

"No, but Pinch did," I yelled. "It's in a hole we dug, fifty-one hundred and thirty-six steps down the creek."

"Good boy!" Mr. Batchlett shouted back. "That's usin' your head! You watch herd as best you can while I take the horses down to drink. Listen for my holler in about an hour."

Mr. Batchlett had moved the cattle to the east side of the creek, to give them a little shelter behind a few stunted cottonwoods. As I rode up out of the creek bottom, they looked like great blurry balls of tumbleweed on the prairie. A few were lying down, others stood humped with their tails to the storm, and some were drifting away down the wind. If the drifters weren't stopped before full dark came on, I knew they'd keep right on going all night.

I put Pinch into a trot, to get around the drifters, but before we'd gone more than a mile it turned from deep twilight to pitch darkness. I couldn't see my hands on the reins, and, in the wail of the wind, I couldn't tell whether the bawl of a steer was near or far away. There was only one thing I could do: turn Pinch straight into the wind, knowing that, sooner or later we'd get back to the creek—if he didn't break a leg in a prairie-dog hole, or stumble over a down animal and fall on me.

I knew when we were back near the creek by the roar of the wind in the cottonwoods, but I didn't know we'd reached it until I was almost raked off against a tree. Of course, I couldn't tell just where I'd struck the creek, but most of the drifting cattle were straight downwind from there, so I had to stay to mark the place.

All around me the trees were screeching and groaning. There was a crack like a rifle shot close by, then the crash of a falling tree or a heavy limb. I was afraid to stay where I was, but I didn't dare leave for fear of missing Mr. Batchlett and losing the cattle. It seemed as if I waited in the blackness for at least two hours—expecting a tree to fall on me every second. I'd made up my mind that we'd missed each other in the dark a long time before I heard Mr. Batchlett's "Hi-ya! Hi-ya!" It sounded as if it were half a mile away the first time, but a couple of minutes later it came from almost beside me.

"Here I am!" I yelled back into the wind, and a moment later a horse bumped into Pinch.

"You all right?" Mr. Batchlett shouted, almost into my ear.

"Yes, but I couldn't stop the drifters," I hollered. "It got pitch dark. They're straight downwind from here. Did you find the water hole?"

Mr. Batchlett's hand found me, and he called out, "Yeah, by countin' steps! Here, take holt of this lead line! Hang tight; there's horses on it!"

He didn't give me the end of the line, but a hold somewhere along it. Then it pulled tight in my hand as he moved his horse slowly downwind. We left the creek bottom at a creeping walk, but some horse behind me must have got his head on the wrong side of a tree. The lead rope snubbed short and slipped a foot or two through my fist, burning as it went. Then it slackened as the snagged horse came back into line, and we crept on.

I thought we'd gone about a hundred yards when the rope fell slack in my hand. In a minute or two Mr. Batchlett was beside me, and shouted, "Sit tight! We'll tie the horses to old Pinch! He'll stand and ride out the wind!"

One by one, Mr. Batchlett brought the horses up, feeling his way along the lead line. Each time, he found my hand and showed me how short to tie the drag line to my saddle horn. When I'd counted seven ties, he shouted, "Give me your throw rope, and sit tight till I come back!"

I couldn't keep track of time, but it seemed to me that Mr. Batchlett had been gone an hour when, from out of the blackness, his hands touched me, took me under the arms, and lifted me out of the saddle. He carried me three or four steps, stood me down, and guided my hand to a rope that hung like a low, loose clothesline. Then he shouted, "Follow me!"

I'd taken fifteen or twenty steps when I bumped into Mr. Batchlett. "There's a hole here," he shouted. "Lay down and follow the rope into it! Go feet-first!"

I'd only wriggled a few feet when Spanish-dagger spears pricked and stung my legs. The rope led into a hole among them. It was smaller than I, but I kept flat to the ground and pushed myself back with my elbows. In another minute or two I felt as if I were in a cave—with Spanish daggers all around me. There was no wind, and the roar of it outside was muffled. When I stopped to feel around, Mr. Batchlett's boots pushed past my head.

I didn't need to be told where I was or what Mr. Batchlett had done. In some way he'd taken the tarpaulin off one of the trail packs, and had lashed it over and around a big hollow clump of Spanish daggers, almost in the shape of a giant mushroom. There was so little room inside that we had to curl up like kittens, and every time I moved a dagger pricked me, but it seemed almost like getting home.

We didn't have to shout in our little tent, and as soon as Mr. Batchlett was in beside me, I said, "I'm sorry I let the cattle get away."

"Done all you could, didn't you?" he asked.

"Yes, sir," I said, "but . . ."

"That's all any man can do, ain't it?" he asked.

"I guess it is," I told him.

"Dang right!" he said. "We done our best, and when a man's done his best he's got nothin' to bawl over if he loses. Wouldn't doubt me we'll round up most of the herd when this wind breaks. How 'bout some cold beans and raw bacon? It ain't fancy, but there's worse where there's none."

23

Diamond Crosses

IT WAS pitch black in our little tent when Mr. Batchlett woke me. "Wind's let down a bit," he said. "It's time we was up and at it. Reckon you could water the horses while I pull camp and rastle up some grub?"

When I crawled outside, the air was thick with dust, and the wind was still blowing from the southwest, but it wasn't roaring as loud in the trees as it had the night before. In the dim gray-brown light I could make out a blurred mound that looked like a small haystack. As I walked toward it, I could make out a huddle of horses, standing with their tails to the wind. Pinch stood with his head hanging nearly to the ground, and the others were crowded close around him.

I retied the ropes so the horses could string out. bridled Pinch, mounted, and turned him toward the creek. Except for Blueboy, no horse moved until its lead rope pulled tight, and old Pinch walked as though he were still half asleep.

The water hole had seeped only half full, and digging it deeper didn't help, so I could let the horses have only a few swallows apiece. Blueboy was the only one that fought for it.

The rest let me lead them away easily, and stood with heads drooped and tails to the wind.

When I got back to camp, Mr. Batchlett had the packs made up, coffee boiling, and beans and bacon fried. There had been no dawn, but the light had grown strong enough that we could see nearly a hundred yards through the dust. As we ate, Mr. Batchlett watched the horses, and said, "Beat-out lookin' bunch of horseflesh, ain't it? Old Pinch won't last out another day and night like this. Drink good?"

"No, sir," I told him. "There wasn't much water, so I could only let them have a few swallows. Blueboy was the only one that fought for it."

"Wild horse in him! He'd stand up to a month of this. Reckon you'd best to try usin' him today. You'll need to save your mare—case old Pinch don't make it. I'll take the sorrel; hobble the rest and turn 'em loose!"

When I came back from hobbling the horses, Mr. Batchlett was tramping out the breakfast fire. The first thing I noticed was that he was wearing his six-shooter. He saw me looking at it, and said, "Reckon we'll have need of it. Want I should help you saddle up?"

I told him I thought he'd better, and as we carried our saddles to the horses, he said, "Blue devil might turn out worth his salt on this trip! Never looked to see the day he would! Glad you fetched him along!"

Then, when I was ready to mount, he told me, "You'll have to fight him if need be this time! Don't dast let you get out o' sight in this dust! Like as not the wind'll veer, and there's no landmarks to go by."

Blueboy reared when I went into the saddle, and came down in a driving run, but I brought him around in a fairly close circle. After that he bobbed his head and sidestepped, but let me hold him to a walk.

When I brought Blueboy back, Mr. Batchlett called out, "Wind shifted a couple o' points to westward about midnight! Reckon we'll find the stoutest drifters well north of downwind

—eighteen to twenty miles out. But we'd best to do our dirty work first—'tain't right to let 'em suffer! We'll spread out to hunt 'em, but don't get out of sight!"

I didn't need to be told what to hunt for, and was the first to find one. It was a tender-footed steer I'd had trouble with the day before. He was stretched out with his legs stiff, his eyes closed, and half buried in sandy dust—but there was a light breathing in his flank. A shudder ran through him when Mr. Batchlett pulled the trigger, then he lay still, for the blowing dust to finish its burying. We found eleven more, but six were past the need of bullets.

I'd never have been able to find any of the drifting cattle in that storm, but Mr. Batchlett led off across the prairie as if he were following a road. He spurred his sorrel into a canter, and Blueboy swung along beside it. After a mile or two, Mr. Batchlett had to ease his blowing horse to a jog, but Blueboy fretted, bobbed his head, and side-danced. Two nights and a day without grazing hadn't sapped his strength, and the driving need to run was still in him.

We'd cantered and jogged a dozen more times before Mr. Batchlett drew his horse close to me, and called, "Keep a sharp lookout to the right! Ought to be seein' some of our stock most any time now!"

The way he said "our stock" made me forget that my mouth was dry and my lungs burning with dust. "Had I better pull away a little?" I shouted back.

Mr. Batchlett nodded, and called, "But keep an eye on me! Give a high-sign if you see anything!"

We'd jogged and cantered twice more when I thought I saw a blurry shape off to my right. My eyes were burning and watering, so I couldn't be sure I'd really seen anything, but I waved my hat to Mr. Batchlett and drew Blueboy around. He'd hardly taken a dozen strides when two of our smaller steers loomed out of the dust in front of us. Their backs were humped, their heads low, and they were barely creeping along —as if they were walking in their sleep.

"About done for," Mr. Batchlett shouted, as he rode up. "But they might make out yet if this wind lets down. It's shifted another point to the west. Did you take note?"

I shook my head. With the dust blowing and no landmarks in sight, the wind could have veered all the way around without my knowing it.

Mr. Batchlett pulled his sorrel around to the up-wind side of Blueboy, so he wouldn't have to shout, and told me, "Leave 'em drift; we'll know where to find 'em on the way back. The stout stuff'll be ten or twelve miles further on—off more to the north. Wouldn't doubt me some of it's drifted as far as South Rush Creek."

We left the steers to drift sleepily on, and went back to jogging and cantering. We rode about a hundred yards apart —just so I could keep Mr. Batchlett in sight. I waved each time I saw cattle, but he only waved back and rode straight on. After what I thought was about an hour and a half, trees stood like dark shadows against the curtain of dust in front of me. When I looked for Mr. Batchlett he was motioning me to him. "South Rush Creek, I reckon!" he shouted as I rode up. "Ought to hold the drifters if it ain't dry! They wouldn't move on and leave water!"

South Rush Creek was as dry as Big Horse had been, but we found twelve of our better steers huddled in the lee of a little cottonwood thicket. Mr. Batchlet looked them over carefully, and shouted, "Ain't bad off, but they got to have water before another day's out! Reckon the rest has drifted on to the Middle Rush. If I ain't mixed up, it branches off a few miles south of here. Ought to be two, three miles to eastward! Better creek; might have water in it!"

Mr. Batchlett was right about the distance to Middle Rush Creek, but there wasn't a drop of water in it. He rode it four or five miles to the north, and I rode south to its joining with the South Rush, but we found only ten of our cattle. We herded them into what shelter the few cottonwoods offered, and Mr. Batchlett sat looking off glumly toward the east. "If my recollection's good," he told me, "there ain't another creek in twenty miles. After crossin' two dry ones, cattle would scatter like blowed leaves. Reckon you could hold a course to ride diamond crosses?"

"I could try," I shouted, "but I don't know what they are."

"Light down!" he told me, then took a stick and drew a long straight line in the sand. "That's the wind." Then he drew three or four diamonds straddling it, with their points meeting along the line. "Them's diamonds. You ride this zigzag; I'll ride this one! Keep the wind blowin' your horses' mane acrost his right ear till you think you've gone a quarter mile, then turn him so's to bring it acrost his left! Go a quarter mile and stand still till I meet you!"

Mr. Batchlett took off his gun belt, buckled it around my waist, and told me, "If I don't meet you at a point by the time you've waited ten minutes, fire once! Count a hundred slow and fire again till I do meet you! Keep a sharp lookout; the best cattle are the ones that goes the farthest!"

When we were back in our saddles and ready to quarter away from the wind in opposite directions, he shouted, "Take a slow lope; you can see best at that gait!"

To ride those diamond crosses in the dust, I needed to know when I'd gone a quarter mile, or Mr. Batchlett and I wouldn't meet at the points. I used to go a mile and a half to school when we lived on the ranch, and usually rode Lady at an easy lope. Just for something to do, I often counted her strides, and they always came to few over 1,300. Blueboy took a little longer stride, so I figured that 200 of his strides would be a quarter mile, counted them off, and made a right-angle turn. I'd counted up to 190 after making the turn, then Mr. Batchlett rode in from an angle to meet me.

"See anything?" he shouted.

I waved a hand back and forth, and yelled, "No!"

"Keep goin' another quarter, and turn left!" he called out as he crossed my line and rode on.

We made three diamonds and met almost perfectly on each

of them before I saw any cattle, but they weren't ours. They were long-horned, slab-sided range cattle. When I met Mr. Batchlett at the point, I held up my hand for him to stop. "There are other cattle around here!" I hollered. "I saw four steers, but they weren't ours."

"Seen some, too!" he called back. "Keep a sharp lookout, but don't stop or turn off course if you see cattle you know! We'd miss one another at the point."

Before we met at the next point I'd seen two of our White Face bulls, drifting along slowly, but not looking too bad. On the next diamond I saw three more. I reached the next meeting point well ahead of Mr. Batchlett, and when he rode up he seemed nearer excited than I'd ever seen him. "We're right in amongst 'em!" he shouted. "And if I ain't forgot all I learnt in the panhandle, we're due for a change o' weather. Didn't take note how the wind's haulin' 'round, did you? You're near onto a quarter mile off point. Next leg, keep your horse's mane straight right till you turn, then straight for'ards!"

I did as Mr. Batchlett told me, and saw four more of our steers and bulls, but that wasn't what excited me—I could have sworn I heard thunder.

"Hear that?" Mr. Batchlett shouted, as we passed at the next point. Then, before I'd counted two hundred more strides, big drops of muddy rain hit me. In less than two minutes, the thunder claps were almost overlapping, and sounded like dynamite blasts all around me. With each crack, lightning turned the dust in the air bright yellow. Then the rain came down as if some great lake in Heaven had overflowed.

There was no need to count strides any more, and no sense in trying to ride in the downpour. There was only one thing I really wanted to do—and I did it. I jumped out of the saddle, pulled off my muddy clothes as fast as I could, and danced around, and shouted and yelled in the rain. Blueboy stood with his legs braced, snorting and watching me. Then he seemed to get the same feeling I had. He buck-jumped half a dozen times, shook himself as if he were trying to tear off the saddle,

then faced into the whipping rain and let it beat against his upturned head.

The shower didn't last more than ten minutes, but an awful lot of water fell, and when it was over the sun came out clear and bright. It seemed as if I could see almost to the ends of the earth, and all around me the prairie sparkled with drops of water on the buffalo grass. I was on top of a low hill, and, as I pulled my dripping clothes back on, I could see nearly a hundred cattle in the shallow valleys. They were no longer humped up, but stood with straight backs and heads to the ground, sucking up the moisture on the grass. Before I climbed back onto Blueboy, I stood for a few minutes, stretching, looking off across the prairies, and wondering why I'd never before noticed how beautiful they were.

I'd been having so much fun in the rain that I didn't think about Mr. Batchlett till he rode out from behind a little knoll, half a mile to the north. I guess he'd taken a bath the same way I did. When we met, his face was shining, his hair was wet, and he was smiling. "That done it!" he sang out. "Doubt me we'll lose another head—if Rush Creek ain't rose too fast and caught a few of 'em. 'Bout ready for some grub?"

While I unsaddled and hobbled the horses, Mr. Batchlett laid out the grub he'd brought in his saddle bags. It looked as good to me as a Thanksgiving dinner. There were hardtack crackers, two cans of sardines, a can of beans, and a can of tomatoes. For some reason the tomatoes tasted better to me than anything I'd eaten in months.

The horses hadn't had a bite to eat in two days, so we didn't hurry, but gave them a full hour to graze. While we were lying on a blanket, letting our clothes dry and soaking in sunshine, I asked Mr. Batchlett, "With nothing to go by, how do you know when the wind veers a point? I wouldn't know if it turned all the way around the compass."

"Never's a time when there's nothin' to go by," he said, "exceptin' it's plumb dark with no stars out. Always keep three points in your eye—same as if you was aimin' a rifle: back

sight, front sight, and the spot you're shootin' at. Don't need
to see more'n twenty feet, so long as you pick a new front sight
before you ride up on the back one."

"I can see how that would keep you going in a straight
line," I said, "but I still don't understand how you'd know
when the wind changed as little as one point."

"Watch your horse's mane; that'll tell you."

Mr. Batchlett's sorrel was just about worn out, and an hour's
rest and grazing didn't help him much. He was sluggish on
his feet, his wind was bad, and he got spraddle-legged if Mr.
Batchlett put him into a hard run. Blueboy seemed as strong
as he had been before the dust storm. He didn't fight me much,
and answered the reins pretty well, but he wasn't much good
with cattle. He acted as if he hated them, and when I'd try
to cut an animal out of a bunch, he'd charge in like a wild
stallion, raking in all directions with his bared teeth.

It was nearly sundown before we had our cattle sorted out
from the range stock and driven back to Middle Rush Creek,
but it didn't make any difference. The creek had turned from
a dry ribbon of sand to a brown, raging river, that frothed
and boiled through the cottonwoods along its banks.

The ten cattle we'd rounded up along the creek that morning were still bunched, and had grazed their way half a mile
to the north. The creek was too high and fast to ford, so there
was nothing to do but to throw the ten in with the twenty-
three we found on the prairie, and go into night camp. With
the cattle half-starved and weary from the dust storm, there
wasn't much work to herding them. I kept watch while Mr.
Batchlett slept three or four hours, then he took over for the
rest of the night.

By morning the Middle Rush was low enough to ford, and
we had no trouble in finding the twelve cattle we'd left on
the South branch. The drive from there to the Big Horse was
slow, because we had to range far out in both directions to be
sure we didn't miss any of our stock. When we reached Big
Horse Creek in the late afternoon we were driving fifty-seven

cattle—all in pretty fair shape—and there was only one un-accounted for. We might have missed a living one somewhere, or one might have drifted far out and died in the storm.

Mr. Batchlett's sorrel was hardly able to cover the last few miles to our old camp, but Blueboy seemed none the worse for the storm and hard work. The full day and a half of rest and grazing had done wonders for the horse string. Even old Pinch was his ornery, crabby self again.

There was no sense in trying to start out until the sorrel had a night's rest and grazing, so we spent the rest of the day loafing, while Mr. Batchlett changed his plans for the trip. "No use in us tryin' to make the Purgatory after losing two days," he told me. "I said we'd be back to the home ranch by a week come Saturday, and I aim to be there. Reckon we'll follow the Big Horse till we sight Nero Hill, then cut south to hit the valley east of Rocky Ford. Ought to be some good tradin' up along the valley. If we've made our trades by the time we hit the mouth of Black Squirrel Creek—and if there's water in it—we'll trail up it towards the home place. I'm sure sorry I fetched you along on so rough a trip!"

"I'm not a bit sorry!" I told him. "I'm only sorry we lost thirteen head of stock."

"Turn of the cards!" Mr. Batchlett said. "No man can hope to draw aces every time, and if them range cattle we seen are anything to go by, we might still hold a winnin' hand. That kind o' herd needs improvin', and young White Face bulls ought to be pretty good trade stock. Did you take note that we didn't lose a single bull?"

Mr. Batchlett was as right about the demand for White Face bulls as he had been about where to find them in the dust storm. Before we'd reached the Arkansas Valley, he'd traded fifteen of them for fifty head of range steers, and he sold the steers for cash at Rocky Ford.

Of course, I didn't have anything to do with the trading, but Mr. Batchlett went to every ranch we passed in the valley. I'd hold the herd while he was gone, and when he came back he'd usually have the rancher and a couple of milk cows with him. Sometimes they'd haggle and talk for an hour or two before the deal was made, and sometimes Mr. Batchlett would give a few dollars to boot, but the rancher always left his cows and drove back one of our bulls or a couple of steers.

I had to hold the herd for three or four hours while Mr. Batchlett was selling the range steers in Rocky Ford. But after he came back I told him I needed to ride into town for half an hour. I'd brought my sixty cents with me, and fifty-five of it was money that Hazel had won from me the first day we hunted cows and calves on the home ranch.

Mr. Batchlett didn't ask me why I wanted to go into town, but told me to take my time. I didn't need very much time, because I knew what I wanted. The first store I went into had some real nice calfskin gloves, with long gauntlets that had big red stars sewed on them. There was a pair that I thought would be just about Hazel's size, but they were sixty-five cents. When I said I guessed I'd have to look at something else because they cost too much for me, the man in the store asked, "How much did you aim to spend, Sonny?"

"Sixty cents," I told him; "that's all I've got."

"Want 'em for your best girl?" he asked.

"Well—" I said, "I haven't got a best girl—but—for a girl —she's my best friend."

While he listened, the man began wrapping up the gloves, as if I'd said I'd take them. "If she was your best girl, they'd be four bits," he told me, "but bein' she's only your best girl *friend* they'll cost you sixty cents."

I didn't have any saddle bags, so I carried the gloves back inside my shirt, but that night I stowed them in my war sack.

Mr. Batchlett found the trading good all the way up the valley, and before we reached the mouth of the Black Squirrel, he'd traded what was left of our young stock for forty-seven milk cows. The creek had water in it until we were nearly to the place where we'd crossed on our way east, and from there we turned west toward the home ranch.

After the dust storm, Blueboy wasn't of any use for herding, because he hated cattle too much. But Pinch and Lady held up in better shape than either Mr. Batchlett or I expected. By early twilight on Saturday we came in sight of the home ranch, and Mr. Bendt and Hazel rode out to meet us.

Hazel didn't say she was glad to see me back, and I didn't tell her I was glad to see her either. I didn't even give her the gloves until after Sunday School the next day.

24

Four-Flush

WHEN Mr. Batchlett and I got back to the home ranch, we found Zeb and Sid there ahead of us. They'd come in during the afternoon, both had missed the dust storm, and they'd had pretty good luck trading—but Sid wasn't happy. Trinidad had taken his guitar to the chuckhouse at suppertime. He was still there, playing and singing, when Mr. Batchlett and I went in to eat. I didn't like Trinidad any better than I had from the first minute I saw him, but he could really sing and play that guitar—and it was easy to see that Jenny liked to listen to him.

Sid and I sat on the bunkhouse steps for a long time after the other men turned in, but Trinidad was still at the chuckhouse, playing and singing to Jenny and Mrs. Bendt. I tried to talk to Sid, and tell him about the dust storm and the gloves I'd bought for Hazel, but I don't think he heard a word I said. He just sat looking glum until the moon rose. Then he got up, and said, "Might as leave turn in, I reckon. With the moon up, that coyote'll prob'ly howl all night."

It was lucky that Mr. Batchlett decided not to go all the way to the Purgatory, and that we got back to the home ranch

Saturday night. Sunday noontime, when we were cutting out trail herds for the next trips, the station agent from Castle Rock rode in on a lathered horse. He brought a telegram, saying that Mrs. Batchlett was very sick, and that Mr. Batchlett had to get to Littleton as fast as he could. The agent had wired to have the one o'clock Santa Fé express stop at The Monument, and had nearly run his horse to death so Mr. Batchlett would have time to make it.

I'd seen men catch a fresh horse and change saddles fast, but I never saw one do it as fast as Mr. Batchlett did that Sunday. We could all see that he was worried and scared, but he didn't lose his head a bit. As he cinched his saddle onto Starlight, he called to Mr. Bendt: "Send Sid into the west end of the Arkansas Valley! Let Zeb work between The Springs and Pueblo! If I ain't back by Tuesday noon, turn my herd back to grass! I'll get word to you!" Then he flipped into his saddle and raced away to the east.

Maybe it was Mrs. Batchlett's being sick, or Trinidad's singing, but everybody seemed touchy and irritable that Sunday afternoon. Twice, Sid and Trinidad ran their horses together when they were taking away the trade cattle that Clay and I cut from the big herd. Even Zeb lost his temper. He told Hank to "Shut up," when he was yelling at me for being slow in cutting out a steer.

After dinner Hazel and I rode out to the secret spring, but she was just about as ornery as the men. She said she liked the gloves I'd brought her, and that they were beautiful, but two minutes later she called me a fool for spending every cent I had and going broke. I'd had about all the riding I wanted in the last couple of weeks, and would have liked to stay at the spring and rest a little while, but Hazel couldn't sit still a minute. She wanted me to ride back and ask her father if we could practice the somersault trick. Then, when he said we couldn't, she got peeved—but at me instead of him —and went to the house, where Trinidad was playing his guitar and singing for Jenny and the other girls.

When I went to the bunkhouse, Sid was mooning around like a sick calf, and he kept it up all afternoon. He wouldn't talk, and three different times he got his pieces of leather out to work on, but he'd only fiddle with them a few minutes, then put them back into his war sack. But he must have found a chance to talk to Jenny before the rest of us went to the chuck-house for supper. Anyways, he waited at the kitchen door after we'd eaten, and when the dishes were done, Jenny came out and went for a walk with him.

I tried to write a letter to Mother after supper, but all I could think of was our trip, and I knew she'd worry if I told her about that. I spoiled two or three pieces of paper, but, with the men all sitting around glum and working on their gear, I couldn't write anything worth mailing, so I gave it up and turned in early. I think I'd drowsed off once or twice before I heard Sid coming toward the bunkhouse, whistling like a meadow lark. A minute later, I thought we were going to have a free-for-all fight.

Sid was hardly through the bunkhouse doorway when Trinidad looked up from the bridle he was polishing, and told him, "Stay away from that little heifer, Redhead! I'm runnin' my brand on her!"

Sid was as feisty as a little terrier, and yipped right back, "You're workin' with a cold iron, Big Boy! I don't reckon your brand'll take!"

Trinidad's voice had sounded real mean when he told Sid to stay away from Jenny, but, except for looking up, he hadn't made a move. He came up like a wild stallion when Sid answered him. Before I could do any more than catch my breath, he'd leaped to his feet and swung the bridle, with its heavy bit, above his head. It would have caught Sid right across the face if Zeb hadn't grabbed it in mid-air.

Trinidad whirled at him with a fist drawn back, and hissed, "Stay out of this, *Old Man!*"

When Zeb grabbed the bridle, it jerked out of Trinidad's hand and dropped to the floor. As Trinidad whirled toward him, Zeb didn't say a word or make any quick move, but just stood there—crouched a bit, and with his arms hanging loose at his sides. Before Trinidad could make a move, Tom and Ned grabbed his arms and pulled them behind him. He kicked and tried to jerk away for a minute, then stuck out his jaw at Sid, and rasped slowly, "You heard me! I won't be tellin' you again, Redhead!"

I don't think Sid weighed more than half as much as Trinidad, but he didn't scare worth a dime. He set himself, with his fists up and his chin tucked in behind his left shoulder. "Turn him loose!" he told Tom and Ned. "He's got a four-flush, and he's yella to the liver!"

Trinidad made a few more jerks, as if he were trying to pull away, but it didn't seem to me that he was trying very hard. And when Tom told him he'd break his arm if he didn't behave, he just said, "All right! All right! I know when I'm bein' dealt to out of a stacked deck! Next time I'll play with my own cards!" Then, when they let go of him, he went back to polishing his bridle.

I was up before dawn to help Sid and Zeb get away on their trips. Until Sid left, he and Trinidad walked around stiff-legged—the way dogs do when neither of them quite dares to fight, but both want to look as if they did. Jenny didn't come to the chuckhouse at breakfast, and I think Mr. Bendt knew there'd been trouble. He always managed to be around when Sid and Trinidad were near each other.

Mr. Batchlett came back to the home ranch some time Monday night. I didn't hear him come into the bunkhouse, but when I woke up at dawn Tuesday, he was dressing. The first thing, I asked him how Mrs. Batchlett was. "Out of danger," he told me. "Out of danger, but not too good! Had Doc Crysler worried Sunday mornin'! Your maw's goin' to look after her for the next few days. Told her you was doin' fine, but I didn't say nothin' about the dust storm. Reckoned you could tell her if you had a mind to."

"I was going to write Sunday," I told him, as I pulled on my overalls, "but I was afraid she might worry. Will we get started away early this morning?"

Mr. Batchlett nodded, but said, "Reckon I'll be takin' Tom along—not that you didn't do as good as any man could, but I aim to work close around Pueblo for the next couple of weeks. Got to be where Doc can get word to me in a hurry —aim to sleep in town and leave Tom with the herd nights. Watt's got plenty for you to do right here on the home ranch —calves ain't been fetched in for three weeks—lot of cuttin' and sortin' to be done."

25

Swing-Over

WHEN Mr. Batchlett hired me I thought I was going to spend the whole summer on trading trips. And when we'd picked our horse strings I thought Sid was going to be my partner. But things didn't work out that way. After the dust-storm trip, I spent most all my time on the home ranch, and things just sort of worked themselves out so Hazel was my partner. While Mr. Bendt and Ned rounded up the stock in the forenoons, Hazel and I hunted out the new calves and any sick or lame cattle. Then, in the early evenings, we'd all work together—cutting, booking, and making up the trail herds for the trading crews.

Hazel had ridden with her father ever since she was big enough to sit on a horse, but that summer was the first time she ever worked as a hand. Mr. Batchlett had her father put her on the payroll at fifty cents a day, and she didn't have to wash dishes or help take care of the baby. And, even if she was a girl, she was a good partner for handling milk cows. She didn't play around when we were working, and she didn't try to push all the dirty jobs off onto me. There was never a day when my job at the home ranch wasn't fun, but the evenings were even better than the days.

When the trading teams were away, we had supper as soon as the day's sweep of cattle had been cut and sorted. Sometimes there was an hour or so of daylight afterwards, and Hazel always pestered me to teach her more riding stunts. Mr. Bendt didn't want me to show her any new ones unless he was with us, and he didn't have a spare minute during the first week I was back from the dust-storm trip.

Most of the really good tricks I knew were ones that Hi Beckman and I had done together. I couldn't teach those to Hazel, because I was neither big enough nor strong enough. But there were a couple of solo tricks that I thought she might learn.

One of them was done by crawling all the way around a horse while he was at a full gallop. All it took was two loops of strap on the cinch, a little timing, muscles strong enough to keep tight against the horse's belly, lots of practice, and not being afraid. Hi had made me practice the trick on a standing horse until I could do it like a squirrel going around a cage. After that, I'd never had any trouble in doing it on a running horse.

If the horse was well-trained for the somersault trick, there wasn't much to the other solo stunt. With the horse in a hard run, I'd take a shoulder stand on his neck, bracing my chest against the saddle horn. When I'd hiss, the quick stop of the horse would throw me forward, feet first. By arching my back a little and spreading my arms wide, I'd travel in a quarter circle, and land on my feet in front of the horse. Neither of the tricks was hard, but, of course, there was always danger of being trampled if I fell.

Every evening that first week, Hazel and I practiced the somersault trick a dozen times or more. But the better she could do it, the more she pestered me to show her new stunts. I wouldn't do it, but finally I told her that when she could do five somersaults in a row without a bobble, I'd talk to her father about new tricks. Saturday evening she did seven somersaults, and landed on her feet every time.

After I told Hazel I'd talk to her father, I riveted straps on my cinch, and practiced a little with Pinch—when everyone had gone to bed—first standing, and then running. With his being used to the somersault trick, it didn't take much teaching for him to learn the new ones. Then, Sunday forenoon, when Mrs. Bendt, Jenny, and all the children were at Sunday School, I asked Mr. Bendt if he'd go down to the little practice meadow with me while I showed him a couple of new tricks.

At first he shook his head, but then he said, "Bein' it's Sunday, and after you kids done such a good job this past week, I'll go along with you for half an hour, but don't get no idees this is goin' to be a regular thing. Trick stunts is fine for roundups, but they ain't no good around a cow ranch— kill too much of a man's time. If I let you show Hazel another trick, you tell her to quit pesterin' the life out of me to come watch her practice."

"Well," I said, "I told her she couldn't even see me do these tricks unless you saw them first and said she could learn them. They wouldn't take but a little of your time. Most all the early practicing has to be done with a standing horse, so you wouldn't have to spend hardly any time with us."

"Get your horse saddled, then!" he told me. "I'll spare you half an hour. But, understand me right, this ain't goin' to be no regular thing!"

Mr. Bendt watched me do both tricks three or four times, then he shook his head, and said, "Don't you never let Hazel see you do them stunts, and don't you be doin' 'em yourself while you're around here! They're too danged dangerous! One slip and you'd be a goner."

"All right; I won't," I told him, "but I could teach Hazel to twist a little in the air on the shoulder-stand trick, and to land at one side. Then a horse couldn't run over her if he failed to make a full stop."

"Ain't one trick enough?" he asked a little bit crossly. "You kids get all het up over trick stunts and you won't be worth a nickel as cowhands. Short-handed, with Tom away, there won't be no time for playin'. Besides, them tricks is too dangerous for any girl."

It looked as if our trick-riding was just about over, and I knew Hazel would be mad at me for not doing a better job with her father. We'd turned the horses and were riding out of the little meadow when I got an idea. "I know how busy we are now," I told Mr. Bendt, "but I know a couple of tricks that aren't very dangerous—ones you could teach Hazel yourself after the busy season is over. I can't explain them very well, but if you could spare a few more minutes I could show you how they work."

Mr. Bendt was riding along with his face set hard when I started to talk, but when I'd finished he was looking at me as if he were real interested. "Betcha my life!" he said, "If it won't take more'n five or ten minutes. Helen's due to raise hob if I don't have the kettle on and spuds boilin' when she gets home from church."

The two tricks I wanted to show Mr. Bendt were ones that Hi Beckman and I had done together at the Littleton roundup. They depended a lot on timing and horse training, but even more on one rider's being twice as big as the other. I was pretty sure that if Mr. Bendt tried them once he'd want to be able to do them with Hazel, and that he might be a bit more willing for us to practice a little.

As we rode back to the bottom of the meadow, I said, "For the easier trick, I stand on the ground facing you, with my left arm held out at a high angle. You race your horse past me, with your left arm held out and down to meet mine. If our wrists hit right together, our hands will grab hold all by themselves. I'll have kicked my right leg up just a split second before our arms met, then all you have to do is to hold on tight, and I'll go flying up and land behind the cantle of your saddle. If our hands miss I'll take a tumble, but it isn't any worse than falling down when you stub your toe, and by the time I'm down, the horse will have run past, so there's no danger of being stepped on."

The pickup trick wouldn't work when Mr. Bendt tried to use his bay. It shied off when it passed me, and our hands missed. But old Pinch was getting used to tricks. When Mr. Bendt tried him, he ran past me perfectly. Our wrists met, our hands grabbed hold, and I went sailing up behind the saddle smoothly. I'd barely landed when I asked, "Don't you think that would be a good trick for you to teach Hazel?"

"Betcha my life! Betcha my life!" he sang out. "Want we should try it again . . . so's I get the hang of it good?"

I guess Mr. Bendt forgot about the potatoes. Anyway, we tried the pickup trick at least a dozen more times, and on five of them I went up behind the saddle. I took a few nose-dives when our hands missed their hold, and I broke open the cracks I'd got in my lips during the dust storm, but they didn't bleed much or bother our practicing.

After the fifth time I'd gone up behind his saddle, Mr. Bendt turned his head back, and asked, "Didn't you say there was two tricks I could maybe learn Hazel?"

I nodded, and said, "The other one is harder to learn. You'd have to practice a lot before you could do it good."

"How does it work?" he asked.

"Well," I told him, "it has to be done with two horses running side by side at a high gallop and in perfect step. I ride at your left, and we lean toward each other, with our arms up and bent into an arch. After we've taken a good tight double wrist hold, you straighten up, jerk me out of my saddle, and swing me over your head in a half circle. As my feet touch the ground on the far side of your horse, I bounce hard, so you'll be able to swing me back into the saddle. All I have to do is the bouncing, but you'll have to hold the saddle real tight with your knees or you'll get pulled off balance. It's better to practice with the horses standing still until we get used to doing it together."

I thought we might try the trick a couple of times, but Mr. Bendt didn't want to stop until we could do it smoothly. "It will never be very smooth until we do it with the horses running," I told him. "If they're going real fast, I can bounce hard enough that you can swing me back as smooth as a stream of oil. Hi Beckman says that when I land with them running, it winds the muscles in his back and shoulders up like a mainspring. I think that's a good part of what makes the trick work."

"Wouldn't doubt me none! Sounds reasonable!" Mr. Bendt said. "Want we should give it a try?"

We ran the horses together a couple of times, but Mr. Bendt didn't try to swing me out of the saddle. Old Pinch didn't like having another horse run close to him. He kept snapping at Mr. Bendt's bay, and driving him far enough away that we couldn't get a wrist hold. Right after the second run, Mr. Bendt looked up at the sun, and sang out, "Great bulls o' Bashan! Where do you reckon the time's gone to? Helen'll skin my hide off for not gettin' them spuds on to boil."

From the first high hill, we saw the buckboard coming— way off to the east—and Mr. Bendt raced to the house in time to have a fire built before Mrs. Bendt drove in.

That Sunday the dairyhands had driven off to town as soon as the morning's milking was done, and Ned had gone when we finished our forenoon's work, so I was the only hired hand on the home ranch at dinner time. Jenny didn't bother to set the table in the chuckhouse, and Mrs. Bendt invited me to eat with the family.

We were hardly down at the table when Kenny began trying to tell me things Hazel had said about me, but she got so mad that Mrs. Bendt had to tell him to keep still. He sat for quite a while, just calling out, "Pass the meat!" "Pass the spuds!" "Pass the gravy!" Then he looked over at me, and said, "Betcha my life you *can't* ride better'n Ned! You fell off Jack and he didn't."

"Ned was never on your old donkey!" Hazel yapped.

"If you children can't behave, you can both leave the table," Mrs. Bendt said sharply. "I won't have no squabblin'!"

For a while the talk was about the minister's sermon that morning, but when Jenny was bringing in the pie, Mr. Bendt asked Hazel, "Want I should saddle up Pinto after you've helped with the dishes, gal?"

Before Hazel could answer, Mrs. Bendt cut in, "Ain't she rode enough this past week! Why didn't you keep Ned to home if you needed an extra hand this afternoon?"

"Oh, I wasn't aimin' to work her none," Mr. Bendt said; "just wanted to see if we had some horse that would hold a gait along with Pinto. Old Pinch, he's too ornery to work double, and there's times it comes in right handy to have a matched pair to work close alongside one another."

"Well, I guess that's all right," Mrs. Bendt said, as if she weren't quite sure, "but I don't know what's got into the child of late! She wouldn't stay off a horse long enough to sleep if I didn't put my foot down."

Hazel's toe touched my leg under the table, then she looked up at her father, and said, "This little dab o' dishes won't take over five minutes. I'll be right out."

As soon as Mr. Bendt and I were outside, I said, "If you were thinking about that swing-over trick, Lady has done it lots of times with Hi and me, and it doesn't make much difference about the other horse; she'll keep pace with it."

"How's she on the pickup trick?" he asked.

By that time, I was sure that Mr. Bendt wanted to show Hazel the new tricks, but Lady was only good for the swing-over one, so I said, "I guess we'd better take both Lady and Pinch along; she's not very good at the pickup trick."

"Wouldn't want to ride Pinch down to that little meadow, and lead your mare, would you?" he asked. "I don't generally ride no horse that ain't in my own string—and the women folks might get to wondering."

I rode Pinch and led Lady down to the little meadow. We hadn't been there three minutes before Mr. Bendt and Hazel came racing in. He was on the same bay he'd ridden that morning, and stepped down as he slid it to a stop beside Pinch. For a second or two I wished I had been wall-eyed, so I could watch both Hazel and her father at the same time. She was making hand-shaking signs behind his back, while he winked and motioned for me to get down off Pinch.

I could only guess that Hazel was telling me I'd done a good job in getting her father to let her learn new tricks. But I knew what Mr. Bendt wanted all right; he sort of kicked a foot up when he winked at me, so I winked back as I stepped down out of the saddle.

When Mr. Bendt put his saddle on Pinch and rode off toward the end of the valley, Hazel watched him as if she thought he'd gone crazy. She looked at me, puzzled, and asked, "You ain't goin' to learn Paw my somerset trick, are you?"

I wanted to surprise Hazel as much as I could, so I stepped in front of Pinto, looked up at her, and said, "No, he's going to show you a trick of his own."

As I spoke, I nodded my head to show Mr. Bendt I was ready, but I didn't take my stand or raise my arm until he was nearly abreast of me. Then I shot it out, and kicked high with my right foot. Hi Beckman and I had practiced that way, but without the rider's having a target to aim for, it was pretty hard to get a wrist hold. Mr. Bendt and I were lucky that time. Our wrists slapped together squarely, our hands grabbed their hold, and old Pinch didn't even slow down until well after I was sitting behind Mr. Bendt.

I was kind of proud of the way our trick had worked, and thought Hazel would be proud of us both, but when her father pulled Pinch around, she was beating her fists on her saddle horn. "You cheat! You cheat! You cheat!" she shouted. "You're both cheaters! You're too busy to go to Sunday School, but I have to go, don't I? Then, while I'm gone, you ain't too busy to learn Paw the tricks you promised to learn me. You're cheaters! You're cheaters!"

"This wasn't any trick I was going to teach you," I told her.

"I'm not big enough to do this one with you. I showed it to your father so you and he could do it together."

Hazel could change quicker than any girl I ever saw. She'd been madder than a cat with a clothespin on its tail when I began explaining to her, and by the time I'd finished she was off Pinto and hopping around like an Indian in a war dance. "Can we do it now, Paw? Can we do it now?" she almost shrieked. "I seen everything he done, and I can do every bit of it! Can we do it, Paw?"

"You just keep your garters tight!" he told her. "This trick ain't one you can learn in no half hour."

Hazel buttoned up her lips so tight they turned white, and looked from one of us to the other. "Then you're even worse cheaters than I thought you was!" she told us. "You've been practicin' behind my back ever since . . . ever since . . ."

"No we haven't either!" I told her. "We only tried it a few times this morning, but I've been practicing it for three years. In this one, the rider doesn't need to have very much practice."

When I said that, I didn't think about its sounding as if Mr. Bendt wasn't very important in the trick, but I guess that's the way it sounded to him. "That's right as rain, gal," he said, "but we got another one where most of the job's the old man's. Want we should show it to you?"

The swing-over trick looked to be the hardest of all, but if the horses ran shoulder to shoulder there wasn't much to it. With Lady trained to keep pace, I wasn't much worried about our having trouble, but I had Mr. Bendt put his saddle on her, and I rode Pinto. He'd be the horse Hazel would ride when she did the trick, and he needed to get used to my leaving the saddle and coming back to it.

We only tried the trick once with the horses running, and it didn't work too well. Pinto shied off when he saw me coming back toward him through the air, and I almost missed the saddle. It scared Mr. Bendt a lot more than it did me, and after that he wouldn't even let Hazel try it with the horses standing. But he promised her that he'd come out and practice with us after supper on evenings when we got through with our work early.

Maybe we all worked harder and faster after that Sunday, but, when the trading teams were away, there was always time for an hour's trick practicing after supper. At first, Hazel had to practice the swing-over trick with a standing horse. But she learned so fast that she'd done both the new tricks at a hard run by the end of the first week.

26

Bunkhouse Fight

THAT week-end was sort of a bad one—one I'll remember for a long time. Saturday noon the creamery driver brought a letter from Mr. Batchlett. Mr. Bendt read it at the dinner table, then told Ned, "Batch has took the train from The Springs to Littleton to see his missus. You hightail on out and help Tom in with the herd!"

He looked up at Mrs. Bendt, who was listening anxiously in the kitchen doorway. "She ain't bad off," he said; "just poorly. Batch, he'll be back Sunday night. Wants I should meet the nine o'clock train at Castle Rock. Wants a lot bigger trail herd than what I've got ready. Aims to keep three teams out, plumb up to Labor Day."

I could see that we'd be plenty busy that afternoon, and with Ned away, I thought we'd be awfully short-handed, but we weren't. I was just finishing my second piece of pie when Jenny came into the kitchen doorway. She was wearing a blue shirt, overalls, chaps, the belt Sid had made her, boots, and a five-gallon Stetson. "Forgot I had these, didn't you, Watt?" she laughed. "If you'll let me have Juno, I'll bet I can still hustle a steer as well as I could three years ago."

I was so surprised that I sat there with a mouth full of pie and forgot to swallow it. I'd never thought of Jenny as anything but a pretty schoolteacher, who could nurse, cook, sew, and wait on the chuckhouse table. But, when we got out into the brush, I found that she could ride and handle cattle almost as well as Hazel—better than some cowhands.

With Jenny and Mr. Bendt working as one team, and Hazel and I as another, we made a clean sweep of all the stock within three miles of the buildings. By sunset, we had the big cutting corral the fullest I ever saw it.

Tom and Ned came into sight with their trail herd just after we'd closed the gate on our last sweeping. I don't think Jenny wanted the men to see her in her working clothes. She stepped down from her saddle, passed the lines to Mr. Bendt, and said, "It's time Hazel and I went to help Helen with the supper." Then, as they started toward the house, she looked back at me and laid one finger across her lips.

At twilight, we heard Zeb's herd bellowing, far to the east, and rode out about three miles to meet it. The trail-weary cattle were trying to scatter, and I had the bad luck to head off a cow that had slipped past Trinidad. Before I knew he was anywhere around, his knotted rope-end bit me on the leg. I thought it was a rattlesnake, and jerked Pinch away quick enough that the second snap of the rope missed me. The knot whizzed past my shoulder with the same kind of a hiss a bullet makes. There was the same hiss in Trinidad's voice as he said, "Keep out o' my business, Smart-aleck!"

I wished I could have been as brave as Sid, and told Trinidad he was a four-flushing coward, but I found that I was a coward, too, and got away from there as fast as I could. I kept an eye on Trinidad until it was too dark to see him, but he really didn't need much help with the cattle. Whatever he wasn't, he was the best man I ever saw with a knotted rope-end, and he was a real rider—not the kind that works as a partner with his horse, but one who rides rough and keeps his horse scared into trigger action.

It was full dark before we had Zeb's herd in the corral, and Mr. Bendt called out, "Reckon we'd best hightail back to find Sid! Wouldn't doubt me he's run into trouble!"

My leg still stung where Trinidad's rope-end had bitten it, and when I put my finger on the spot, my overalls were sticky with blood. The first thing that came into my head was that, out there in the dark, Trinidad could sneak up on Sid and kill him with one snap of that knotted rope. He could snap it hard and straight enough to hit a man's head or neck at ten yards, and the only sound would be the cracking of bone. Nothing could ever be proved, and, in the dark, Sid wouldn't be missed until we got back to the home ranch.

I wasn't going to tattle on Trinidad for clipping me, but I wasn't going to let him get out there in the dark with Sid if I could help it. I pulled Pinch around and headed for Mr. Bendt, but I was only half way when he called out, "Reckon you'd best to stay here, Trinidad! Cut the horses out of the trail herds and run 'em to the creek for water!"

It was nearly nine o'clock when we met Sid, and he was still more than five miles east of the home ranch. He was having plenty of trouble, too, but I think most of it was with Hank. I heard Hank shouting and yelling from a mile away, and he was raving mad when we reached the herd. When Mr. Bendt rode over to quiet him down, he shouted, loud enough to have been heard in Castle Rock, "This here red-headed kid don't know no more 'bout bossin' a trail herd than . . . by dogies, if he'd a-listened to me . . . why, I knowed more . . ."

It didn't take Mr. Bendt long to quiet Hank down, but it took us till nearly midnight to get the scattered herd rounded up and into the corral at the home ranch.

Trinidad was nowhere in sight when we brought in the herd, but when we went to eat, he was sitting on the chuck-house steps—playing his guitar and sort of crooning. I don't know if Jenny and Mrs. Bendt had been listening to him, but they had a good hot supper ready for us. And when Jenny passed Sid the meat and potatoes, I noticed that she brushed against his shoulder. Everybody was too tired to do much talking, and we turned in as soon as we'd eaten.

That Sunday there was no time to practice trick-riding, and we had to work as hard as we could go until nearly seven o'clock. While the other riders swept in more cattle, Mr. Bendt, Sid, and I did the cutting and sorting. Hazel even stayed home from Sunday School to keep the herd book.

Ned and Tom changed their clothes and rode off to The Springs as soon as they'd brought in the last sweeping. Then, after supper, I helped Mr. Bendt harness a team to the buckboard. As he drove away, Jenny came out of the kitchen, took Sid's arm, and they walked toward the beaver pond.

I was afraid Trinidad might follow them, but he didn't. He went to the bunkhouse with Zeb and Hank. When I got there he was shining the silver studding on his saddle.

I tried to write a letter to Mother, but didn't have any better luck than I'd had the week before. Zeb was darning socks and Hank was stretched out on his bunk—talking his head off about a cloudburst being due any day, and telling how much better he was at trading and trail-herding than Sid, but nobody was listening to him.

After I'd started my letter over for the fourth time, I heard Sid's meadow-lark whistle, coming nearer from the direction of the house. If anybody else heard it, he didn't make a move, and Hank kept right on talking.

As Sid came in, Trindad got up with his fists cocked. He started across the floor slowly, and said, just as slowly, "I warned you, Redhead!"

Hank stopped talking, my hand shook so much that I drew zigzags on the paper, and Zeb rose in that half-crouch of his, but Sid didn't seem a bit afraid. He jumped to one side, and lit balanced on his toes, with his fists up and his chin tucked in behind his shoulder.

Trinidad took a quick step and swung a punch at Sid's head that would have knocked a mule down, but Sid bobbed under it. Trinidad's back was toward me, so I couldn't see Sid's punch, but it must have been a sharp one to the stomach with his left fist. Trinidad grunted, doubled over a little, and lunged forward from the force of his missed swing. As Sid danced out from in front of him, his right fist shot up and caught Trinidad square on the nose.

Trinidad whirled and rushed at Sid with both fists flailing, but all he hit was air. That time I saw Sid's punch. As he ducked and sidestepped, he shot his left into the soft spot under Trinidad's wishbone. Then, without raising his head, whipped his right up to the face, and danced away.

I've never seen a man look so much like a bull as Trinidad did when he whirled back from that punch in the face. He was nearly twice as heavy as Sid, a full foot taller, with arms as big and long as Sid's legs. For a moment he stood with his head and shoulders hunched down—then he charged. It was almost exactly the way the ugly White Face bull had charged Clay when we'd had our fight in the cutting corral. And Sid handled Trinidad just as Clay had handled that bull.

He stood teetering back and forth on the balls of his feet, ducking and dodging his head, but never moving his eyes from Trinidad's face. Each time the big man rushed he ducked and slipped around him, but each time his fists flashed out like the heads of striking rattlesnakes—one to the soft spot under the wishbone and the other to the face.

The only sounds in the bunkhouse were the scuffling of feet and the grunts that Trinidad made when Sid's fist knifed into his stomach. The whipping rights to the face were so quick I couldn't see where they landed, but after the third one, blood smeared across Trinidad's nose and mouth.

Trinidad charged seven or eight times, swinging punches that would have broken Sid's neck or mashed his face to a pulp, but not a single one of them landed. Around and around they went in the middle of the bunkhouse floor, Sid waiting for the charge, ducking under the blows, and ripping in a shot with each fist as he danced away.

With each charge Trinidad looked madder and swung harder,

but he might as well have been trying to hit a fly in mid-air, and the harder he swung the farther he missed. His last swing was so wild and hard that it threw him off balance and he nearly fell. He staggered as he turned to face Sid, stood a few seconds with his feet spread wide, his shoulders heaving, and his head stuck forward. Then he charged again, roaring like a range bull, but he didn't swing.

As Sid ducked low, Trinidad threw his arms out wide and drove a knee up. Sid saw it coming and tried to jump back, but he wasn't quite quick enough. The knee caught him square in the stomach and threw him higher than my head. He came down in a crumpled heap, and Trinidad swung a foot back to kick him as he landed.

I'd been so excited as I watched Sid rip his punches in and dance away that I hadn't moved from my chair or noticed Zeb. Then, when Trinidad kneed him, I caught my breath and froze, but Zeb didn't. A split second before Trinidad's boot would have smashed Sid's ribs, Zeb's shoulder slammed into him and nearly knocked him out the doorway.

Trinidad caught himself against the door jamb and didn't go down. He whirled and charged at Zeb, with his fists held wide apart and high. Zeb neither fisted his hands nor put them up, but just stood there in front of his bunk—crouched a little and with his long arms hanging as his sides, as if he were bewildered.

The punch Trinidad threw at Zeb's face would have killed a man—but Zeb's face disappeared. He dropped, almost as if he'd been shot. Then he came up like a wild bull. His head rammed into the pit of Trinidad's stomach so hard that it threw him flying back onto the table in front of me. There was a ripping, tearing sound as the table legs buckled, then a crash as Trinidad hit the floor, and the ringing of broken glass from the lamp.

When the table went down I got knocked over, and scrambled for the corner where Sid lay holding his stomach and gasping for breath. I pulled him farther back into the corner, then realized that the bunkhouse had become so quiet it almost hurt. I looked around and saw Zeb and Trinidad facing each other across the broken table. Zeb was motionless, in that half-crouch, with his arms hanging loose at his sides. Trinidad was on his feet, edging around the table toward him. Blood trickled from his nose and a small cut high on his cheek.

Zeb didn't move a muscle or blink an eye as Trinidad edged around the broken table, creeping toward him like a mountain lion ready to spring. I was behind Trinidad then, and could have knocked his knees out from under him, or thrown something at his head, but neither my body nor my head was working. I just knelt there, holding my breath and feeling my heart pound against my ribs. I couldn't even yell for Zeb to watch out when I saw Trinidad pull his foot back to kick.

How Zeb did it I'll never know, but he caught that flying foot in mid-air, flung it high, and sent Trinidad crashing back over the broken table.

I'd been scared plenty of times before, and I'd seen men plenty scared, too. But I'd never been so frightened as I was then, or seen a man show fear the way Trinidad did when he crawled to his feet. Zeb had moved around the table and was standing motionless in front of him. Trinidad backed away until he was against a bunk post—with his eyes darting this way and that, hunting for any sort of weapon he could get his hands on.

Sid gasped, only half-conscious, but I hardly noticed him. Zeb was closing in on Trinidad, inch by inch. I could no more have stopped watching him then a cow can stop watching a rattlesnake that is coiled in front of her. Trinidad was watching, too. His lips were white, and, even under the blood and tan, his face was a muddy gray. Once he pulled his foot back to kick again, but changed his mind and crowded tighter against the bunk post.

Zeb crouched lower and lower, then drove up and forward. His shoulder caught Trinidad square in the chest—crushing him against the post. He crumpled, but before he could fall

Zeb's arms were around him in a grizzly bear hug. I've heard
horses scream in a burning barn, and it's a sound that no one
can ever forget, but there isn't the fear in it that was in
Trinidad's shriek. I was afraid Zeb was killing him, and my
voice squeaked when I yelled, "Don't kill him, Zeb!"

My yell seemed to bring Zeb to himself. He dropped Trinidad
in a limp heap, turned, and in his usual slow drawl, said,
"Don't reckon he's worth it nohow. You all right, Sid?"

Sid was still yawping for breath, but pulled himself to his
feet, saying he was all right, and trying to thank Zeb for
helping him.

"Ain't got no thanks a-comin'," Zeb told him, then went
back to his darning. A couple of minutes later he was mumbling, "*She wore a yella ribbon around her neck. She wore it
for her lover who was far, far away.*" That was the first and
only time I ever heard him sing the second line.

As soon as Trinidad could get up, he gathered his stuff and
took it outside. Even if Sid wouldn't admit he was hurt, he
could hardly straighten up, and began getting ready to turn in.
Hank had been so far back in his bunk during the fight that I
hadn't seen him, and I'd forgotten all about him till he shouted
at Sid, "Why'd you let him knee you in the belly? By dogies, if
he'd a-raised a hand agin me, I'd a- . . . ."

If I hadn't been so nerved up—and ashamed of myself for
having been a coward—I'd have kept still. But, before Hank
could go on, I'd blurted, "You'd have run, like I would!" Then
I pulled off my clothes and turned in, too.

I was hardly in my bunk when I heard the sound of horses'
hoofs coming toward the bunkhouse. Zeb shuffled to the doorway, and stood leaning against the jamb until I heard the hoofs
again. As the sound faded away, he went back to his darning,
but all he said was, "Reckon them six-guns Batch is a-holdin'
ought to be worth a lamp and table. 'Pears like Trinidad's
moved on."

27

Cloudburst

Mr. BATCHLETT never mentioned the fight in the bunk-house, nor asked any questions that I know of. I didn't hear him come in during the night, but he was dressing when I woke up Monday morning. At the breakfast table, he looked over at Mr. Bendt, and said, "Reckon you could spare Ned to go along with Zeb till I pick a new hand? The way the trade's goin', I don't like to pull a team off the trail."

Mr. Bendt winked at me, and said, "The way old Little Britches and me had our crews workin' Saturday, I reckon we'll make out—find a new hand or no."

That was the last of our having a regular home ranch cow-hand. Mr. Bendt, Hazel, and I were in the saddle every morning at sunrise, and, until it went down again, we were only out long enough to eat. But we seldom missed a half-hour's practice on the tricks, and it wasn't too long before Hazel and her father could do them as well as Hi and I ever had.

Little by little, Lady learned to handle cattle in brush as well as on open prairie, but Blueboy was almost useless. I tried him at cattle-sweeping a dozen times when I had both Pinch and Lady worn down, but I could never stop him from plunging and ripping. I knew he should have been turned out to the mountain pasture, but I couldn't seem to give up on him. Night after night, I rode him at a high run for eight or ten miles, to see if I could work some of the drive out of him, but it never did any good.

Most of the time Mr. Bendt, Hazel, and I worked as a team —sweeping the canyons and gullies during the day, bringing in the stock we'd gathered before the sun was too low, then cutting, sorting, and booking in the early evening. If we got behind with our work, Jenny would come out and help us for part of the day.

Jenny didn't know anything about our naming cows until she began working with Hazel and me. She thought it was a lot of fun, and helped us until we had nearly every cow on the home ranch named. Of course, we ran out of last names after the first few weeks, so we had to name some of the older cows, "Mrs. Arthur Jones," or, "Mrs. Frank Smith," but we saved all the girls' names for the heifers.

By mid-August we'd used up all the trading stock on the home ranch, so Mr. Batchlett decided to bring in the best yearlings from the mountain pasture. It was about twenty miles up there, and we started out at dawn on Sunday morning—taking spare horses, grub for two days, and Clay to do the cutting. I was riding Lady, and as I led Pinch and Clay out of the horse corral, Mr. Batchlett said, "Why don't you take Blueboy along and leave him up there? It won't be long till Labor Day, and you'll have to be goin' back to school anyways."

I didn't know I cared so much about Blueboy, but a lump came into my throat when I tried to say, "All right."

My feelings must have showed in my face, too, because Mr. Batchlett grinned, and said, "Aw, leave him stay! We'll run him out with the rest of the horses when the tradin' season's over."

I remembered to say "Thank you," but I hurried away before he could change his mind.

Our ride up to the mountain pasture would have been fun if Hank hadn't got on everybody's nerves. He was wound up tighter than I'd ever known him to be, and couldn't keep still two minutes at a stretch. First he was bragging about things he used to do when he was young, then about how much better trader and trail herder he was than Sid, and in between he kept telling us that a cloudburst was coming.

"By dogies, Batch," he shouted, so loud that the echoes overlapped each other in the canyon, "I'd be danged careful 'bout a-puttin' men and hosses up this here canyon with a sky the likes of that there one yonder to the east! Cloudburst sky! That's what it is! Why, I recollect when . . ."

"Aw, recollect to yourself!" Tom called to him. "You wouldn't know a cloudburst if you was caught in one!"

"By dogies, I'm a-tellin' you!" Hank yelled back, but Mr. Batchlett looked around hard at him, and he kept still a few minutes. When he began again, it was about my being a fool for not bringing Blueboy along to pasture.

The mountain ranch was really Government land that Mr. Batchlett leased. I don't know how many miles square it was, but, if it had been smoothed out flat, I think it could have covered the whole state of Delaware. There were no fences, but old Tom Haney lived up there in a little cabin, and kept the stock from drifting. With the mountains and canyons for natural fences, old Tom didn't have much to do. He was deaf and old, with long white whiskers, but he knew every foot of that mountain ranch, and just where we'd find the stock Mr. Batchlett wanted brought in.

Mr. Bendt knew the mountain ranch almost as well as old Tom. They bossed the roundup crews, while Mr. Batchlett, Hank, and I did the sorting, cutting, and holding. Mr. Batchlett told me which yearlings to cut out, took them away from the herd, and ran them into a box canyon for Hank to hold. I think he gave Hank that job just to keep him from bothering the other men. We worked until full dark Sunday night, then were at it again by dawn Monday. By mid-afternoon, we had a hundred and sixty yearlings ready to move back to the home ranch.

Even with young stock, there isn't much work to driving cattle through mountain canyons. There's hardly any place for them to go except where you want them to. After a hard day and a half of rounding up and cutting cattle, we were all tired and wanted to rest a little, but Hank kept up a steady stream of howling about a cloudburst coming.

When we were within a mile of the canyon where I'd first heard Zeb sing, "Yella Ribbon," I saw Mr. Batchlett wink at Mr. Bendt. Then he stopped his horse and called out, "Where's them three brindle steers that was laggin'? Hank, you let 'em slip past you! Go on back and hunt 'em! And don't show up again till you've found 'em!"

Hank pulled in a lungful of air to shout something, but I guess the tone of Mr. Batchlett's voice changed his mind. He let his shoulders sag, turned his horse, and jogged it back up the creek bed.

I couldn't have been the only one who saw Mr. Batchlett wink. As soon as Hank was out of hearing, all the men—except Zeb—began to laugh, and called back and forth to ask if anybody had seen three brindle steers. Sid had wanted to visit with Jenny that week-end instead of going to the mountain pasture, and he'd been a bit grumpy. But, as soon as Hank was gone, he started to clown and act as if he were trying to do trick-riding stunts.

Sid had everybody, even Zeb, laughing when the lead yearlings headed into high-walled Yella Ribbon Canyon. Suddenly, we heard shouting and the pound of a horse's hoofs in the dry creek bed behind us. In another minute, Hank raced his horse around a shoulder of the mountain, waving his arms and shouting, "It's a-comin'! It's a-comin'! Cloudburst! Cloudburst! Flood's a-comin'!"

The sky above us was clear and bright, but there was no mistaking the terror in Hank's voice. And, above the sound of his shouting, I could hear a low, dull rumbling—kind of like thunder that's a long way off. I had never heard that exact sound before, but Mr. Batchlett and Mr. Bendt seemed to know all about it. Mr. Bendt spurred his horse out of the creek bed, and ran it along a narrow, rocky ledge—racing to get in front of the herd and turn it back from the narrow canyon. Mr. Batchlett was right behind him, shouting orders as he spurred: "Split 'em! Split 'em, boys! Turn 'em back and up the mountain side!"

With ropes flogging and spurs flying, we fought our way through the frightened, bewildered yearlings; splitting the herd, stampeding it, shouting, yelling, and driving it up a mountain side that was steeper than a church roof.

I was lucky to have my saddle on Pinch. He seemed to sense the danger as well as any man in the outfit, and he was no longer pinching. His bare yellow teeth ripped and cut, driving the frightened yearlings in a swarm before him.

There were only two men who were not shouting at the top of their voices—Zeb and Hank. A dozen or more times I saw Hank, striking with his rope-end as a rattlesnake strikes with its head, but his mouth was clamped tight, and there was no fumbling. Each time his rope flashed out, the knot caught a yearling on the rump, and no man in the outfit kept his head any better.

We had most of the stock out of danger when I saw a wall of water come around the shoulder of the mountain where Hank had raced three minutes before. It didn't look very dangerous, or as if it were moving very fast, but within another three minutes the creek was a racing, raging river, ten or twelve feet deep. Where it sucked in to shoot through Yella Ribbon Canyon—the one we'd have been in if Hank hadn't saved us—it leaped and plunged, with white foam whipping back and forth like the mane on a fighting stallion.

Mr. Batchlett stepped down from his horse, took off his hat, and with it in his hand, climbed along the mountainside to where Hank sat his horse. We couldn't have heard him if he'd spoken, but I was watching his face and knew he didn't. He just reached up, shook hands, then turned and put his hat on as he went back to his own horse.

There was no way out of the mountains except through Yella Ribbon Canyon, and any stock that went through it that night would be coyote food. Three or four of our yearlings did go down fighting wildly for a minute or two, then being rolled and swept along with the deadwood that rode the crest. There was nothing to do but cling to our perches on the mountainside until the flood passed and dawn came.

I think all the men expected, as I did, that Hank would brag of his having been right about the cloudburst's coming, and of his saving our lives—but he didn't. One by one, they climbed to where he was perched, took off their hats, and shook hands. When I put my hand out and told him he'd saved my life, he said, "Reckon that leaves us even. I ain't forgot the time I got us lost up here."

I know I dozed off a little during the night, wedged behind a boulder so I wouldn't roll into the flood, and I think most of the others did, too. A heavy dew fell, and toward morning a chilly wind came down the canyon. It made our teeth chatter and our legs and stomachs cramp, but I didn't hear anyone complain. I guess they were all thinking, as I was, that we might have been tumbling and rolling like the dead calves and driftwood on the crest of that flood.

By dawn the flood had passed, and the creek was only a sprawling brook again. But the high-water mark showed, black and far above my head, as we pushed the nervous yearlings through Yella Ribbon Canyon. When we'd passed through and come out between the hogbacks, the buildings of the home ranch came into sight across a sea of brush-covered ridges. They were little more than specks among the brush, but few places have ever looked better to me.

It had been less than two and a half months since I'd first come to the home ranch, and then it had meant little to me. I'd looked forward to being a real cowpoke, like the ones who brought the Longhorns up from Texas, but it hadn't worked

out that way. Instead, with the exception of the dust-storm
trip, I'd only been a ranch boy, doing the things that hundreds
of other ranch boys were doing—and my partner had been a
freckle-faced little girl with pigtails.

As I rode along behind the bawling calves, I tried to feel
sorry for myself, but I couldn't. After the first week, there'd
hardly been a minute all summer when I'd have traded my job
for anything in the world. I didn't care if I did have a girl for
a partner; there were few cowhands who could do a better job
with milk cows—or that I liked to work with any better. Much
as I wanted to see Mother and the children at home, I found
myself being a little bit sorry that I'd have less than three more
weeks on the home ranch.

It was mid-forenoon when we brought the yearlings into the
big cutting corral, and there was no chance for any rest before
we got the trading herds cut and ready to take the trail at dawn
next morning. Mrs. Bendt and Jenny had breakfast waiting for
us, and as we ate, Mr. Batchlett told us what his plans were.

"This'll be the last go-round," he said, "and I aim to strike
out for the Purgatory again. There's need for good young bulls
to improve the range stock in that country, and they'll take
yearlings if they can't get older stock. Zeb, how about you and
Ned takin' a bunch of steers along the foothills between The
Springs and Pueblo? You could figure on tradin' two for one.
Take farrow cows if you have to; there's grass enough here to
winter 'em through."

Zeb was stuffing away flapjacks, half a one at a mouthful,
but he nodded, and Mr. Batchlett went on. "Reckon I'll let you
and Tom go back into the South Park country, Sid. Take heifer
stuff along, and trade out as best you can—two for one; three
for one if you have to. We're getting a late start, but I want you
back here by two weeks from tonight. It'll take a few days to
round up the Denver herd, and I aim to have it in Littleton by
Labor Day."

I'd been listening, but not paying too much attention until
Mr. Batchlett said Tom would be going with Sid. That left only

Hank or me to go on the trip to Purgatory. I knew how much
Hank always irritated Mr. Batchlett, so I was sure he'd pick
me. Hank must have thought so, too; he seemed awfully sober
and disappointed—but not for long. When Mr. Batchlett had
finished talking to Sid, he looked down the table, and asked,
"Reckon you and I could make it to the Purgatory and back in
two weeks, oldtimer?"

Hank's face lit up like a sunflower, and he shouted back,
"Reckon so, Batch! By dogies, I recol . . ." Then his voice
dropped low, and he went on, "Reckon we could. I rid that
there country some when I was a young fella."

28

A Lot of Horse

THE TRAIL herds got away from the home ranch at dawn Tuesday. At midnight Thursday I was wakened by a horse racing into the dooryard. I jumped to the bunkhouse doorway as the rider slid the horse to a stop at the house. A minute later a light came on, and the man shouted, "Telegram for Batch! His wife's bad off! Where's he at?"

Just as ribbon unwinds from a spool, the trail Mr. Batchlett and I followed across the prairies and down the Big Horse unwound in my head. With yearlings instead of two-year-olds, I knew he couldn't travel quite as fast as we had, and, if he'd found water in Black Squirrel Creek, he wouldn't have driven on through the night. That ought to put him not far beyond the spot where we'd spent the night in the dust storm. I forgot to pull on my overalls, and went running toward the house, barefooted, and shouting, "I know where to find him! I know exactly where to find him!"

Mr. Bendt hadn't thought about dressing any more than I had, and came out on the kitchen porch in his long underwear. He didn't ask me where I thought Mr. Batchlett would be, but called, "Get dressed and throw a saddle on! I'll be with you in a minute."

I pulled on my overalls, buckled the chaps over them, and kicked my feet into my boots. As I did it, I made up my mind that I'd have my saddle on Blueboy before Mr. Bendt got to the corral and told me I couldn't take him. Seventy miles at one stretch would kill old Pinch, and Lady would have to take it in easy gaits.

I didn't dare run to the horse corral for fear of exciting Blueboy, but I'd saddled him enough times in the dark that I knew he'd stand if I took it easy. He did, and I was in the saddle by the time Mr. Bendt reached the corral. He didn't pay any attention to what horse I had, but shook out his catch rope, and called, "Stop by the house! Jenny'll have grub and water ready."

The excitement in Mr. Bendt's voice set Blueboy off like a skyrocket. He pitched and crow-hopped all the way to the house, and was still rearing when Jenny passed me the grub sack and canteens. In the lighted doorway behind her, I got a glimpse of Mrs. Bendt and the children, huddled in their nightgowns. They all looked frightened, and the freckles on Hazel's white face stood out in a spatter.

Blueboy rounded the corrals and hit the wagon road with his head low and legs driving, as he always did on our night rides. Mr. Bendt was on his tall buckskin, the fastest and toughest horse in his string. He spurred in behind me, shouting, "Spare your horse! Spare your horse! Hold him in!"

I drew Blueboy in little by little, but I couldn't take a chance on his fighting or possibly throwing me. Mr. Bendt caught up with us at the end of the straightaway, and called again, "Hold him in! That pace would kill him in ten minutes! We got a night's ride ahead!"

"We've got more than that," I called back, "but he'll settle down in a mile or two; he always does."

It was all of two miles before Blueboy's head came up and he settled into the long, swinging stride that I'd become used to. Mr. Bendt still called for me to hold him in, but when I did he bobbed his head and side-danced. Mr. Bendt watched him a minute or two, and said, "Fool maverick! All he knows is run! Leave him have his head and he'd kill hisself! I should'a put you on Juno." Then, after another quarter mile, he pulled alongside of me, and said, "Don't you reckon we'd best to go back and trade off for Juno? That blue devil won't last out twenty miles."

I'd seen Blueboy at the end of twenty fast miles when he looked and sounded fresher than Mr. Bendt's buckskin did right then, so I said, "He'll settle down pretty soon, and he breathes good on a long-run. You lead and I'll follow, but I'd rather go on with him if you'll let me."

"Fair enough!" Mr. Bendt told me. "You know him better'n I do, but I doubt me he'll last out till daylight."

There was no moon, but the stars were bright, and we could see fairly well. After we'd passed the thickest of the scrub oaks, I called, "This is where we left the road on the dust-storm trip! I think we headed almost due east!"

"Reckon you remember how you went?" Mr. Bendt called back.

"I can see it in my head," I told him. "I think I can remember most of the landmarks as we come to them."

"Lead off, then," he called back, "but leave me set the pace! Where you reckon we'll catch up to Batch?"

As I let Blueboy come up beside the buckskin I reined off the road, and said, "It'll depend on whether or not he found water in Black Squirrel Creek. If he did, he'll probably follow it down a ways, then cross to the Big Horse. If he didn't, he'll go straight east across the divide. Either way, I think it will be about seventy miles."

As soon as I said seventy miles, Mr. Bendt pulled his buckskin down to a jog trot. After half a mile, we loped again. In the starlight, I couldn't be real sure I was following the same route we'd taken before, and there were no trails. But when we reached the Colorado Springs-Denver highroad we heard dogs barking at our right. They were at the ranch with two windmills. We stopped just long enough to let the horses take a few swallows of water, then loped on.

East of the highroad, our old route wasn't too hard to follow, and Blueboy swung along in an easy, reaching gait. I'd pulled my cinch tight when I saddled him, but I didn't have to be afraid of his rearing or bucking any more, so I loosened the knot till my fingers would slide under the ring. Before moonrise the buckskin was blowing a little on the rises, and Mr. Bendt let him down to a walk whenever the climb was a bit steep. I'd been keeping a sharp ear on Blueboy's breathing, but he hadn't blown once since he'd caught his second wind, and he was running with his head well up.

Mr. Bendt guessed it to be about three o'clock when the moon rose. It was just a saucer of yellow light, and seemed to be resting, tilted, on a dark row of hills to the east. Soon after, we came into the round valley with the little pond and the cottonwoods, and stopped to let the horses drink. There were yearling tracks all around the pond, showing that Mr. Batchlett had stopped to water and graze his herd.

From the pond east, the hills flattened out, and, even with a little moonlight, it was harder to pick out landmarks that I remembered. It had been afternoon when I'd gone that way with Mr. Batchlett, and the roll of the low hills looked different in the moonlight. Even Mr. Batchlett had missed the head of Black Squirrel Creek, and in daylight. But he would have reached the creek where it turned south if we'd kept on going. If I should get too far north, we'd miss it altogether, and then I'd be completely lost. After I'd worried about it for a few miles, I told Mr. Bendt, "I'm not too sure that we're going just exactly the way we went before. If we are, and hold this pace, Black Squirrel Creek ought to be about an hour ahead and a little to the south."

"I ain't so worried about the Black Squirrel as I am about

the pace," he told me. "That danged blue mav'rick's got a gait that throws a man off pace! Fools him into over-runnin' his horse! Listen to the way Buck's blowin'!"

"Do you want to trade off?" I asked him. "I'm a lot lighter than you are; my weight would make it easier for him."

"Nope! Nope!" he said, almost sharply. "A man's horse is his horse! I ain't never took another man's horse, and I ain't goin' to now!" Then we jogged on without talking until the buckskin stopped blowing.

With me, hills are a lot like people: when I'm waiting to meet someone I've only seen once or twice, it's hard to remember just what he'll look like. But when he comes along, I couldn't mistake him. It was that way with the hill that Blueboy had run up when the jack rabbit spooked him. The moment I saw it, I knew that the cottonwoods along Black Squirrel Creek stood just beyond it.

There was water in the Black Squirrel, but yearling tracks showed that Mr. Batchlett had only followed it a little way before he turned east. It was gray dawn when we turned east with the yearling tracks and put our horses up the divide toward the Big Horse. It had been almost black night when I'd gone over the route before, and I'd been too sleepy to remember landmarks if I could have seen them. But that didn't worry me; I knew the Big Horse ran toward the southeast, and that Mr. Batchlett would be at least twenty-five miles down it. There was no longer any reason for our following the old route; I reined to my right, to cut across the angle and save every mile we could.

The prairies stretched out in front of us like a great table with a brown velvet cover dropped over it in careless wrinkles. Beyond, the sky arched up in a deep, cloudless blue. And between, the sun rose naked—as if a giant hand were pushing a giant orange slowly above the edge of the table. Not a breath of air moved, and the sun threw out its heat before it was hardly above the horizon.

By an hour after sunup, Buck was dripping sweat, and blowing hard at every rise of ground. Mr. Bendt eased him, leaned low in the saddle to put a hand on his chest, and came up with his face set and worried. We jogged a half-mile, then, after we'd reached a flat tableland and were loping again, the buckskin began to weave in his stride, but Blueboy was running as steadily and quietly as ever.

Mr. Bendt drew the staggering buckskin to a stand, and as I brought Blueboy around, he called out, "Go on! Go on, boy! Don't scare Batch no more'n you need to, but tell him he's got to make the one o'clock train out of The Springs." Then he waved, and I turned Blueboy back toward the southeast. I didn't try to hold him in, but let him take his long, reaching, half-wild-horse, half-thoroughbred gait.

Among those low rolling hills, and with the sun moving steadily to the south, it would have been easy to ride in a curve, but I couldn't afford to waste a minute of Mr. Batchlett's time, or Blueboy's strength. Setting a course that I was sure was due southeast, I kept three check points picked out ahead, and never let my sight wander from them. I knew that would keep me in the same direction as the upper Big Horse, but that I should reach it soon after it turned south, not far below our dust-storm camp.

Of course, I couldn't tell Blueboy that we still had twenty or twenty-five miles to go—so he might gage his own strength. I could only keep a sharp ear to his breathing, feel for any tremble in his shoulder muscles, and let him know that I wasn't pushing him.

I kept low on Blueboy's neck, holding my weight forward on his withers, and talking the soft-talk I'd learned from Hi. It didn't make any difference what it was—poems, psalms, Mother Goose; anything to let him know I was trying to help him. I don't remember much about it, except that I said the Twenty-third Psalm over at least a dozen times. I wasn't a bit afraid, but for some reason I couldn't get the Psalm out of my head. And it seemed to have just the right rhythm to keep Blueboy's hoof beats steady and even.

Blueboy's stride began to shorten on the rises, now and then a nerve twitched in his shoulder, and his breathing whistled a bit in his nostrils. I was worried for fear I'd let him run himself out, or that I'd broken his wind, when, above the brown of the prairie, a dark line of green showed ahead and to my left. Columbus couldn't have felt happier when he sighted the shores of America than I did when I sighted that row of cottonwoods along Big Horse Creek. Before I knew I was even thinking it, I was chanting, "We made it! We made it! We made it!" in time with the beat of Blueboy's hoofs. Ten minutes later we topped a rise, and Big Horse Valley lay below us—with a herd of yearlings strung out along the creek.

I ya-hooed as loud as I could yell, and watched Mr. Batchlett whirl his chestnut away from the herd and come racing toward us. When he slid it to a stop beside us, his face was set, and there was a gray tinge under his tan that I had never seen before, but his voice was low and steady when he asked, "What's the news?"

"You had a telegram; it came at midnight," I told him. "You've got to catch the one o'clock train from The Springs."

"Good boy! Good horse! I can make it! Sixty miles; six hours!" was all Mr. Batchlett said before he spurred away.

As I jogged Blueboy down the slope, I watched Mr. Batchlett race his chestnut toward the horse string that was grazing along the front of the herd. His catch rope was swinging before he reached it, and in less than a minute, he'd switched his saddle onto Starlight. The rest of the horses spooked away, but he had his iron-gray snubbed to the saddle horn.

We met where Hank was sitting as motionless in the saddle as if he'd been stunned. If Mr. Batchlett was frightened or nervous, he didn't let it show in his voice or actions. As he tied his catch rope into a lead halter and slipped it over the gray's head, he said, "Little Britches, you know the trail we followed before—hittin' the Arkansas Valley below Nero Hill, and workin' up towards Rocky Ford. Take what's left of my horse string, and show Hank the same trail!"

Then he looked over at Hank, and said, "Trade where and how you can. I trust your judgment. If I ain't in Rocky Ford by the time you get there, trade on up to the Black Squirrel. Little Britches, here, knows the trail back to the home ranch." Then he swung into the saddle, but before he set spurs, he turned to me, and said, "Cool Blueboy out good! He's too much horse to let founder!"

With a glance at the sun, Mr. Batchlett set Starlight's head a little to the north of west, and took off at a brisk canter, quartering up the slope beyond the creek valley. I knew that every ten miles he'd be changing horses, that somewhere in front of him there'd be three check points picked out, and that Colorado Springs would be sixty miles straight down that line of check points.

29

Lucky on Every Pick

AFTER Mr. Batchlett had ridden out of sight, Hank still sat motionless on his horse, and asked in a dull voice, "Is she dead?"

"I don't know about now," I told him, "but when the rider brought the telegram he said she was bad off."

Hank sat looking at his saddle horn a minute or two without saying a word, then he mumbled, "Poor child . . . poor child . . . she wa'n't never stout enough to a-born him them four little young'uns."

I'd never guess that Hank knew anything about Mr. Batchlett's wife, or his family—or that he was anything more than a worn-out, windy old cowhand who couldn't get any better job than working with milk cows.

I had been afraid, just as I could see Hank was, that Mr. Batchlett would be too late, but I didn't want Hank to worry any more than I could help, so I said, "Dr. Crysler is an awful good doctor, and my mother is the best nurse in Littleton, and we live right close to the Batchletts, so I know she's going to be all right."

Hank still sat, staring at his saddle horn and mumbling as if he were talking to himself. "Don't seem no ways right . . . The Lord a-takin' away them as is needed . . . and a-leavin' them of us as ain't no need to nobody."

The only thing I could think of to say was what Mother had said when Father died, "Maybe He needs them in Heaven." Then I added, "And we needed you last Sunday about as much as anybody was ever needed."

"Wa'n't nothin' nobody else couldn't a-done," Hank said quietly, then turned his horse back toward the herd.

I found myself sitting and staring at my own saddle horn. I couldn't make out what had come over Hank since the cloud-burst. Ever since I'd known him, he'd bragged his head off about things that everybody knew he'd never done. And now, when he'd really done something worth bragging about, he didn't even want to take credit for it.

Whatever had happened to Hank seemed to have happened for keeps. All the way down the Big Horse, and along the Arkansas Valley to Rocky Ford, he was as good a partner as I could have asked for. He didn't boss me, he didn't yell at me when I made mistakes, and he didn't once "recollect" about when he was my age.

I didn't think that some of Hank's trades were as good as Mr. Batchlett would have made, but I kept my mouth shut about those. I did tell him, though, when I thought he'd made a real good trade.

Hank had traded out about half of our yearlings, and we had some pretty good cows when we came into sight of Rocky Ford. We were still a good ways out from the edge of town when I saw a rider coming toward us. At a quarter mile, I knew it was Mr. Batchlett, from the way he sat his horse. We pushed the herd off to the side of the road, and when Mr. Batchlett rode up there was a broad grin on his face. "It's a boy!" he called out. "Had us all scared stiff for a while there, but they're both doin' right fine now."

Mr. Batchlett fished in his shirt pocket, gave Hank a cigar, and started to pass me one, but he put it back, and said, "Made

the one o'clock train with five minutes to spare. Watt's back
to the home ranch. Ruined the buckskin; had to put him under
grass. You done all right when you risked your pick on Blueboy! Know how many miles you two covered in seven hours?
Seventy-eight, as near as I can reckon it."

Then he looked around the herd, and told Hank, "You done
fine, Mister! Couldn't have done better myself!"

Mr. Batchlett had hired the horse he was riding from a livery
in Rocky Ford. When he'd shifted the saddle to his chestnut, he
flipped me a five-dollar-gold-piece, and said, "Want to run this
cayuse back to town and pay the man? Big stable near the
depot; ought to be about two dollars—I had him since yesterday."

I didn't like to draw anything ahead on my pay, but I didn't
like to go past Rocky Ford without buying another present for
Hazel, either. It must be that my face is awfully easy to read.
While I was sitting there, trying to make up my mind whether
or not to ask Mr. Batchlett for an advance of a dollar, he said,
"Ain't no rush now; why don't you look around for some trin-
kets to take on back to the Bendt kids? There'll be change
enough left over from the horse hire; that's your cigar."

The belt I got for Hazel wasn't quite as fancy as the one Sid
made for Jenny, but it was a real pretty one. And I got something for Kenny and Martha and the littler girls—but I liked
the belt best of all.

It was twilight on the Monday before Labor Day when we
brought our trail herd in to the home ranch. Of course, it was
too late then for Hazel and me to ride out to our secret spring,
but we did walk around the corrals, and looked at the new
cows, and named some of them; and I gave her the belt.

While we were feeding pieces of biscuit to Blueboy, Hazel
got tears in her eyes, and when I asked her what the trouble
was, she said, "I got to take back what I said to you at the
horse-pickin'. It was a lie! I said you'd be sorry all the rest of
your life if you ever picked Blueboy, but not you, nor nobod
. . . nor anybody else could be sorry now."

"I guess I was just lucky," I said. "I guess I was lucky when I picked every single one of my string. Did you ever think of it: if I hadn't picked Clay and Pinch I'd have been out on trading trips all summer?"

Hazel didn't really lean against me, but we were standing sort of close together, and we touched when she turned her face up to look at me, and asked, "Why do you think I told you which ones to pick, Ralph?"

That was the first time I ever wanted to kiss a girl, but I didn't. Hazel whirled away and raced for the house. With my high-heeled boots and chaps on, I couldn't run fast enough to catch her.

About the Author

RALPH OWEN MOODY was born December 16, 1898, in Rochester, N. H. His father was a farmer whose illness forced the family to move to Colorado when Ralph was eight years old. The family's life in the new surroundings is told from the point of view of the boy himself in *Little Britches*.

The farm failed and the family moved into Littleton, Colorado, when Ralph was about eleven. Soon after, the elder Moody died of pneumonia, leaving Ralph as the oldest boy, the man of the family. After a year or so—described in *Man of the Family* and *The Home Ranch*—Mrs. Moody brought her three sons and three daughters back to Medford, Mass., where Ralph completed his formal education through the eighth grade of grammar school. This is the period of *Mary Emma & Company*. Later, Ralph joined his maternal grandfather on his farm in Maine—the period covered in *The Fields of Home*.

A new series of books, about Ralph's experiences as a young man, starts with *Shaking The Nickel Bush*.

In spite of his farming experience, Ralph Moody was not destined to be a farmer. He abandoned the land because his wife was determined to raise her family (they have three children) in the city.

"When I was twenty-one," he writes, "I got a diary as a birthday present and I wrote in it that I was going to work as hard as I could, save fifty thousand dollars by the time I was fifty, and then start writing." True to his word, he did start writing on the night of his fiftieth birthday.

—Adapted from the *Wilson Library Bulletin*